Hunting Aquila

by

James Hume

Hunting Aquila

.

For

CALLUM

My grandson

Who will continue the family line

And make things happen!

Chapter 1. Porritt

Commander Jonathan Porritt hurried through the dim, dank London streets. His rolling gait hinted of many years at sea. His old boss from Naval Intelligence days before the war, Sir John Halton, had a problem and wanted him, as head of Special Branch in the UK, to help solve it.

Halton had been a great mentor. They had often used tiny slivers of info to catch some very nasty people who wanted to harm Britain. It had led them to set up code breaking operations at Bletchley Park that were now, in 1942, doing so much to turn the war in Britain's favour.

Porritt skipped up the steps of a drab building in the Strand. He still got a thrill at a new challenge. Here, no one used names in public. Only 'sir' or 'madam'. A security man showed him up a wide staircase and along a dark-panelled hall to an unmarked door. He knocked and opened it. 'Your visitor, sir.'

Halton came out from behind a desk at the window, smiled and shook hands. 'Jonathan. Great to see you again. Thanks for coming in. How are things at Special Branch?' They sat at the conference table.

'Very well, sir. Got rid of the dead wood. Now we have the right people in the right jobs. Haven't had a complaint from the top for a long time.'

'You're right. I can tell you the PM is very happy with what you've done there. They needed you, Jonathan. That's why I proposed you.'

4

He liked meeting Halton. Always so positive. At least with him. And still alert and active, though greyer now and more stooped. 'And how about you, sir? I thought you'd retired.'

'I did, Jonathan, I did. But when Churchill became PM a couple of years ago, he wanted me back on some key War Office committees. For my experience, of course. But also to give him the inside story of what's going on. Too many people tell him what they think he wants to hear. He needs people he can trust to tell him the *real* story. The one that's not carried in the minutes.'

Porritt nodded, but stayed silent. He knew Halton was a long-time friend of Churchill.

'And that brings me to my problem, Jonathan. The PM thinks there's a leak from one of our committees. Wants us to find and fix it sharpish.'

'Blimey, what makes him think that?'

'I meet the PM once a month. Six weeks ago, I told him I'd missed the August meeting of the Strategy Review Committee because of illness. But I was unhappy at an item in the minutes.

'They had assessed Normandy beaches for landings and rated one near the village of Yport in the top five. Now, I know that area well from my bird watching days. It's absurd. Boggy terrain and limited access roads beyond the beach. So I told the PM I'd force a review of the assessment criteria at the next meeting.

'However, two days ago, the PM saw, in one of the many notes that pass across his desk, that the Germans had moved a full division of troops to that spot near Yport. He wondered what had prompted the move. The assessment I'd mentioned? Had our info leaked?

'So he asked me to probe the other eight committee members, plus their staff. See if we can find a mole. We have to be very discreet, of course. And I need your help to do it. The PM also wants to plan a new strategy, so we need to do it pronto.'

Porritt felt the buzz of a new hunt building inside him. He agreed, of course. An exciting case. Even if Halton hadn't been the one to ask him.

They analysed their options and agreed a two-step action plan. They'd first try to confirm a leak.

Halton sat on another committee that approved sabotage acts by the SAS and SBS on foreign targets. They had looked at an attack on the huge ACL–Penhoët shipyard in France, which now built German warships. Their agent there had noted they could enter the site through a disused gate at its south-west corner.

Halton would mention this at the next SRC meeting and include it in the minutes. He would then ask the agent to check on the gate and report any activity.

Their second step assumed there *was* a leak. The Germans would want evidence from the leaker, such as a copy of the minutes.

Halton showed Porritt the minutes from last month as an example. The front page had a summary and a table with the distribution list at the bottom. The example had an 'X' against Halton's name.

Porritt agreed to have Special Branch teams tail all staff who had access to the minutes. This gave a total of eighteen targets.

But he then realised that someone taking a photo of the front page just had to cover the 'X' column to hide the member's identity. So he set up a secret third step.

He went to see the machine supplier and got them to insert an extra feature. As before, the machine marked an 'X' against the first name on the list on the first copy, against the second name on the second copy, etc.

But now it would also mark a small dot at the first line of summary text in the first copy, at the second line of text in the second copy, etc. A casual reader would never see the dot among the other spots on the page.

Porritt kept this secret feature to himself.

***

Eight weeks later, Halton showed Porritt a note from his agent in Saint-Nazaire. A squad of builders had removed the disused gate and replaced it with a new fence with no gate. They agreed this confirmed a German mole had leaked info from the committee.

On the second step, Porritt had his SB teams in London monitor each of the eighteen targets. But after eight weeks, they'd cleared all of them.

Porritt puzzled over their conclusions. But the mole hid himself well. Unless they could look over each person's shoulder 24/7, they wouldn't find him.

And without catching the leaked info as it left the country, he had no chance of checking his third step. His secret dot.

He went through the evidence with Halton. 'We can't see who it is, sir, without blowing our cover. And we don't want to do that and lose him.'

Halton thought for a moment. 'He'll make a mistake at some point, Jonathan. Stay alert and then pounce.'

Chapter 2. Jane

Jane glanced up as her supervisor, Mags, approached. 'Jane, would you go and see Mr Anderson at eleven o'clock, please?'

'You mean Mr Anderson, the technical director?'

'That's right. His secretary just called.'

'Do you know why?'

'Sorry, I don't.'

Jane sat at her drawing board and looked around. It all still seemed normal. The feeble February sunlight from the roof windows had little effect on the gloom in the huge drawing office of Stewarts & Lloyds Ltd, near Glasgow. The draughtsmen and tracers still needed their individual lamps on.

She cleaned her pen. She needed focus to trace the draughtsmen's drawings in ink. Her work provided copies for the shop floor. But now she'd lost it. Why would the technical director want to see her? She was among the most junior of the hundred or so people in the drawing office. She hadn't met him before. Nor any director. The most senior person she'd met in her three years there was her boss's boss. She glanced at the clock. Forty minutes to go.

She finished off a small part of her trace. Then went to the ladies' room. She checked in the mirror. Stepped back to make sure her blouse tucked neatly into her skirt. Wartime rations had helped keep her slim and shapely. Even after two children.

But she felt nervous about meeting Mr Anderson. She looked a bit pale, so applied a light touch of rouge to her cheekbones. Lipstick to her full lips. Touched her hair on each side and patted down her blouse and skirt.

Just before eleven, she tiptoed along 'Mahogany Row' and knocked on Mr Anderson's office door.

'Come in.'

She opened the door and peeped in. Mr Anderson, tall and grey-haired with glasses, his shirt sleeves rolled up, stood beside a drawing board. He came forward with a smile. 'Come in, Mrs Thomson. Thanks for coming. Please sit down.' She sat at the conference table and he sat beside her.

'I've a paper here in German that I'd like translated. But we've no one who can do this. A girl in Personnel said you were born in Prague. So, may I ask whether you know any German?'

Jane hesitated. She kept very quiet about the fact she knew German. And knew it well. While her mother was Czech, her father had been born in Germany, though he now had a Czech passport. When she was alone with him, they preferred to speak German. Since the war started though, people in Britain were hostile to anything German, and she didn't want to stir up trouble. She wasn't sure how to answer.

Mr Anderson cut in. 'I know it might be sensitive, Mrs Thomson. But I'd value your help.'

She thought it better to be honest. To some extent. 'Well, I do know German. We got it at school. Happy to help if I can. As long as we keep quiet about it.'

'Not a problem. We'll keep it secret.' He reached for the document, and gave it to her.

There were three stapled pages. She read it through. It described a test on a special pipe coupling, with the results. 'Okay. I've got most of it.'

He smiled. 'Good. Now, I'd like my secretary to note what you say. Okay?'

'Yes, of course.'

He called her in, and Jane read out her translation. Partway through, she stopped and grimaced. '*Dichtung*. It's like a thing inside a water tap that stops leaks.'

'Seal?' he asked.

'Yes, seal.' She went on and finished.

He sat back with a smile. 'Betty, would you type that up for me, please? And keep quiet about this.' She nodded and left the room. He turned to Jane. 'Well, my dear, I'm very impressed.'

'Thank you, Mr Anderson.'

'How many languages do you speak?'

'Well, Czech is my mother tongue. But I'm fluent in English, German, and Serbo-Croat.'

'Wow. Very good. Would you translate again?'

'Yes, of course. I'd be happy to help.'

'Well, thank you so much.' He stood and shook her hand. 'Can you find your way back okay?'

'Yes, I'm fine.' She left the room, and went back to the drawing office.

She sat and thought about what she'd just done. Something no one else here could do. And with such good results. *Ah well, back to the drawing board*. She picked up her pen.

***

A week later, Jane gathered her things at stopping time. Her husband, Tommy, waited at the door. Dressed in a grey suit, white shirt and tie. His dark wavy hair untidy. Wore glasses with thick lenses.

She smiled at him. 'Hello, love. Had a good day?'

'No. Pissed off. Fed up with this job.'

'What's wrong?'

He snarled. 'Ach. That's young Jack away tonight to join the RAF. Lucky bugger. I hate being stuck here. Want to be out there fighting as well.'

'But you *are* doing your bit here, love. We do important work for the war effort. Lots of it top secret. That's your bit. Not everyone can join the RAF. And it just wasn't for you.'

'Bloody eyesight. Oh, come on, let's go.'

They walked out of the office block and through the gate. She took his arm. Tried to snuggle into him to make him feel better. But it was a constant battle. His anger at the RAF rejection had become bitter as more of his mates joined up. They strolled towards the bridge over the river, past the City of Glasgow sign, with the giant Dalmarnock power station looming on the left. They rented a flat in the first tenement block on the right. At only half a mile from the office, they were lucky to get it.

They waited to cross the road, as trams rumbled past each way. Tommy said, 'How about a drink to cheer us up a bit?'

She glanced at the Boundary Bar at the next corner. 'Let's just go up, love. I need to talk to you.'

'Oh? Sounds serious.'

They went up to their flat. Tommy sat at the kitchen table without taking his coat off. 'What's the problem then? You're not pregnant again, I hope.'

She sat opposite him. 'No, not that.'

'Okay, what is it then?'

'You remember last week I told you I had translated a paper for Mr Anderson?' He nodded. 'Well, he asked to see me again today. And this time he had another man with him. Called Stevenson. A chief superintendent from the Special Branch.'

Tommy's eyebrows lifted in surprise.

'They want more German translators. He asked if I'd do it with them full time. What do you think?'

He frowned. 'Is your German that good? I thought you only had school German. Would that be enough?'

'Well, I did it all through school. He said that's good enough.' She couldn't tell him she spoke fluent German. It was still too sensitive. 'But it would mean me having to leave home for three weeks at a time. It would be three weeks on, one week off.'

He sat quiet for a moment. 'What about me? What would I do for three weeks while you're away? What about the kids? How would they get on without you around for three weeks? How long would it last? Would the company keep your job open? Is there more money in it? Need to think about all that, doll. And more.'

'Well, that's why we need to talk about it.'

'When do they want an answer?'

'A couple of days.'

'We need to think about this. Do you want to do it?'

That was the question, she thought. 'I'd like to give it a go. They need German speakers. And it would give me a chance to do a bit more for the war effort.'

'Do your bit, huh?' Tommy scoffed. 'I'll have a drink and think it over.' He stood up.

She tried to stop him. 'What I thought we'd do is have a quick fish supper and then go and see the kids. We haven't seen them this week yet.'

'No, you go if you want. I'll have a think. See you later.' He walked out.

She sat for a minute, angry at him. Then left to catch a tram to her in-laws in Cambuslang. She had moved the children out of the city for safety after a German bomb, aimed at the power station, wiped out a tenement block nearby.

As the tram passed the factory, she looked up at Anderson's window. In that office, she'd had a glimpse of another world. One that might lift her out of this sense of being in limbo. Where she might gain more personal satisfaction. But could she really do that sort of thing? An ordinary girl like her? And what about her husband and kids?

She thought about her marriage. They had to get married after she drank too much at a Glasgow Fair party in July 1936 and let his usual sexual fumbles go too far. It upset both families. But Tommy's father told him to stand by her, and a couple of months later they married. They had the two boys in less than two years. Her life had changed in a very short time.

She tried to keep some love alive. But he couldn't cope with regrets about his life. His answer to everything lay in the pub. And he could get nasty with her when drunk. She wanted to feel excited again. Escape from her dreary life. She didn't seem to have any impact on anything. Not on Tommy. Or the kids. Or even her job.

The translation had been great. She had at last felt useful. And this job might give her more of that.

She bathed the children and then read them a story. They fell asleep in no time. Over a quick meal, she talked about the job with her in-laws. It surprised them. They hadn't realised she spoke German.

They asked what it would mean for them and for the children. Jane answered as best she could. To her relief they were happy to support her in doing something extra for the war effort. Even better, they agreed to cope with the children during her three weeks away.

***

She came home before nine. Tommy still out at the pub. So she thought about her visit. Her in-laws had become more pleasant to her since they started looking after the children. And the kids seemed happy too. But she still found it hard at times.

At first, she and Tommy tried to see the children every night. To bath them and read their bedtime stories. But then they missed a night. And then two or three. Now when she arrived, the kids didn't even run to her for a hug. And that upset her.

She'd suggested to Tommy they go and live with his parents. But he vetoed it. 'I got out of there when I married. I'm not going back. No way.'

His father, a manager at the Colville's Steel plant, had been strict with Tommy. But he doted on the kids.

Stephen was five now. George almost four. They could still cope with change. At least, that's what she kept telling herself.

Just after ten, Tommy arrived. He'd had a few drinks and become surly. She could hardly remember when he could make her laugh. He'd just changed so much.

He spoke with a slur. 'You should take the job. It'll do you good. And do the country good as well, we hope. I'll get by okay while you're away. And the kids'll be fine. Just take it and do your bit. Become more useful to someone for a change.' He laughed with a sneer.

She ignored his insult. 'I'll tell them tomorrow then.' *What he changed his mind?*

They sat in silence. Then he picked up a newspaper and began to read it.

She gazed at him with a mixture of disgust and anger. 'I'm going to bed then. Oh, by the way, the kids are fine. And your mum and dad asked after you. I told them about the job too.'

He grunted.

'Right, see you in the morning.' She went through to their bedroom. In the past, when he came in drunk, he would demand his 'rights'. And she had to lie there trying to avoid his boozy breath. But now even that had stopped, thank God.

She got ready for bed and thought what she'd need to cover when she met Stevenson.

***

Jane sat outside Stevenson's office. Her mouth felt dry. She tried to moisten it. She now wanted this job, but wasn't sure she could do it.

His door opened. He walked over to her with a smile. Bags under his eyes and looked tired. About six feet tall with hair going grey.

'Jane. Many thanks for coming in.' They shook hands and moved into his office. 'Meet Inspector Sandra Maxwell. One of my team.'

The women shook hands. Maxwell, tall, with dark hair and a pretty face, had hard eyes. In her mid-thirties?

Stevenson waved to a seat at his conference table. 'Would you like some tea?'

'No thanks, I'm fine.'

'Good. Well, first of all, do you mind if we record this meeting?'

'That's okay.'

'Great.' He switched on the recording machine. 'Why don't we start with you telling us about your life to date? How you came here from Czechoslovakia?'

She took a deep breath. 'I was born in Prague in 1918, and brought up there. My dad and his brothers, all master tailors, grew up in Dresden, Germany. They each had their own business in the cities where their wives came from. The oldest in Dresden. My dad in Prague, of course. And the youngest in Zagreb, Yugoslavia.

'We all got together three times a year. In Prague at Easter. Opatija in Yugoslavia in July. And in Dresden at the end of September. They were happy times. We all spoke German. My dad and uncles solved the problems of the world. The wives cooked. And we children just had endless fun.

'But it all changed in 1933 when Hitler took control in Germany. His followers became very nasty towards Jewish people. We were atheists. But someone said we came from Jewish stock. It just wasn't true. But they began to harass Uncle Will in Dresden.

'Dad realised we could be targets in three ways. The false Jewish links. Being atheists. And having a socialist outlook. Hitler hated all three.

'He also thought Hitler would go on and take over all the countries bordering Germany if he could. So, we had a choice if we didn't like it. To fight or leave. He chose to leave.

'Dad talked the others into moving to Britain. They opened accounts in Swiss banks so they could access their money from anywhere. Then sold their businesses.

'Dad and Uncle Will brought their families to London in July 1935. Their younger brother had a few problems. But in the end, moved to Greece in 1936. I don't know if I'll ever see them again.

'But business would be hard in London. Too many tailors had already come here. So we headed north. Dad settled in Glasgow. Uncle Will in Manchester.

'We naturalised and changed names. Our surname became Wiseman from Weissmann. My father Georg became George. I changed from Jana. And my brother Marek became Mark. He's a bomb aimer in the RAF.'

She paused, and Stevenson smiled. 'Please, go on.'

'We did well here. Set up Wiseman Tailors in Byres Road. Rented a flat in Lawrence Street nearby. I took dad to the university and the BBC to offer an on-site tailor service. He did best of all the brothers.

'I made friends with a girl called Rhona who lived up the same close. We spent time in each other's houses. Listened to music. Talked about life. She taught me to dance, and we went to the Locarno on Saturday nights.'

She thought back to those days. *What would have happened if she'd never gone to the Locarno?* 'One night we met a couple of boys, Tommy and Billy, and formed a foursome. Tommy and I hit it off. He was a nice lad and made me laugh. We married in September 1936 and have two boys, Stephen and George. Tommy's dad helped us to get a flat in Dalmarnock Road. We moved there just before Stephen was born.

'I tried to keep helping Mum and Dad when I just had Stephen. But with two babies, it was impossible. We brought in a woman to help manage the shop.

'When the war started, Tommy wanted to join the RAF. But they turned him down because of his eyesight. I also wanted to help the war effort. So his mum looked after the kids. They were safer out of the city anyway. And I got a job as a tracer in the same place as Tommy.'

She looked down at her folded hands in her lap. 'I kept very quiet about my German until Mr Anderson asked me to translate last week. Is that enough?'

'It is indeed. I've known Iain Anderson for years. You impressed him. So, what do you think about our job? Have you talked it over with your husband?'

'I have. We think I ought to go for it. Or at least give it a try to see if I can help in a more practical way.' She pushed Tommy's cruel jibe out of her head. 'And my in-laws are happy to look after the kids while I'm away.'

Stevenson smiled. 'That's good. We spoke to Commander Porritt this morning. He's head of Special Branch. And he's very keen to have you.'

'That sounds good.'

'You talked about your father's views on Hitler. How do you see Hitler now?'

She thought for a moment. 'My father has a great name for Hitler. He calls him a . . .' She stopped. 'In German it's *Grössenwahnsinniger*. What's the English word again? Erm, mega . . . megalomaniac. That's the word. He has just gone on and on, as we thought he would. It's going to take a lot of effort by a lot of people to stop him. I could weep when I hear what he's done in my home country.'

'Thank you for that. Now, are there any other details you want to know about the job?'

'Well, I'd like to know what the job entails. How long it's for. The conditions. Whatever you can tell me.'

Stevenson checked his notes. 'Just before we get into that, would you sign this, please? It's the Official Secrets Act. It means you can't talk about your work. Not even to your nearest and dearest. Can you do that?'

She read the paper and signed it. Her life might be on the verge of something much more exciting.

He went on. 'Thanks. Let's see if we can answer your questions. Porritt has set up this new unit, Station BX, near Lincoln. It's an overflow from Bletchley Park, near London. Have you ever heard of it?'

She shook her head.

'Well, this new unit translates longer German documents to ease the pressure on Bletchley. Porritt also thought he could tap into more translators in the north. So he asked his SB teams to check their contacts. Hence my talk with Iain Anderson.

'This meeting is an initial screening. If you go on to Station BX, they'll assess your translating skills in the first week. If you pass that, you can then work there as long as you want. Or until the war ends.

'The hours of work are six days of twelve-hour shifts. Three weeks on and one week off. You'd get an enhanced private rate of nine shillings and three pence per day. We provide all travel, meals, and room. You'd have a single room. Like a hotel. Meals are typical canteen food. They have leisure rooms for use during off-work time. Porritt says most people think it's okay. So, what do you think?'

The rate was better than Tommy earned. So that would be another bone for him to pick. But she didn't care. 'Sounds all right. Better than I thought.'

'Glad to hear it. So, is it a goer then?'

She thought for a moment of Tommy's sneer when he'd come home drunk. Then felt her face break into a smile. 'Yes. Let's go for it.'

'Great. When do you want to start?'

'No point in waiting. Next week?'

'Right. I'll arrange it all with Porritt and Anderson. Sandra will give you a travel warrant for Sunday. Best to travel through Edinburgh to Newark. When you get there, ring this number. A car will pick you up and take you to Station BX. The very best of luck, my dear. Look forward to hearing great things about you. Thanks for coming in. And have a safe journey.'

She left with Sandra, who grinned at her. 'Well done, Jane. Hope it goes well.'

She smiled, and took the warrant. 'Fingers crossed.'

As she left the building, she skipped down the steps. This was a new chapter in her life. She needed to tell her parents. And her in-laws. And, of course, Tommy. And that would send him off to the pub again.

But none of that mattered now. Lincoln might just offer her a new start.

Chapter 3. Emerald 3

Chief Superintendent Malcolm Craig, Head of Special Branch in London, took the call. The duty inspector at Hampstead Police Station. 'Just had an old man in, sir. Listens to overseas stations on short-wave radio. For the last two nights, at exactly 5.30 pm, a strong Morse code signal has cut in. Thinks it might come from a spy in the area. I've said we'll send someone round to check. Do you want to pick this up, sir?'

Craig sighed. Three years into the war and everyone was jumpy. Adverts such as 'Walls Have Ears' and 'Careless Talk Costs Lives' spawned lots of calls. 'How do you rate him on a scale from crank to sane?'

'Came across as sound, sir. Served in the last war.'

Craig pursed his lips. Had to follow the inspector's hunch. 'Okay, give me the details. We'll check it out.'

'Right, sir. Here you are.' The inspector gave him the name and address.

Craig needed some comms experts. So arranged for a couple from MI5 to join him in the old man's home the next evening. They set up a recording machine next to the radio.

Sure enough, at 17.30, the Morse code cut in. Very fast. For only a few seconds. They had to replay it four times to catch the message.

'Bsxmqg 2 todvfmk 4 fwfl.' A gap. 'Bnoix pm.'

The comms men thought they'd heard only one side of a chat. Craig studied the coded message. *The old man*

21

could be right. Let's do first things first. He looked up at the old man. 'Thanks for your help. But I need you to tell no one about this. Do you agree?'

The old man nodded, eyes wide. 'Of course.'

Craig knew what he then had to do. 'I need to make a phone call. Could I ask you all to leave, please?' The old man and the comms men left. He turned to Brian Walker, his second in command. 'Here we go.'

He picked up the phone and asked for the number. The familiar voice answered. 'Porritt.'

'Good evening, sir. It's Malcolm Craig here. On to pick your brains.'

'Oh, hello, Malcolm. Won't get much, I'm afraid. But go ahead anyway.'

He described what had happened. Then asked the best way to get the message decoded.

There was a pause. 'Here's a name and number, Malcolm. He's at Bletchley Park. Tell him I said to call. He'll do what he can, I'm sure.'

'Thanks, sir. Leave it with me.'

'Good luck.'

Craig called the man. Told him the situation. Then asked if he could help decode the message.

'How soon can you get here?'

'A couple of hours at most.'

'Bring the note with you. Ask for me at the gate.' He rang off.

Craig turned to Walker. 'Could you ask the comms men to come back, Brian?'

They returned and sat down.

'We've got to go now,' Craig told them. 'But I want to check with you first where we go from here. How would we find the sender's location?'

The senior comms man replied. 'Well, first we need to know the frequency he's calling on. We can get that tomorrow night. Then triangulate his location the next night. Probably to within about twenty yards.'

'Is that all? And so much time?' He paused for a moment. 'Do you need approval for this?'

'Well, we should. But let's just set it up. We'll get approval at the last minute. Avoid reams of form filling.'

'Okay. Let's do it.'

'No problem. We'll get right on to it.'

As Craig and Walker left the house, they passed the old man and thanked him again.

Craig stood for a second and looked up and down the road. Both sides lined with terrace houses. Three floors with a basement. 'There's a nasty bugger here, Brian. We've got to get him.'

***

The security man guided them from the gatehouse to a wooden hut, just visible to Craig in the darkness. They went inside. The man knocked and opened a door. 'CS Craig, sir,' and stood aside to let them enter.

'Ah, come in, Craig,' said a tall, young man with glasses. 'I'm Hugh. We spoke earlier. And this is Ernie. One of our top decoders.'

Craig introduced Walker. And they all shook hands. He thought the coders looked in their early twenties. So young to be such senior staff.

Hugh held out his hand. 'Right. Do you have the message?'

Craig passed it over. Hugh and Ernie looked at it together. Then Ernie took it to a table at the side. He sat for a moment. 'Okay. I've got it. It's a simple cipher some German groups use for agents in the field. Means they don't have to carry code books. Let me see.'

He wrote on a sheet of paper. They all watched him. After a couple of minutes, he stood and gave the paper to Hugh. He read it and raised his eyebrows. Then handed it to Craig. He and Walker read it.

Code –
bsxmqg 2 todvfmk 4 fwfl
bnoix pm

German –
Aquila 1 Smaragd 3 euch
Alles OK

English –
Aquila 1 Emerald 3 over
All OK

Craig whistled. 'So it *is* a spy.'

Hugh pursed his lips. 'It's more important than that. Can't say more. Need-to-know and all that. But I suggest you let Porritt know.'

'Really?'

'Yes. You should do it now.'

Craig paused. *Need to get this right*, he thought. 'May I use a phone?'

Hugh gestured to the door. 'Use the office next door. All our lines are secure.'

'Thanks.'

Craig and Walker went next door, and Craig called Porritt. 'Sir, it's Malcolm Craig again. Sorry to bother you. But Hugh's chap has just decoded our message. He's said we should let you know.'

'Okay. What've you got?'

Craig read out the message.

'Well, now. That's *very* interesting, Malcolm. Where are you with catching this guy?'

'I've got a couple of comms men from MI5 to help. They'll get his frequency tomorrow. Then set up a triangulation the next night. And with a bit of luck, we'll catch him.'

Everything went quiet. Craig knew better than to interrupt Porritt's thinking.

'Wonder if there's any way to do that faster? Are you sure our man's only sending at five thirty?'

'I don't know, sir. Our short-wave radio man seems to listen at all times. But says this only comes in at five thirty. Short and fast. Lasts about ten seconds.'

'They'll do well to get the frequency in that time.'

Craig cleared his throat. 'I know it's very secret, sir. But can you tell me anything that might help us?'

'Okay. Keep this to yourself, Malcolm. About nine months ago, we upgraded our signals detection. Picked up messages from an Aquila 1 in Germany to an Aquila 3 and an Aquila 4 over here. But we couldn't detect any return signals. So we don't know who or where they are.

'The signals also referred to couriers called Emerald, who moved in and out of the UK at will. Maybe via Ireland, given the name.

'About six months ago, the signals ceased. Or we couldn't find them. Maybe they changed their method. Since then, we've heard nothing. Now your old man in Hampstead seems to have stumbled over them. We need to use this to find out more. And break them.'

25

'Does that mean you don't want us to lift him if we do find him, sir?'

'I'm tempted to just keep a watch on him. Find his contacts. Then pull them all in. But I think, on balance, if we do get the chance, we just lift him. It'll send a message we're on to them. And he could have something on him that leads us to others. What do you think?'

'I'm happy to go either way, sir. But even if the triangulation works, we only get to within twenty yards. We'd have to search lots of rented rooms to find him. Hard to do that without alerting him.'

'Yes, that's true. Right, let's agree. If you get the chance, lift him. And we take it from there. Keep me informed as you go please, Malcolm.'

'Of course, sir.'

'One other thing. Keep it all within SB. This lot seem clever. Just might have contacts on the inside.'

'Well, I'm using these comms men from MI5. We just don't have anyone of that calibre.'

'Fine, but tell them to keep quiet about it.'

'Will do, sir.'

'Okay. Good luck.' Porritt rang off.

Craig turned to Walker. 'Let's get back next door.'

Hugh looked up as they entered. 'Did it go okay?'

'Yes. You were right. We needed to tell him.'

'So, what else can we do for you?'

'Well, if the coding's as simple as you say, Ernie, could you tell us about it? So we can work it out for ourselves. I'm sure you've lots of other things to do.'

Ernie smiled. 'You could say that.' He took the original note and held it up. 'It's a progressive word-based code. Each letter moves on through the alphabet depending on its position in its word.

26

'For example, the first letter in the word moves on by one. The second by two. And so on. So, for this first word, b-s-x-m-q-g, you have to count back the right number of letters. And so you get a-q-u-i-l-a. And so on. The numbers follow the same rule. Once you decode it, you get the message in German. Then translate into English. Simple.'

Craig laughed. 'It may be simple to you, but it's clever to me!'

Hugh chuckled. 'Well, anyway, do you follow that okay? If you have trouble, you can always call us.'

Craig took the note back. 'Thanks very much. Appreciate all your help and advice.'

They all shook hands and the security man showed Craig and Walker back to the gatehouse.

***

The next morning, Craig called the comms men to his office. Bob, the senior of the two, in his forties, had a careworn look about him.

Craig asked them to keep this job secret.

'Right. But we'll have to use lots of equipment. So it won't be easy.'

'Well, do what you can, please. It's crucial.'

'Will do.' His partner, Don, nodded.

Craig then raised two points. First, could they do it faster? Second, could they be more precise?

Bob explained they had no automatic way to find the frequency or the location. The first would take about ten seconds at best. The second about fifteen minutes. And be no better than within twenty yards. That was the best they could do.

He placed a detailed map on the table. The old man lived on the east side of Gayton Road at number 42. Bob reckoned, with such a strong signal, the sender was close to the old man's home. On the west side of Gayton Road or on the two streets behind that. Spencer Walk or Flask Walk. The twenty yard range meant the sender could be in any one of three terrace houses.

Craig sighed. He had to rely on the two comms men. They were the best he could get. They agreed to meet again later in Gayton Road.

Just after 17.30, Craig and Walker, in coats with 'Savoy Electrics' on the back, walked up Gayton Road to a plumber's van. They met Bob and Don and stood as though discussing a job in a nearby house.

Bob kept his voice low. 'Well, we got it. Just. The lad's fast. But we got his frequency. Same message as last night.'

'So we're all set for tomorrow, then?'

'Yep. Would be good if we have parking spaces free for our vans.'

Craig looked at Walker. He nodded. 'We'll send in our roads squad early in the morning. Where do you want them?'

Bob looked around. 'Three locations. Near the top of this road. Down there near the Crescent. And in the lane off Flask Walk behind there. Big enough for vans like this.' He pointed at his van.

'Okay, will do.'

Craig turned to go. 'Right, we'll get back and start planning. See you tomorrow. Fingers crossed.'

The 'electricians' gave the 'plumbers' a wave and walked back to their van.

***

Early next morning, Craig met Walker to discuss their plans. Walker already had the roads squad at the three points. All taped off ready for vans.

Craig worried about the fifteen minutes delay to get the sender's location. He didn't want the spy to stroll off. Good spies would just blend in and vanish in that busy area. He'd block off three roads with 'Gas Board' barriers. Gayton Road, Spencer Walk, and Flask Walk. A 'gas leak' to keep everyone off the streets for these fifteen minutes.

Walker had pulled in extra staff from Hampstead and Camden forces to form five search teams. All in plain clothes. They could then hit five houses at the same time. He planned to brief them at three o'clock. But they had to agree what to say.

Craig picked up the phone. 'A radio transmitter would take up how much space, Bob?'

'About the size of a small case. But heavy. Maybe thirty pounds? Wouldn't be easy to hide in a rented flat. And on a first or second floor to get the best signal.'

'Thanks. See you later.'

Craig thought the spy would be a man on his own. A courier coming in and out all the time. With enough clothes for just a week. Most likely in a small bag.

'Do you think it's a safe house?' Walker asked.

The discussed it. In the end, they agreed it would make more sense to put someone here for a week into an area where lots of others did the same. A busy area near a tube station. Just like Hampstead. He wouldn't stand out there.

Craig pursed his lips. 'This lot have been running for months, Brian. I'll bet someone here books a room for a courier to stay. And pays in advance. Maybe a month in advance. So when he goes early, no one complains.'

Walker checked his notes. He could now brief the search teams later.

***

Just before 17.30, Craig and Walker joined Bob in his 'plumber' van. The signal came through right on time.

Bob stared at his instruments. 'Shit. I don't think he's here, sir.'

Craig grimaced. 'What? You sure?'

'Let me do my calcs and I'll tell you.' He took notes and worked his slide-rule. A few minutes later, 'He's not here, sir. Reckon he's in central London.'

Craig closed his eyes. 'Damn, damn, damn!' He dropped his head, thought through his options, then turned to Bob. 'Has Don got the message?'

'Yep. I'll get it for you, sir.' He left the van.

'Right, Brian. We won't find our man today. But we still need to find out where he's been at this time every day for the last week or so. Let's still do the search. To our guidelines.

'So, the old man's home is at 42. And the signal was strong there. Let's follow Bob's logic. Start across the road. What's that number?'

Brian checked his pad. 'Number 15.'

'Right. Let's do the searches as planned. Start at 15. We can do five houses at a time. So let's also do 14 and 13 to the south. And 16 and 17 to the north. Then spread from there. Don't open the street just yet. Brief the teams, Brian. Let's go.'

'Okay, sir.' Walker left the van.

Craig waited for Bob to come back. Then decoded the message. It took him a lot longer than Ernie.

Aquila 1 Emerald 3 over.
Package received. Return plan changed.

Craig wondered what had changed the return plan. He left the van and strolled up the road. The 'Gas Board' barriers were still in place at each end. Now with a small crowd behind them. He could see police officers trying to keep traffic moving in the High Street. Couldn't hold the road block much longer.

Walker emerged from a house and waved. He hurried towards him. 'Is this it, Brian?'

'Looks like it, sir. Number 12. First floor. But it's clean. Our bird seems to have well and truly flown. Landlady says he's been here a week. Always here at this time. But she hasn't seen him since this morning. Oh, and paid his rent a month in advance.' He looked at Craig and raised an eyebrow.

They climbed the stairs to the flat. 'Have a look at this, sir.' He pointed to an open drawer in the table with a gloved hand. 'See the imprint of writing on this pad? Mean anything to you?'

Craig bent and studied the pad at an angle against the light. He could just make out the imprint: bsxmqg 2 todvfmk 4 fwfl bnoix pm.

He pulled the original piece of paper from his pocket. Same letters.

'Right, this is it, Brian. Let's get it all back to normal outside. Thank everyone for their efforts.' He scanned the room. 'Cordon off this flat. Check every last inch for prints. Don't miss a thing.'

'Okay, sir. Will do.'

'Who else is here in the house?'

'Landlady in the flat below, sir. Pretty upset at all this. Also a man in the upstairs flat. We haven't talked to him yet.'

'Let's speak to her first. Oh, and get a police artist over here, Brian. Let's build up a picture of our man.'

***

Mrs Palmer, the landlady, sat at her kitchen table twisting a dish cloth. A small, slim woman with dark hair pulled back into a bun. Craig had to find out more about her tenant in the flat above. And whether she or the house were part of the spy gang. *It didn't look like it. But let's not rush it.*

He sat opposite her. 'Mrs Palmer, I'm Chief Superintendent Craig. You've met Chief Inspector Walker. We're from the police. And would like to ask you some questions. Is that okay?'

She nodded.

'We'd like to know more about the man who rented your first floor flat for the last week.'

Mrs Palmer stuttered at first. Then took a drink from a glass of water. 'He's a nice young man. Maybe mid-twenties? Very polite. Keeps himself to himself, really. Came here last Thursday.'

Craig coaxed a vague description from her. Quite tall. Fair hair. Square face. Nice smile. Good looking. Well built. But with no distinctive features. *Typical spy. Could fit hundreds of men in the area.*

The man spoke with an accent. But Mrs Palmer wasn't good on accents. She couldn't say which. His name was Tim Convery, and he showed an ID card.

Craig asked if she knew where he came from. She didn't, but his aunt had said he was from up north.

He exchanged glances with Walker. 'His aunt? When did she come?'

'She came Tuesday morning last week. Booked the room for him and paid a month in advance. Well dressed. Nice grey tailored suit. Matching hat and shoes. Wasn't cheap. Expensive handbag too. Very pleasant. Hair going grey. Medium height.'

She agreed to help the police artist create a picture of Convery and his aunt.

He asked her about the house. Did she own it? More relaxed now, she gave her life history. It had been in her family for several generations. *This was no safe house*.

Craig began to draw things to a close. 'May I just come back to Convery again? Did he ever have any visitors, letters, or phone calls?'

'As far as I know, he had no visitors or letters. And only one phone call. That was this morning.'

'Oh? That's interesting. Who took the call?'

'Well, I answered it. Went upstairs and told Mr Convery. He came down and took the call.'

'Who was it that called? Did they give a name?'

'No. Just asked for Mr Convery.'

Craig leaned forward. 'Was it a man or woman? What kind of voice? Any accent at all?'

'It was a man. Very pukka English. Very posh.'

'And what time was that?'

Mrs Palmer thought for a moment. 'I'd say around half-past nine. Maybe a bit earlier?'

Craig turned to Walker. He knew it was almost impossible to trace a call, but said, 'See if we can get any info on that call, Brian.' Then he turned back to Mrs Palmer. 'And did you see him after that?'

'No, I didn't. Heard him coming down and going out. Maybe fifteen minutes later? But I haven't seen him since. Which is unusual. He's always in at this time.'

'Have you used the phone since he took his call?'

She shook her head. 'No.'

'Good. Well, thank you, Mrs Palmer. If you think of anything else about Mr Convery, give me a ring.' He gave her his card.

'Is he a criminal?' she asked, as he got up to leave.

'Well, we can't say. We'd just like to talk to him.'

Craig and Walker left Mrs Palmer and went upstairs to see the man in the top flat. 'Make sure the prints boys give the phone a dust, Brian.'

Grogan was a thin man in his early thirties. Worked with the GPO, and had come down to London from Manchester for a month to train on new phone systems. He hadn't ever spoken to Convery. Had only seen him a couple of times in the house. But he agreed to help the police artist with a picture.

Craig asked him if he had ever seen Convery outside the house. In a pub or restaurant, for example.

'Yes. He was in The Flask saloon bar on Saturday night. I was there with a mate from work. Saw him chat up a couple of girls. Think he fancied himself as a bit of a ladies' man.'

'Was he on his own?'

'Yeah.'

'What about the girls? Would you know them again?'

34

'I would. Quite pretty. Dark hair. Looked like sisters. The three of them left the bar around half eight. Didn't see them again after that.'

'Could you help the police artist get a picture of them as well?'

'Sure. Be glad to help.'

'And if you see them again, could you call me, or just tell the nearest policeman? We'd like to talk to them.' He gave Grogan his card. 'By the way, when did you last see Convery?'

Grogan drummed his fingers on the table as he thought. 'This morning, about quarter to ten. I left here at ten to ten, and it was just before that. Bit unusual, though. He walked away across our backyard and then across the next yard. Then went into the street behind us here. Spencer Walk, I think it's called.'

'Was he carrying anything?'

'Yes, a small brown suitcase and a soft grey bag.'

'And how was he dressed?'

'Dark coat and cap. Maybe dark blue? Dark trousers, I think. Sorry I can't be more helpful.'

'That's all right. Thanks for your help so far. And please call me if you see him or these girls again.'

'Is it very serious, then?'

Craig stood. 'Well, it might be. We'd just like to talk to them to find out.'

They shook hands, and Craig and Walker left him.

One of their team stopped them as they came down. 'Got a partial print off the side of the basin, and from the back of the pad. But that's it, sir.'

Craig sighed. 'Okay. Check with what we've got. Let me know as soon as you can.'

***

Back at the office, Walker went off to type up his notes. Craig sat at his desk, angry that Convery had got away. He wracked his brains over what he could have done better. But couldn't think of anything. He made the dreaded call.

'Porritt.'

'Hello, sir. Craig here.'

'How did it go?'

'We missed him, sir. Had it all set up. But the target got a phone call this morning and scarpered.'

'Did he now? That's interesting.'

'Yes. Pukka English voice. We're trying to trace the call. But you know how difficult that is. And it was probably from a public phone box in any case. Bloody annoyed, sir. All that good work undone because . . . I hate to say it . . . because of a leak.'

'Who were you using, Malcolm?'

'My own team. Rock solid, I'd say. We also used teams from Hampstead and Camden to help with the searches. But they didn't know the set up. The only outsiders were the comms men from MI5. That must be where we leaked.'

'Mmm. Not good.'

'The comms men themselves seemed okay. But they had to get approval to use the equipment. That's where the leak must have come from.'

'Did you find anything in the end?'

'Well, we still got the signal at five thirty. But sent from central London. It read: Package received. Return plan changed.'

'Sounds like he's got what he came for. That's a pity. Wonder what changed his return plan.'

'We also found the flat, sir. Wiped clean. But we got a couple of partial prints. Checking them now. We've also pulled in an artist to draw a picture of the target. I'll send you a copy.'

'Okay, Malcolm. Too bad it didn't work out. Don't blame yourself for that. Keep me posted.'

Craig thought about the call. Bastard leaks from MI5? How the hell were they going to deal with that? A few months ago, Porritt had them tail a bunch of members from a Whitehall committee. And that had come to nothing. Let's hope this didn't end the same way. *Shit*. It was hard enough fighting the bad guys, without having to fight the so-called good guys as well.

He went to find Walker. 'Time for a pint, Brian.'

Before going home, Craig went back to the office and found a message on his desk. 'No match for partials so far. Update tomorrow.'

Shit. Another dead end. Far too many on this job.

Chapter 4. Convery

Tim Convery loathed the English. With a deep passion. Always so stuck-up and superior. Treated everyone else as second-class. His granddad had told him stories about the English hunts back home in Ireland before the First World War. They just squashed farmland, crops and fences in their path. He had a long scar on his face from a huntsman's whip. 'Don't speak back to your elders and betters.' *Bastards. All of them.*

Above all, they had killed his gentle, beautiful Liesl. In a bombing raid over the Ruhr. It still brought tears to his eyes. He missed her so much. Her touch. Her smile.

He sat in a tearoom, and watched people passing along the narrow street in central London. Bent forward with collars up against the wind. How many of *them* had met Hitler? Maybe a few old politicians. But none of them twenty-five years old like him. Hitler would change the world. As the English would soon find out.

In 1925, at the age of seven, he and his dad moved to an uncle in Germany to find work and ease the burden on the family farm. But in 1934, his dad went back to Ireland. He stayed on, joined the Hitler Youth, and thrived in it. With his fair hair, good looks and build, and super self-confidence, he sped up through the ranks and became an area leader. He'd met Hitler once at an HY rally. Awesome. A magical man. He would do anything for him.

His fluent English was also a great help. Abwehr, the German military intelligence group, soon chose him to travel to England as a courier.

He also watched the shoe shop across the street. That morning, he'd had a surprise phone call at his flat in Hampstead. The man told him to wipe it all down, clear out, and get here before five o'clock.

He caught the tube down from Hampstead. Made a couple of careful route changes along the way. Always last on, last off, to throw a tail. He now waited for the signal to go into the shoe shop.

Lyall Shoes had a large window on each side of the door. The display on the right carried a bust of Homer among the shoes. It now sat at the side nearest the door. His sign to go inside. He left the tearoom.

Inside the shoe shop, a woman approached him. 'Yes, sir? How can I help you?'

'Mr Lyall, please.'

'And your name?'

'Convery.'

'Ah, Mr Convery. Let me take you to him.'

She led him through an arch at the back into another smaller showroom. Lyall sat at a desk, writing. A stout man with silver hair. He glanced up and smiled. 'Mr Convery. Nice to see you again. Your shoes are ready. Thanks, Becky.' The woman left. 'Try them on. Make sure they're comfortable.' Lyall passed him a box.

Convery sat and put the shoes on. This is what he had come to England for. He'd been in a week earlier to have his feet measured. The shoes were just right.

He stood and tested them. 'Fine. Perfect fit.'

'Excellent. Will you just keep them on?'

'Yes. I'll do that.'

'Good. I'll send the bill on to you.' Lyall put Convery's old shoes in the box and laid them aside.

'Thanks.' Convery leaned forward and whispered, 'Why the sudden change in plans?'

Lyall's voice dropped to a whisper too. 'We think they were on to you in Hampstead. We had to get you out fast. But we'll put you in a safe house. Also, your usual exit route is not ready right now. So you may have to wait a few days for a way back.'

'Fine. Can I transmit from here at five thirty?'

'Sure. Use this back office here.' He opened a door.

Convery glanced into the room. 'Thanks.' He took his case, bag, and gas mask box with him.

'I'm just going to close up the shop and let the staff away. You all right here for a minute or two?' Lyall went off through to the main showroom.

He opened his case, set the aerial up around the wall, plugged it into the transmitter, and waited for five thirty. Then studied his new shoes. They looked well-made. Must contain a secret. But couldn't see where. He put them back on and planned his message.

He set the frequency, turned the power up because the room had no windows, and began to transmit with the agreed code. 'Aquila 1, Emerald 3, over.'

An immediate response. 'Emerald 3 send.'

'Package received. Return plan changed.'

'Roger Emerald 3. Out.'

He repacked it all. Then put the case at the wall.

Lyall popped his head round the door. 'Everything go all right?'

'Yes, fine.'

'Leave that here.' Lyall pointed to the case 'I'll deal with it later.'

40

They moved back into the other room. Lyall picked up a piece of paper from the desk. 'Take a taxi from here to King's Cross and catch a train to York. There's one leaving at seven. At York, phone this number.' He passed over the paper. It read: P 437. 'They'll send a car for you and take you to a safe house. We'll get you out from there as soon as we can.'

He squinted at the page. 'What does P mean?'

Lyall opened a map and indicated a town.

'Okay.'

'Right, get going, Here's some cash.'

'Thanks.' He picked up his bag and gas mask box.

Lyall walked him out of the shop, and shook hands. 'Have a safe trip.'

***

The journey from York seemed endless. And with capped headlights, he saw little of the road.

After an hour, they turned off through some woods and entered a long, low garage. He got out and stretched. The driver walked him across a garden to a large house, outlined against the night sky.

As they approached, a door opened. A tall, slim, grey-haired man with glasses greeted them. 'Come in, Mr Convery. Good to see you. I'm John Kay' He shook hands, then turned to the driver. 'Thanks, Ted. See you in the morning.'

'Right, Mr Kay. Good night.'

Kay closed the door, pulled the curtain over it, and put on the light. 'Welcome. And this is Elizabeth, my wife.' An attractive, slim woman in her fifties stood at the kitchen table.

41

He walked over and shook her hand. 'Tim Convery.'
He clicked his heels.

She smiled. 'I know it's late, and you've had a long
journey. But can I get you something to eat or drink?'

'That would be nice, thanks. Just some tea and
maybe a sandwich?'

Kay pulled out a chair. 'Come on, sit down here and
let's talk.'

He sat and relaxed.

Kay went on, 'It's going to take us a few days to get
you out. So just relax and be comfortable while you're
here. Is that okay?'

'Yes, fine.'

'Good. So how was the journey?'

'Packed train. Lots of soldiers travelling on north of
here. But everything went fine.'

'Yes, we've a few big army camps up north. And
every train's packed these days.'

Elizabeth put down a mug of tea and a sandwich.
'Hope that suits you.'

'Thanks. Tastes good.'

They chatted for a while. But his eyes kept closing
with tiredness.

'Let's get you up to your room,' Kay said.

He rose, picked up his bag and followed Kay
upstairs. They went into a bedroom at the back of the
house. 'I hope you find this comfortable. Bathroom's
just next door. I'll leave you to it.'

He felt exhausted yet excited at the sudden change
of plan. He used the bathroom and started to read in bed.
Within minutes, he was asleep.

Chapter 5. Station BX

Jane liked the look of Station BX on Sunday evening. It had an airy feel. In pastel shades. Nice room. A single bed, wardrobe, and dressing table on one side. An easy chair, lamp, and radio over by the window. The bathroom had a shower. But that was okay with her.

The next morning, she went to Meeting Room C. She found four other new starts there. All looked as nervous as she felt. Two other Czech girls, Dianka and Kristina. And two Swiss men, Andrej and Martin from Bern. All in their mid-twenties, now lived in Britain. They seemed a pleasant bunch, and she began to relax.

At eight o'clock, a man and woman entered. The man about six feet tall. In his late forties, maybe? Well-built, with dark hair and a tanned face. Wore a blazer and flannels, white shirt and striped tie.

The woman. Also quite tall. Very slim, with glasses. Hair going grey. In her fifties? In a casual beige uniform.

They introduced themselves. Commander Jonathan Porritt, head of Station BX, and Sophie Silverman, head of admin. They all shook hands, and he welcomed them.

He talked about his background. Joined the Navy at seventeen. Worked his way up. Commanded destroyers for many years. Then to London with MI5. Then helped set up the signals decoding unit at Bletchley Park. This had become very busy and had to expand. Hence the need for Station BX.

He was also head of Station 19, based in the large house just seen above the trees beyond the fence. Also ran Special Branch in the UK. A busy man, thought Jane, though lots of people did multiple jobs in wartime.

He left to get on with other things, and Silverman showed the Station layout on the screen. She told them they would have a tour later and collect their uniforms. Then moved on to discuss the job itself. This covered the basics Jane had heard in Glasgow.

'You'll translate German documents into English. You need to be both accurate and timely.' Jane hoped she'd be accurate enough.

'We'll use real documents during this stage. And on Wednesday, assess your progress. If you pass, you move to the workroom. If not, you remain here till Friday.

'Now, we realise your fluency in German varies. So we suggest, while you're on site, you talk together in German to improve it. Off site, of course, you must speak only in English.'

She ended by telling them a free bus ran into Lincoln in the evenings and all day Sunday. But they must always go with someone else for security.

After their tour, they got their uniforms, and went to their rooms to change. Then back to the meeting room.

Silverman looked round the group. 'That's good. Look the part now. We'll move next door. We've set up two sections of tables just like in the workroom.'

Next door, she gave out a document in German. 'This is just to get you familiar with the process. Not to assess you. Write your translation on the blank form, as neat as possible, please. Remember, someone has to type it. Okay? Start now.'

Jane read the document. Just over a page long. It gave instructions to a courier. Go to an army camp in woods near Dortmund. Get a document from a Captain Weber. Take it to an office in Dortmund. And give it to a Mr Schmidt. Lots of detailed directions and procedures. She had no problems with any words, and started writing her translation on the blank form.

Within a few minutes, she finished, read it through, and signed the form. The others were still writing. And some seemed to use their dictionary a lot. She checked her work again. A new day. A new way. A new life. She'd found her niche in this war. Magic.

Silverman gathered in the forms. They then broke for a quick lunch. The five recruits took their lunch trays outside to a picnic bench in the garden. They chatted to the background noise of aircraft engines from the RAF base on the other side of Station 19.

***

By Wednesday, Jane had done over a dozen test papers. Each longer and harder than the one before. They then in turn went into Meeting Room C to meet Porritt and Silverman, and hear their fate.

They told her she'd hit the top rating, and should join the twenty translators in the workroom. Three others in her group had also passed. Next morning, they settled in an island of four tables near the window.

She found a large Czech group gathered in the evenings. They spoke only German. But she was among the most fluent. She therefore became much more confident within the group.

The three girls from her sub-group went into Lincoln on the two middle Sundays. They liked the city and climbed up the hill to admire the cathedral.

Her work days passed in a flash. In the first couple of weeks, she missed her children in the evenings, and phoned her mother-in-law a few times to speak to them. But, by the third week, she'd settled in, and relished her new part in the war effort.

Before she knew it, she was on her way back home on the Saturday night at the end of her first stint.

Her flat lay empty. And it wasn't as much of a tip as she'd expected. Tommy seemed to have tidied up. Which was rare. She picked up an old newspaper and put it in the bin. Then noticed some cigarette butts already in the bin had lipstick on them. She froze and sank onto the sofa. Her mind reeled.

Sure enough, he came in just after ten. 'Oh, you're back?' He gave her a casual wave.

'Yes, I *am* back. And wondering what's been going on here while I was away.'

He frowned. 'What you on about, woman?'

She picked up the bin. 'I'm on about these cigarette butts with lipstick. Have you had a woman in here?'

He shrugged and looked away. 'No. Well, yeah. I had a few friends in last night. Had some drinks. Played some cards. Nothin' to worry about.'

'Who was she?'

He'd had a few drinks, and slurred his words. But tried to speak clearly. 'Peggy. From the pub. And Doug and his wife. Nothin' bloody creepy about it. Are you sayin' I can't have anybody in when you're no' here? Is that what you're sayin'?'

She pursed her lips and turned away. 'No, that's not what I'm saying.' Then she turned back with a pointed finger. 'But I don't want you to have any lone women in here while I'm away. And that's just being sensible.'

After a moment, he nodded. 'Of course. You're right. It won't happen again. Trust me. I'm just not interested that way in anybody else. I only love you. It would be nice to get a wee kiss and a hug, though. Haven't seen you for so long.'

She watched him slump into his easy chair. *That's the problem. I don't trust him anymore.* She walked over to him. 'Look, it's been a long day for me. I need to get to bed.' She leaned over and kissed him on the forehead.

Tommy looked up with a laugh. 'Is that an invite, darlin'? Come on, let me feel these tits.' His hands came up onto her breasts. 'Let me see these beautiful tits. That's what I've been waitin' for.'

She pulled back from him. 'Leave it till tomorrow. It's too late for me tonight. I need to get some sleep.'

He leaned back in the chair. 'All right, doll. See you in the mornin'.'

She went to the bedroom and sifted through her bag. She'd had a contraceptive cap fitted after George's birth without letting Tommy know. He just refused to use anything. She took it out of her bag together with the cream, and inserted it in case he demanded his 'rights'.

She was sound asleep when he came to bed.

***

Next morning, she got up and made herself breakfast while he slept on. Afterwards, she heard him going to the toilet, and went through to see him as he came back to the bedroom.

She smiled at him. 'Ready for breakfast?'

He laughed. 'I'm ready for my tits,'

She knew it had to happen and forced a smile. '*Your* tits? They're *my* tits.'

'Oh no. They're made for my pleasure. Come here.'

She pulled off her nightdress and straddled him on the bed. Within a few minutes, he had come and lay breathless with a big smile. 'That was great, doll.'

Jane rolled off him. Every time it happened, she thought back to her friend Rhona in Lawrence Street. *She* had much more experience in sexual matters, and Jane had learned everything about the ways of men from her. 'Men just ride you and come. And think they're doing you a favour. Will I ever meet a man who'll give me more pleasure than I can give myself?' As time went on, Jane asked herself the same question.

She got up off the bed. 'Tell you what. Let's get ready and take the kids out today. Just be a family again? What do you say?'

To her surprise, he nodded. 'Okay, let's do that,' and got out of bed.

They caught a tram out to Cambuslang, took the kids to a park, let them play on the swings for a while, then got them an ice cream. Jane was just so glad to see them again. They went back to Tommy's parents' house for a meal, put the kids to bed, and headed back home.

It had been a good day, Jane thought. More like how it should be. When he was sober and in the right mood, Tommy could still be good company. Maybe there was still hope for them yet.

***

The week passed in a flash. Jane deep-cleaned the house, took the kids out, and spent time with her parents. As the week went on, though, Tommy spent more time in the pub. And his nasty side reappeared. Then it was Sunday. She headed south, ready to start again.

Halfway through Monday morning, Brenda, her team leader, came over and whispered, 'Commander Porritt would like to see you in Meeting Room C.'

Jane lifted her eyebrows. 'Really?'

Brenda nodded and put a hand on her arm. 'Just as soon as you can.'

Jane tidied her papers away, locked her table drawer, and left the room. Porritt was on his own in the meeting room and waved her in. 'Come in, Jane. Nice to see you again. How are you settling in?'

She smiled. 'Very well, sir. Enjoy it very much.'

'Good. Well, sit down. I want a word with you.'

Jane sat and waited.

'I'd like you to join me over at Station 19. We interview captured Germans there. I need someone beside me to translate my questions, and the answers I get back. But it's more than that. It's also to sense if his reply doesn't sound right. And let me know. We think you've got that extra maturity we need.

'I've used the same girl, Gloria, since we started. But she's called in sick and will be off for a while. So I need someone to replace her now. The hours are more flexible over there. We sometimes work in the evenings or even late at night. But you'd be on a higher pay rate. An enhanced sergeant rate. Thirteen shillings and three pence a day. What do you think?'

Jane exhaled. She found it hard to stay calm. *Wow, could she really do that job?* 'I'm very surprised – honoured, in fact – that you think I could do it.'

'Well, you're one of our top translators. And I've heard you're the most fluent German speaker here. So, Sophie and I thought it right for both you and us?'

Jane took a deep breath. Then smiled. 'Yes, I'd like that, sir. Bit nervous. But I'd like to give it a try.'

'Great. I'm very pleased. So, finish off the document you're working on. Then call this number. A car will pick you up at reception here and take you over to Station 19. I'll meet you there and show you round.

'And please don't talk to anyone about this. You'll work between the two stations for a while. If you're not required there, you'll work here. Is that okay?'

She nodded. 'Look forward to it, sir.'

'Good. See you later.' Porritt stood and shook hands.

She left the room excited. Desperate to tell someone. But knew she couldn't. *What an opportunity.*

***

Jane arrived at Station 19 just after lunch. To get there, she had to show her pass at a gatehouse. The large mansion house had extra wings built on each side.

The hall was massive. A wide stair split into two to reach the upper floor. She stood at the desk on the right.

A few moments later, Porritt and another man appeared. He welcomed her with a warm handshake. Then introduced her to Alison, at the desk, who 'knows everything about everything that goes on here.'

Then to Mike Williams, his second in command, 'without whom this place would not function at all. Good to have you with us. Let's get you started.'

Jane took a deep breath to relax. Porritt led her into a large office with two desks at the windows. They all sat at a conference table in the middle.

Porritt explained Special Branch, the part of the police that looked after national security, ran Station 19. They also worked with other government agencies. But SB had the powers of arrest.

The building kept staff and prisoner areas separate. The only link between the two was at the interview rooms, with guarded access from both sides. Porritt wanted her to translate his questions and the answers. But if she sensed the answer didn't feel right, she should bump his leg under the table. They would then break to discuss it. 'So, what do you think?'

She nodded. 'So far, it's fine. Should I take notes?'

'Well, have a pad to note any points you want. But we record all interviews. Okay?'

'Yes. I'm ready.' She took a deep breath again.

'Good. Then the next one we have is a young flier shot down about three months ago. Hardly a scratch. Very lucky. He's Oberleutnant Hans Krieger. Twenty-four. Born Berlin. After a hospital check, we sent him to a POW camp in County Durham.

'Two nights ago, he escaped. But we caught him hiding just off the main road to Bishop Auckland. It's not clear at this stage how he got out. But we have a local witness who saw him use a phone box. We've searched him, but can't find a phone number in this country.

'So we'd like to know more about Herr Krieger. How he escaped and who he phoned? I want to know if there's a network these people phone that gets them out of the country. Shall we go see?'

The guard on duty at the interview room checked their passes, switched on a red light, and let them enter. Jane looked round. The room was bare except for a table in the centre with a microphone. Two chairs on the long side nearest them. A young man in an open-necked shirt sat at the other side. A smaller table with a chair against the wall to the left with a recording machine. A guard on each side of a door in the back wall that must lead to the prisoner area.

She and Porritt sat down opposite the young man. She was amazed how young he looked. Even though he was about the same age as her. He had fair hair, blue eyes, and a fresh face.

Williams switched on the recorder. 'Interview of Oberleutnant Hans Krieger. Monday fifth April 1943 at Station 19. Led by Commander Porritt. With CS Williams and Sergeant Translator Thomson. Guards, Sergeant Brown and Corporal Henry. Time 14.45.' He nodded to Porritt.

'Good afternoon, Herr Krieger.' Jane stepped into her role and translated to and from him. 'The reason for this meeting is to find out how you escaped lawful custody at our Windlestone POW camp.'

Krieger cleared his throat. 'I have nothing to say to you,' he said in German.

'Well, of course, that's your right. But I'd just like to point out we try to make life as pleasant as possible for you there. It's one of our best camps. And only for officers. Which is not the case with all our camps.

'Now, if you don't want to talk, that's fine. I'll then move you to one of these other camps. And remove some comforts from your fellow officers. I'd make it clear to them it was because of your lack of cooperation.

'But if you do cooperate, both you and I will be a lot happier. And none of these painful things will happen.'

Krieger looked from her to Porritt and back again. After a few minutes silence, he said, 'If I talk, will I be sent back and no one would know?'

Porritt nodded. 'Yes. You'd lose some comforts for a short time. But we'd say nothing about this.'

He pursed his lips. 'Okay. I'll talk to you.'

'Good decision. Now, would you like to tell me how you escaped?'

He paused for a moment. 'We used ground-floor rooms in the old house for games and leisure in the evening. One night, when I was going to the toilet, I tripped and fell against a door. Although locked, it opened as I hit it.

'It led down to a basement. And this had an outside door close to the gardens where we worked during the day. The fence around the estate was on the far side of these gardens.

'Once I knew how to get out the house, I planned an escape. It took about two weeks to get it all ready. I left a covered trailer we used to move vegetables near the fence. With a coat I could put over the barbed wire. Two nights ago, it was dark and cloudy. So I took the chance. It was really quite easy.'

Porritt glanced up from his notes. 'Did you tell anyone about your plan?'

'Well, not at first. But once I knew I could do it, I told my senior officer.'

'And who was that?'

'Hauptmann Werner. About a week before I went, I showed him the exit route. He arranged some British money for me. And would cover my absence.'

'And what did you plan to do after you were out?'

'I thought I could catch a truck going south. Maybe get to the sea or the Channel and steal a boat.'

'And what about papers? Do you speak English?'

'No, my English is not good. But I spent some time in Poland before the war. I could get by as Polish. So I forged Polish papers as backup.'

Porritt sat silent for a few moments. 'You've been at the camp for three months. Right?'

'Yes.'

'During that time, what British people have you met? Like the guards or officers at the camp? Or others?'

'Well, not many. A guard called McKenzie. Worked with us in the gardens. And there were the people who served meals. Also Captain Wilkinson, the head of the camp. There was another. A priest, I think. But I didn't get involved.'

'Tell me about McKenzie. What was he like?'

'Tall. Heavy built. Red hair. From Scotland. I think he'd been a gardener before the war. He had a wounded leg. Walked with a stick. He was okay.'

'And Captain Wilkinson? When did you meet him?'

'When I arrived. Told me the rules of the camp.'

'And how would you describe him?'

'Tall. Mid-forties. Dark hair. Handsome. Good build. Just a nice, pleasant man.'

'Okay, thanks.' Porritt paused. 'We'll have a break. Get him a drink, Sergeant. Back in ten minutes.' He stood and led the way back to his office. 'Well, Jane, what did you think of your first session? By the way, you did very well.'

'Thank you, sir. I found it fascinating. But one of the things that struck me was that his voice changed when he talked about Captain Wilkinson. It seemed like he was talking about a woman, sir.'

Porritt raised his eyebrows. 'Well now. That's interesting, Jane. What do you think, Mike?'

'I didn't pick up on that. But I wondered why he described Wilkinson as "handsome". Was it the right word, Jane?'

She thought for a moment. 'He used the words *gut aussehend*, which means "good-looking". I'd say for a man that means "handsome". For a woman, I'd have used "beautiful". But his tone of voice changed when he said it. That's my point.'

'And it's a good point, Jane. Exactly what we want from you.' He turned to Williams. 'Mike, call Durham. Let's find out more about Wilkinson. Married? Family? The usual. Quick as you can, please.'

Williams picked up a phone and talked for several minutes. Then updated Porritt and Jane on his call. 'He lives in Bishop Auckland with his mother. Mid-forties. Not married. No family.'

'What do you think, Mike?'

Williams shook his head. 'Krieger's ideas of going across the country using Polish papers and pinching a boat are crazy. There's no way that would work. We'd nick him the first time he went anywhere. It's nonsense.

'I'm a wary bugger as you know. Sorry, Jane. My apologies. But I think, from what Jane said, our man was closer to Wilkinson than he's making out. Maybe very close, if you know what I mean.'

Jane wondered what he meant.

'The escape sounds possible. But let's think for a moment that these two want to get together for some hanky-panky. They can't do it at the camp. So they work out a way Krieger can escape and get to Wilkinson's house to stay. We'd all search for him. But none of us would dream of looking for him there.

'I think they planned for him to escape. Then picked up by Wilkinson and taken home. The pickup point was probably the phone box our witness saw Krieger using. And our notes here say when our team pulled up at the crossroads, Krieger came out from behind the phone box as though he was waiting for them. Then when he saw it was the police, he scarpered.

'I'll bet Krieger phoned Wilkinson. To let him know he was out. But because our witness called our boys so quickly, we got there first. Wilkinson maybe had a car problem or was just late in arriving. Does it fit?'

'I think it does, Mike. Let's go and see.'

They went back to the interview room. Williams spoke into the recorder. 'Resumed 15.57.'

Porritt smiled. 'Right, Herr Krieger. Let's go back to when we picked you up. A police patrol caught you at the Leasingthorne crossroads, a mile from Windlestone. Is that correct?'

Krieger nodded.

'Now, no one at Windlestone knew you had gone. Why do you think the police got there so quickly?'

He looked from Porritt to Jane and back again. She thought his eyes looked scared. He shook his head. 'I don't know.'

'Well, you see, we have a witness who lives in the cottage at that crossroads. He was in his garden in the

56

darkness. Getting some fresh air before going to bed. He saw you scurrying along the road from Windlestone. In fact, when you turned down the side road past the phone box and stood against the hedge, he was standing less than ten feet – three metres – from you in the dark.'

Krieger stared at Porritt.

'And this witness is an ex-army man. An ex-MP. So he suspects anything out of place. But do you know what else made him really suspect you?'

He sat as though frozen.

'You used the phone box. Then walked down and stood against the hedge. Now, who did you phone?'

A faint sheen of sweat appeared on his forehead.

'And just to complete our story. While you stood there, our witness tiptoed back into his house and called the police. Now the County Durham police have new in-car radio telephones. So the control room alerted a patrol car on its way to Bishop Auckland. And that's why they were there so quickly. Good for us. But bad luck for you, I'm afraid.'

Krieger dropped his head.

'So, would you like to tell me who you phoned? We've already asked the phone company to trace the call. So we'll know by tomorrow. But it would help your position if you told us now.'

Porritt waited. Total silence in the room. The silence lasted several minutes. Then Krieger whispered, 'Captain Wilkinson.'

Porritt leaned forward. 'Are you saying you phoned Captain Wilkinson? Did he help you escape?'

Krieger nodded.

'For the record, please state your answer.'

'Yes. He helped me to escape.'

'How did he do that?'

'He switched off the alarm on the outside door from the basement on the night I escaped.'

'And did anyone else, such as Hauptmann Werner, know about this?'

He shook his head. 'No, he didn't know. He thought I had found the exit route myself.'

'So, you phoned Wilkinson from the phone box and waited for him to come and pick you up. Is that correct?'

'Yes. That's correct.'

'And what was the plan after that?'

'He would hide me at his home. And we could be together. What's going to happen to him?'

Porritt shrugged. 'Can't say. A court will decide.'

Krieger's eyes filled with tears. 'We just fell in love. Is that such a crime?'

'It is in this country, Herr Krieger.' He nodded over to Williams.

'Interview ended. 16.37.'

Porritt looked over to the guards. 'Take the prisoner back, please, Sergeant. Thank you both.'

***

Back in his office, Porritt said, 'Well, you were right, Mike. Well done. What did you think of that, Jane?'

Jane shook her head. The constant translating both ways needed her total focus. But the unfolding real-life story had gripped her. 'I'm shocked, sir. Do men really fall in love?'

'It seems so. Though usually kept hidden.'

She now felt secure in their company. 'But Wilkinson must be crazy to have done that, sir.'

'He sure was. But, you know, the three big emotions that change people's behaviour are greed, fear, and love. And love can be the most powerful of them all. To those on the outside, their actions seem crazy, as you say. But for those involved, it just seems normal. That's life.'

'What will happen to Wilkinson now?'

'Oh, we'll arrest and charge him with aiding the escape of a POW.' He glanced over at Williams. 'Issue the warrant, Mike. As soon as you can, thanks.'

He turned back to Jane. 'Then we'll hand him over to the army. They'll want to deal with it themselves. They'll court-martial him. Send him to prison. For maybe ten years? I think we can assume, no matter how handsome he may be going into prison, he won't be when he comes out. Stupid man.'

Porritt and Williams just took it all in their stride. She felt thrilled at being part of their team. Dealing with people's lives. Sending them to prison, for heaven's sake. 'That was amazing, sir. Thank you so much.'

'Oh, thank *you*, my dear. You were very good at your job. So let's call it a day. Check with Alison. She'll arrange a car to BX. Come back in the morning. I'd expect to start around eight. See you then?'

'Yes, sir.'

She left the room. What a day. Greed, fear, and love changed behaviour? How wise.

Translating at BX had been great. But this was at a higher level. She relished the extra buzz it gave her.

Her impact on the war effort way now way beyond what she thought possible a few weeks ago. She could hardly wait for tomorrow.

Chapter 6. Brenner

John Kay had a headache. In fact, the whole Aquila group had a headache. Tim Convery.

Each night, they talked. Aquila 1 wanted Convery back. And Aquila 4, Kay, wanted him on his way. But it wasn't so easy now. Their usual exit route had just shut down. Kay fumed.

He had joined Abwehr when he worked in South West Africa. When they heard he was going back home in 1937, they asked him to work for them under cover.

He'd backed the fascist point of view and so agreed. Not least because they would set him up wherever he wanted in the north of England. And pay him very well.

They trained him how to work in secret. Blend in. Get the cover story right. Build trust. Surveillance.

He had to support Aquila 2, a British MI5 officer with access to secret papers. And work with Aquila 3, based in London, who ran agents in the south. Kay had to copy this group in other parts of the UK.

Abwehr set him up in a large house in Pickering, Yorkshire, as SMC, a firm of mining consultants. He then called Aquila 3 to find out how to set up his group.

He went to fascist meetings fronted by Sir Oswald Mosley. But kept well in the shade. He thought Mosley a good speaker, who didn't seem to control his rabble of followers. However, there were always some mature fans at the side.

And that's where he found his targets. Those who would blend in. Had an inner faith. Who wanted to do something extra for the cause. And paid well for it.

He built up a network of agents based in the major cities of the north. Trained them how to stay hidden. And gather data on defence matters, which he fed back to Aquila 1 each night.

At first, their actions were not illegal. But the new Treachery Act of 1940 changed the rules. They then had to become even more covert.

Kay mulled over his problem. Aquila 3 dealt with couriers. His entry and exit route used two brothers with a fishing boat on the south coast. They'd go out at night and transfer to and from a French fishing boat arranged by Aquila 1.

But not content with big money from this, the brothers talked the French into selling them brandy to make some extra cash. The police caught them landing it near Beachy Head. They lost their boat and got a month in jail. Aquila 3 was livid. But now had to find a new transfer route.

Meanwhile, Kay had to get Convery out of the UK. He'd fixed up an exit route only once before. Then, he used his links in West Belfast to get the courier over the Irish border. And had to pay plenty to get him on to one of the few Irish cargo ships that did the 'Lisbon Run' to Portugal. The other side had then to get him back home. Once was enough.

As a result, Kay had searched out a fishing boat owner in Scarborough. He was a pal of a pal of Ted, his driver. And agreed to operate an exit route in the North Sea. For a price.

So Kay now waited for Aquila 1 to arrange a boat from the other side. But that wasn't easy either because of British patrols.

Each night, he pushed for an answer. And Aquila 1 told him to be patient. But that was hard with Convery. The man talked on and on about his key role in Aquila, his future role in Abwehr, and how he had met Hitler.

The last straw had come when his wife claimed Convery had made a pass at her. She had pushed him away. But it rankled with Kay. He told him to calm down. Convery had been there almost a week now. It had affected Kay's agent training. He needed him out. And soon.

The next call brought great news. A U-boat would pick up Convery from a point in the North Sea. They would confirm it all at their six o'clock call the next night. Weather permitting, they would do the transfer at midnight UK time.

Kay called his skipper in Scarborough. He was happy with the plan. But security had now tightened at the port. So he'd take Convery out to his boat from a quiet bay south of there. 'Won't be a problem, though.'

Kay went to Convery. 'At last, you're all set to go. They're so keen to get you back, they're sending a U-boat for you.'

'Bloody boats. I hate them all,' he said in his soft Irish accent.

'Well, you don't have much choice since we're on an island.'

'I know. But I get seasick even thinking about it.'

'Oh, too bad.' Kay felt pleased that something could dent Convery's super self-esteem. And something nasty at that. 'Leave your British ID with Ted before getting on the boat. You've still got your German ID?'

Convery dug into his inside pocket. 'Yes, I've got it here.' He showed Kay his papers.

'Well, safe journey when it comes.'

'Thanks. I'm sorry if I was a bit of a pain at times.'

'That's okay. It's not easy waiting like this. Let's see what tomorrow brings, eh?'

***

Convery sat silent in the back of the car as Ted drove through the darkness. Heading home at last. Though sad he wouldn't have Liesl to caress and love when he got there. She'd been the perfect woman for him. The love of his life. And they'd so enjoyed each other's company. Where would he ever find another woman like her?

After an hour, Ted turned left. Went down to a parking area. And got out.

He watched as Ted stood looking around. A large, broad-built man emerged from the dark. Ted gave him an envelope. Then came and opened the door. 'This is the skipper.'

He got out and shook hands. 'Hello.'

'Got any bags with you?'

'Just this.' He showed a small light bag with a long strap. Then put it over his head sash-style.

'Yeah. That's okay. If you're all set, let's get going.'

He followed the skipper down a path to the beach. They then walked to the right until they came to a small boat half in the water. A man stood beside it.

'This is Joe,' the skipper said. 'Let's put these life jackets on and get in. My fishing boat's just out there.'

Joe helped him on with the jacket. Then he climbed into the boat, and faced the bow. Now felt sick. And he wasn't even on the water yet.

The two others pushed the boat into the water and jumped in. Joe started the engine and steered the boat out to sea. At first it was quite calm. But soon the boat rocked and yawed with the waves.

He gripped the sides. Hated this. Took him back to a rowing boat with granddad on Dublin Bay. Almost mown down by a ship coming into port. *Bloody boats.*

Then he felt a thump from below as the boat hit something. He jumped out of his seat. 'What was that?'

The skipper shouted back. 'It's okay. Just some driftwood. Not a problem. We're almost there.' His fishing boat now just about thirty metres away.

He felt his feet wet. Water sloshing in the bottom of the boat. And it was rising. 'Water in the boat!'

The skipper leaned over. 'You'll be okay. Just calm down. Your life jacket will keep you afloat and your head above water. Hold on to Joe. I'll swim on and get my boat. You'll be fine.'

He didn't feel fine. Now shaking. But he kept quiet.

The boat filled with water and sank under them. The skipper swam off. And he held on to Joe.

The swell pummelled them. After a large wave passed over, he put his hands up to wipe his eyes clear. And then couldn't find Joe again. *Shit.* Letting go had been a mistake. *Dammit.* 'Joe? Joe!' he shouted.

He could hear Joe shouting, 'Just over here.' But he didn't know where. He started splashing around.

'Joe! Can you get me? Can you get me, Joe?' But when he looked around when the waves bobbed him up, he couldn't see him.

Soon, he couldn't hear him either. He felt alone and scared. The water was so cold. This was it. This was the end. No golden future for him.

He kept afloat in the life jacket. And as he bobbed up in the waves, he saw the fishing boat move around, searching for him. He waved and shouted as much as he could. But it just kept going round and round.

And he was now drifting away from it. Even at the top of the wave, he couldn't see it any more. He thought he might try to swim back to shore. But now didn't know which way that was.

He tried to keep his head up. But he now felt very cold and tired. Just wanted to rest and sleep. He tried to stay awake and moved his arms to get some warmth.

He'd had some great days, though. Walking in the Black Forest. The magic handshake with Hitler. Loving his beautiful Liesl. Great days. But now so tired and alone. He began to weep.

***

He'd just put on a record of The Four Seasons. Poured a smooth Cognac. Settled in his easy chair. And the phone rang. He waited, holding his breath.

It rang twice. Then stopped. That was a signal. If it had gone on, he'd have answered it.

It then rang again. Four times.

Aquila 4 wants a call back. Must be serious.

He went out to the hall. Put on his coat and hat. Then whistled on his dog, Toby, who came padding out of the kitchen. They went out to the car. A man with a dog looked as though he should be there. A man on his own at night just looked dodgy.

As he drove, he thought about Aquila 4. The man was a bloody good chap. As good as Aquila 3. He hoped it wasn't another glitch with the latest courier.

Last week, he'd picked up by chance, that a major spy search would take place in Hampstead. After a few panic phone calls, he'd got the lad out in time. And sent him up to Yorkshire for onward travel.

He didn't want any more bad news. The lad now carried secret papers that named *him* on the distribution list. He'd checked no one could trace the copy back to him. But he still worried about it.

He pulled up at the side of the village common and watched. All very quiet in the darkness. He could just see the phone box fifty yards ahead. He got Toby out and strolled towards it.

He asked for the number.

'Hello?'

'Aquila 2 here. You wanted me to call?'

'Yes. Just to let you know we've lost Convery.'

'What? How did that happen?'

'He was on a U-boat pickup. But they had a problem with the boat from shore. It hit something in the water, sprung a leak, and they had to swim for it. They all had life jackets and should have been okay.

'Our skipper swam on to get his fishing boat. Came back to collect his mate and Convery. But couldn't find him in the dark. It was a pretty heavy sea with strong tides running. He could finish up anywhere down the coast. They'll go back out in the morning.'

'Do you think he's survived?'

'Our men say yes. He panicked and felt sick on the way out. Which would weaken him. But they think he'd stay afloat and wash up somewhere.'

'What ID is he carrying?'

'That's another thing. He's only carrying German ID. Name of Karl Brenner.'

'Oh?' Aquila 2 thought for a moment. 'Can I call you in the morning? Say around nine?'

'Yes.'

'Right, I'll have a think about it and ring you back then. Bye.' He hung up. *Shit. Another bloody glitch.*

He strolled on round the common back to the car, and stowed Toby. Then sat smoking.

What would happen if the police found Convery with only German ID? What would they do? Probably hand him over to Porritt's people. *Dammit.*

Porritt was sharp as a tack. A bit of a maverick. Didn't always play by the rules. Much admired by Churchill because he got things done. Why he got those top jobs. It wouldn't take *him* long to find out what he had if Convery turned up.

Thank God he had two people embedded in Porritt's new Station 19. If Convery appeared there, he'd know about it quick time. And get him out fast. But he'd need to talk to his key man there in the morning.

Chapter 7. Tuesday

Jane arrived at Station 19 just before eight. She signed in and went through to Porritt's office. Williams put his finger to his lips. Porritt was on the phone. She tiptoed in and sat at a small side table.

Porritt took notes as he listened. 'Okay, we'll come over and have a look. See you in about an hour. Thanks for the call.' He hung up and sat back.

'Well now, there's a thing. That was CI Chris Andrews from Lincolnshire Police. He lives on the coast at Chapel St Leonards. Just north of Skegness. On his usual run along the beach this morning, he saw a man in a life jacket lying partly in the water. He pulled him on to the beach and checked him. Alive, but unconscious. Found ID papers in German. Name of Karl Brenner. Born Munich, twentieth April, 1918.

'He dashed back home, called an ambulance, and the chap's now in Skegness General. Andrews kept the ID to himself. So the man's booked in as John Smith. There's a police guard on him.

'Initial checks show hypothermia. But other than a bruise on the head, all other vital signs seem okay. Got drips into him and waiting for him to recover.'

Porritt packed his notes into his briefcase. 'Let's cancel our meetings and go see. This is more crucial. Jane, you better come with us, just in case. I'll get Alison to reschedule and arrange a car.'

***

Porritt led the way in. Andrews met them in the private room where Brenner lay. Tubes led from arm catheters and he wore an oxygen mask. A dressing over his right temple. Porritt thought the lad looked young. Fair hair. Square face. Steady breathing.

He went over to a side table. Andrews had laid out Brenner's things. And gave him the German ID from his pocket. Porritt handed it to Williams. 'What do you think, Mike? Genuine?'

Williams studied it. 'Yeah. Looks like it, sir.'

Andrews waved at the clothes on the table. 'All good quality. No tags, sir. Also had this bag with these spare clothes. No other papers on him. I assume he'd get a British ID when he landed.'

Porritt looked through the clothes, shoes, and bag. All new. 'You're right, Chris. Enough to stay for a week, I'd say. And there's nothing else?'

Andrews shook his head. 'That's it, sir.'

Porritt sighed. 'Not much. Apart from German ID. Feel there should be something that tells us why he's here. Have the medics said when he'll come round?'

'They said today. The lad's in good shape. It's just a matter of waiting.'

Williams asked, 'You know the beach where you found him, Chris? Is that a common spot to land a small boat? Or could the tide have carried him there if he hit a problem elsewhere?'

'No, it's not. I spoke to Curtis on the door about this. He's a sailing man. There are huge tide races that run north to south across the Humber estuary. So, if he hit a problem heading for Yorkshire, they could easily carry him down to here.'

'So the boat or dinghy could have landed anywhere from Yorkshire down?'

'Yeah. Could be. Or sank.'

Porritt glanced at the bed. 'Get a set of prints off him please, Chris. Possible spy. My authority.'

'Okay, sir. I'll arrange it now.' Andrews left.

They stood in silence. Porritt wondered whether they should stay or go. Always the dilemma when waiting. Then there was a sudden moan from the bed.

Williams went across and pressed the alarm button beside the bed. Within seconds, a doctor and a nurse appeared. The doctor checked his pulse and sounded him. The nurse leaned over. 'Mr Smith!' She touched his cheek. 'Mr Smith! Wake up.' She touched his cheek again. 'Mr Smith? Can you wake up?'

Brenner's eyes opened. They looked blank.

Andrews came back into the room and nodded to Porritt. 'They'll come over within the hour.' He glanced over at the bed. 'Is this him back with us again?'

'Looks like it.'

The nurse leaned over and held a straw in a glass of water against his lips. 'Mr Smith. Will you take a drink, please?' His lips moved, and he began to suck through the straw. His eyes still looked blank. 'That's good, Mr Smith. Well done. You'll feel better now.'

The doctor came over to Porritt. 'I think he's okay. Pulse and blood pressure fine. We'll keep on with the IV liquids for the moment. But he'll want some food soon. On the way to a full recovery.'

'Can we talk with him?'

The doctor looked across at the bed. 'Yes,. You'll get a few minutes. But he'll drift in and out of sleep for most of today. Part of the recovery process.'

'Okay, thanks.'

A few minutes later, the doctor and nurse left the room. 'Maybe ten minutes max?'

Porritt nodded. He and Williams went to one side of the bed. Jane took a seat at the other side. She took his hand. 'Herr Brenner,' in German. 'Can you hear me?'

He stared at her.

'Can you hear me?' she asked. Again in German.

He nodded, his eyes puzzled. He tried to speak. 'Liesl? You're here?' He squeezed her hand. 'Liesl? Where am I?'

'You're in hospital. You've had an accident.'

He frowned. 'In Germany?'

'No, in England.' She repeated each phrase to Porritt and Williams in English. They leaned over, listening.

His eyes closed again. Then he looked at her. 'Can't get Joe,' he said in German. 'Need to hold on to Joe.'

'Who is Joe? Where is he?'

'In the water. Joe in the water.'

Porritt leaned over and whispered. 'Ask him something in English.'

Jane thought for a moment. 'What happened to your boat?' she asked in English.

He frowned and said nothing.

'Ask in German,' Porritt murmured.

'What happened to your boat?'

'Boat sank. Need to hold on to Joe.'

'Who is Joe?'

He was drifting off again. 'Joe in water. Hold on to Joe . . .' His eyes closed.

Jane looked over at Porritt. 'I think he's gone back to sleep, sir.'

Porritt nodded. Then waved for her to come over to the side of the room. They stood next to Andrews. 'What do you think?' Porritt asked.

'Well, there must have been two of them in the boat,' Williams said. 'Him and Joe.'

Porritt glanced at Andrews. 'Sounds like you need to renew your search for another one.'

'Will do, sir.'

Porritt thought for a moment. 'Do you think he only knows German?'

Jane nodded. 'Would seem so, sir. Though, since he's not fully fit, it's hard to say.'

Porritt frowned. 'Why would they send someone over here who doesn't know English?'

'Maybe that's what Joe was for,' Williams said.

'But why do that? It doesn't make sense.'

'Unless he has special knowledge or something.'

The doctor came in and went to the bed. He checked on Brenner then came over to them. 'I think we'll just leave him sleeping now. If that's all right?'

Porritt nodded. 'We'll just wait here for a while.'

The four of them stood together in silence. Porritt looked over at the bed. 'But why would they do that?' he said to himself. The others had no answer.

After a few moments, Porritt stirred himself. 'Right, let's think about what we know. We assume there were two of them in the boat. Brenner and Joe. But the boat sank. Or it threw them out. He had to hold on to Joe. But couldn't, and they drifted apart.'

He looked at Williams and Andrews. 'So what you two should do is combine our forces on this. Mike, get Dave Burnett in Yorkshire involved.

'Let's get our people to scour the coast. From where to where? I don't know the area.'

'Wait. I'll get Curtis. He knows more about the coast than any of us.' Andrews went to the door and came back with Curtis. Porritt asked him the best range of coastline to check for Joe. And maybe a boat, if it had floated on to the coast.

Curtis thought for a moment. 'Hornsea down to Spurn Point in Yorkshire. North of that, it's too busy. In Lincolnshire, Saltfleet down to Skegness. With a couple of boats for each stretch, you could cover the areas in two to three hours tops.'

Porritt thought of the landing. A U-boat or German fishing boat would never come close to shore to unload onto a dinghy. Far too risky. Much easier to offload outside the twelve-mile limit on to a British fishing boat. Which would then come close to unload. So there could be a local fishing boat involved in this somewhere.

They debated where such a boat could come from. Curtis said it would have to come from either Hull or Grimsby, both with huge fishing fleets. Or maybe Scarborough or Whitby further north.

Porritt asked if these fishing boats had ship-to-shore radio telephones. But Curtis said no. Fishing boats used Morse code systems. Porritt pointed out these used open channels. So, other boats could listen in to any signals.

'If a British fishing boat was going to meet a U-boat, they'd would want to keep it quiet. Their only safe line would be a landline. So they wouldn't leave port until they got the "go" signal via a landline. They'd meet at night, probably beyond the twelve-mile limit. And it would take them say three hours to get there. So they'd leave port as late as possible.

'Once they lost Brenner, the fishing boat crew would have to let their bosses know. So they'd need a landline late last night or early this morning. And they'd also have lost a dinghy or a small boat.

'Putting it all together, check from the sea, as Curtis has outlined. But also check from the land over the same stretches for any reports of unusual movements.

'And check on fishing boats that left port at say five o'clock or later last night. Then returned late at night. Had a crew member named Joe. Lost a small boat or dinghy. And didn't land a catch. Since they wouldn't have time to do any fishing during all of this.'

Williams and Andrews took notes as he spoke. 'We'll get right on to it, sir,' Andrews said. 'Want us to call in later?'

Porritt nodded. 'Yes, let's meet here at five.'

***

He loaded Toby into the back of his car and drove to another village. Again, he stopped near the common and watched for a few minutes. Then got out and strolled with Toby to the phone box. He asked for the number.

'Hello?'

'Aquila 2 here. Time for a chat?'

'Yes,' Kay replied.

'I've thought about this. If our lad's found with German ID, he'll be handed over to the police and then to Special Branch. Now, they have a new base near Lincoln, called Station 19. Where they take POWs before sending them off to camp. It's almost certain, if he turns up anywhere on the coast, he'll arrive there.

74

'I've got a couple of our boys embedded there. Part of the security team looking after POWs. So they know what's going on. My main man there tells me who's captured and where they're sent. His name's Brown.

'I need you both to work out how to get our lad out of there before they find out about him, and send him off somewhere else. I'll leave a message for Brown to call you. He'll think he's calling Dr Kerslake, who did a medical check on him a while ago, and got him into Station 19. You need to tell Brown who you are and see him as soon as possible. Work out how to get our lad back to your place. Okay?'

'Yes, I can do that. Do you have any ideas on how we could get him out?'

'I don't know the place. Never been there. But Brown's a good man. A bit rough around the edges. And can get nasty at times. But very experienced and up for the cause. Has worked with me for about a couple of years now. Done some good stuff too.'

'Okay, I'll meet with him and fix it. I'll try to see him today.'

'Good man.'

'Once we've got our lad back here, we'll get him on his way again, asap.'

'Right. Erm, could you hold him for a few days? I'm getting some more info ready for Aquila 3. But it'll take two or three days. With the screw up on the south coast, we don't have another courier coming in. Let's get our lad to take this info out as well.'

'Fine. We'll do that.'

Aquila 2 hung up. Then asked for another number. 'Station 19, good morning,' came the bright response.

'Good morning. This is Dr Kerslake here. Could you pass a message on to one of your staff, please?'

'Yes, of course, doctor. Who is it for?'

'It's for Sergeant Robert John Brown. '

'And what's the message?'

'Tell him I've had another look at his blood tests, and I'd like him to call me to discuss them. The number is Pickering 437.'

'Okay. Is that it?'

'That's it. Could you make sure he gets this as soon as possible, please?'

'No problem, doctor. I'll do it now. Thank you for your call.'

'Thank you for your help. Goodbye.' He hung up. Nothing more to do. He'd better head in to the office.

He walked Toby back to the car, dropped him off at home, and caught a train into London.

***

Kay hung up the phone. He didn't want Convery back. But he realised there were no other options. In fact, the lad might be making his way back on foot. Though if that was the case, he'd probably have phoned by now.

He cancelled his plans for the day and waited for Brown to call. Pulled out his road map of Britain and looked up Lincoln. Then called Ted to bring the car round. The phone rang within ten minutes.

'Hello?'

'Is that Doctor Kerslake?' A strong Northern Ireland accent.

'Is that Sergeant Brown?'

'It is. I've got a message to ring you.'

'Yes. Your message was from Aquila 2. He needs you and me to meet to discuss something. I'm Aquila 4.'

'Oh, I see. When?'

'Today, if possible.'

'I go on duty at two. Can you get here before that?'

'Looking at the map, I'm at least two hours away. Could we meet at, say, twelve o'clock?'

'Yes, I could do that.'

'Where do you suggest?'

'Mmm. We want somewhere quiet. How about the car park of the Windmill Inn?' He gave Kay directions. 'What will you be driving?'

'A large black Austin. Last digits 324.'

'I'll be there at twelve. See you then.'

'Fine. And thanks.' Kay hung up.

***

Just before twelve, Ted turned into the car park of the Windmill Inn. A man standing next to a car at the far corner waved. Ted pulled up alongside.

Kay got out and stretched. 'Sergeant Brown?' He extended a hand. 'I'm John Kay, Aquila 4.' They shook hands. 'Let's talk in your car?'

'Sure. In you get.'

Kay looked around as he got into the car. All quiet. 'We lost a courier last night in the North Sea. We think he'll probably wash up on the coast somewhere. But he's only got German ID in the name Karl Brenner. Aquila 2 thinks if he's found, the police will send him over here to Station 19. He wants us to get him out fast and back to my place. Can you help do that?'

Brown nodded. 'Sure. No problem. We can get him out of the cell block at the back.' He paused. 'Could you create a diversion in Lincoln to keep the cops busy?'

'Yes, I'll do that.'

They discussed the best way of using a diversion and agreed on how they'd do it.

'When do you want it done?' Brown asked. 'I'll need a night to prepare the fence.'

'Well, let's go for tomorrow night, assuming Brenner turns up today or tomorrow?'

'Fine. Plan for nine. Porritt sometimes interviews in the evenings. But the diversion will disrupt that and we'll get him out. I'll show you the pick-up point.'

They got out and moved into Kay's car. Ted drove down to Station 19, about a mile away. Brown took him up a side road and then a disused narrow lane up to a fenced-off wireless mast near the rear of the station. They then drove back to the car park.

Brown got out of the car. 'I'll call you tomorrow.'

Kay shook his hand. 'Good. Look forward to it.'

Kay and Ted studied their road map, and planned how they'd get round Scunthorpe and Goole on side roads back to Yorkshire and home. They tested the route on the way north.

***

Just after one, Porritt got word that Mr Smith was awake again. So he and Jane set off to see him.

To his surprise, he found Brenner sitting up in bed. Still a bit rough looking, but alert, compared with earlier. Brenner still had the dressing on his head and a drip in, but no oxygen mask.

They went over to the bed, taking the seats they'd had earlier. Brenner smiled at Jane and took her hand as before. Porritt wondered why she didn't pull her hand away. But then thought she wanted to keep him relaxed.

They'd agreed on the way over the areas they would cover. So Jane started. 'Herr Brenner, do you speak English?' she asked in German.

He shook his head and waved his free hand. 'Very small. Not good,' he said in halting English.

Jane looked over at Porritt. He shrugged and nodded for her to go on.

'Herr Brenner,' she went on in German, 'this is Commander Porritt from the police. I am Sergeant Thomson, here to translate for you. We'd like to talk to you about how you came here. Is that okay?'

He nodded. 'Yes, it's okay. But why do they call me Mr Smith? You know my name.'

Porritt told her what to say. 'The police gave you the name so the doctors wouldn't know you're German.'

He thought about what she said. 'Now I understand.'

'Could you tell us where you were born?'

He frowned. 'If you know my name, you know that.'

'We would like you to confirm it, please.'

'Munich. Nice city. Do you know it?'

She ignored his question. 'And on what date?'

'You know the date.'

'Again, would you just confirm it, please?'

He sighed. 'Twentieth of April, 1918. I'm now almost twenty-five. How old are you?'

Jane ignored his question again. 'What does your father do?'

Brenner glanced at Porritt for the first time since they'd started. So far, he'd kept his eyes on her.

'Professor of engineering at Munich University.'

'And what do you do?'

'I'm a technician with a large engineering company.'

'What is the name of the company?'

'Siemens.'

'Do you remember talking to us earlier today?'

He frowned again. 'I remember seeing you. But not talking. What did I say?'

'Do you remember how you got here?'

'No, I don't.'

'You said you were in the water. What happened?'

'I don't know.'

'You told us you were in a boat.'

He frowned and shook his head.

'You said the boat sank. And that's how you got in the water. Why were you in the boat? You said Joe was in the boat. And in the water with you. Who is Joe?'

Brenner sighed. 'Don't know Joe.'

'What were you doing in the boat?'

He closed his eyes. 'Landing,' he murmured.

'Landing where?'

'In England.'

'Where in England?'

'I don't know.'

'Why were you coming to England?'

'For a meeting.'

'A meeting with whom?'

'Don't know.'

'A meeting about what?'

Brenner was silent for a moment. 'A new engine.'

'What kind of engine?'

'An aircraft engine.'

'Where were you meeting?'

'In England.'

'Who was taking you to the meeting?'

'Joe.'

'Who is Joe?'

'Don't know Joe,' with more emphasis.

'Was Joe a good swimmer? Better than you?'

He nodded. 'Better than me.'

'How did you get into the boat with Joe?'

Brenner closed his eyes and pursed his lips. 'From U-boat,' he whispered, and looked as though he wanted to go back to sleep.

'Did Joe bring the boat to you?'

Brenner closed his eyes and nodded.

Porritt studied him. He had winkled out the story of how Brenner had got here. But now needed to verify it.

On the face of it, Brenner had offloaded from a U-boat on to a small boat that Joe had brought out to him. Joe would then land him somewhere for a meeting with someone about a new aircraft engine.

Porritt didn't believe the boat transfer story. But the rest was just about plausible. He had to keep an open mind, though. Brenner could have just spun a line about coming here. Might even be a pick-up from this country that had gone wrong. Couldn't reject that just yet.

Just then, a nurse appeared at the door. 'Commander Porritt? Phone call for you, sir.'

Porritt stood up. 'Let's leave it at that for the moment.' He left the room.

***

Jane jumped as Brenner gripped her hand. 'You're so beautiful and gentle. I thought you were Liesl,' he murmured in German.

With Porritt out of the room, she relaxed a bit. "Who's Liesl?'

He smiled. 'She was the love of my life. But she's gone now. You're so like her. You're just as beautiful.'

She blushed. When had anyone called her that? Not the man in her life. She leaned forward and touched his arm. 'I'm sorry about Liesl.'

Brenner smiled. 'Thanks.'

Porritt came back into the room. 'Right, Jane. Let's go and prepare for our meeting.'

She quickly pulled her hand away. Brenner smiled at her as she gathered her things and left.

***

Just before five, Kay's phone rang.

'Brown here.'

'Any news?'

'Not much. Our lad hasn't turned up yet. But the top man ditched his plans. Took off with his pet translator. So something's going on in German somewhere.'

'Okay. Sounds like they might have found him.'

'Yeah, maybe. Call you tomorrow.'

Kay thought about Convery. Even with all his faults, the lad was a highly trained spy. Would handle questions okay. So he'd have the lad back tomorrow night.

That meant, with the delay from Aquila 2, he should line up the Skipper for another transfer at the end of the week. He'd talk to Aquila 1 about that at six.

***

Williams and Andrews joined Porritt and Jane just after five. Porritt updated the others on Brenner. 'On the face of it, his story matches what we thought. But I'm not convinced yet. We need proof to back it up. So, what have you got?'

Andrews said the prints check on Brenner hadn't shown up any matches so far. On the sea check on the Lincolnshire coast, they had picked up one rubber dinghy five miles south of Saltfleet partly deflated. They were doing a prints check on it. The land check had thrown up nothing.

They'd also checked fishing boats from Grimsby. Out of 314 listed boats, 238 had been out last night at ten o'clock. Of these, only six had a listed crew member called Joe. And all of *them* had left port that morning. None of them fitted the profile. But boats listed at other ports also used Grimsby. The harbour master didn't track them. And boats often sailed with unlisted crew.

Porritt sighed. There were always complications. 'I accept these are valid points. But let's stick to our profile. Make sure that's covered first.'

Williams reported on the Yorkshire findings. Their sea check had found no boats or dinghies. The land check had thrown up a call to Hornsea Police at 21.03 last night. Report of a group of men at a car park above the beach at Mappleton. Local police found no one there.

The caller had been walking his dog along the cliff top. He claimed he'd also heard a motor boat going out from the beach in the dark five minutes later. Which was why he had called it in. However, there was no trace of any men, vehicles or boat.

They'd checked fishing boats out of Hull. But found no matches. However, Dave Burnett had checked out the Scarborough fleet. He found one boat with a listed crew member called Joe. It had left port last night at 18.50. Returned just before midnight. It had left again just after six this morning and was still out. The harbour master noticed as it left port that the small wooden motor boat it usually carried at the stern was missing. And to crown all, the boat had not landed a catch the previous night. 'Ticks all the boxes, sir.'

Porritt punched the air. 'Yes! Great stuff, lads. Let's get Dave on the phone.' He asked for the number. 'Dave, it's Jonathan Porritt here. Mike's just told me about your Scarborough fishing boat.'

'Yes, sir. Looks like it could be the one.'

'Great. Well done. Do we know the skipper?'

'We do, sir. Bill Wadsworth. Age forty-three. Done for assault in '37. Part of a pub brawl. Fined for that. Done for smuggling in '38 and in '41. Booze and fags. Locked up for a month. Lost his boat. But with all the pressure on boats up here, he got relisted and started fishing again.

'His crew is his extended family. He has eight listed. But usually sails with just threes. One of them is Joe Armitage, his brother-in-law. The other two are his younger brothers, Pete and Andy. Nothing known on any of these three.'

'Right. They're still out?'

'That's correct, sir.'

'Okay. They'll have been searching for our man. So they'll come back in tonight. Lift all four of them, say around five in the morning. For smuggling booze and fags. Make that known. But don't mention Germans.

'Get warrants to search their homes. My authority, if you need it. Clear everyone out. If they've smuggled our man, they'll have cash. I want to find it. Most likely in their homes somewhere.

'Impound the boat. Do a full print search. Chris Andrews has a full set of prints from our man. We'll need solid proof to make the case against Wadsworth. Unless they confess.'

'Right, sir. What about grilling them? Are you coming up here for that?'

'No, I can't make it. Need to find out more about our man here. We just don't know enough about his story. He says he offloaded from a U-boat to a small motor boat. Which then sank, throwing him and Joe into the water. But it was all too glib. So I need to dig deeper. You need to question the four up your end. Is that okay?'

'Yes, fine, sir. We'll start in the morning and keep you posted. Try to do it without an extension.'

'Don't worry about that, Dave. Emergency Powers. Potential treason under the Treachery Act 1940. Even though they think it's for smuggling. They're not going anywhere soon. No access to phones either. I don't want them to contact their paymasters.

'We need to find out more about them too. So scare the shit out of them. Tell them they're heading for twelve years in jail. We'll go lighter if they confess.'

'Okay, sir. Leave it with us. Call you tomorrow.'

'Thanks, Dave. Goodbye.' Porritt hung up.

'Is he up for it, sir?' Williams asked.

Porritt nodded. 'Yeah. He'll be fine. He's my youngest CS. And it'll be the first time we've worked together. But he's got a good track record. Between us, let's keep an eye on him, though.'

'Okay, sir. Will do.'

'Let's have a look at Brenner's bag before we go.'

They studied the bag. A soft canvas with a hard base. Lined with a light cloth. Porritt brought out a knife and cut into the stitching around the lining. It came away to reveal the inside. No hiding places there.

Then they examined the hard base. Glued together in two layers. Porritt eased the knife between the layers and pulled them apart. Again, nothing.

He shrugged. 'Oh, well. Good day, though. Let's get back to Lincoln.'

***

Kay's phone rang just after nine.

'It's Bill the skipper here.'

'How did you get on?'

'We've searched to Spurn Point. No trace. He's either still mobile and making his way back. Or found and in hospital or clink somewhere. Or carried further down the coast to Lincolnshire.'

'Mmm. We think the police might have him.'

'Oh? What makes you think that?'

'Well, I've got sources. If they're right, we're going to spring him. Get him back here. So, we'd be looking for a re-run of the transfer at the end of the week. Would that be okay?'

'No problem. Just let me know when and where.'

'Okay, thanks. Will do.'

Chapter 8. Wednesday

The next morning, Porritt drummed his fingers on his desk as he waited for news from Burnett. He called just before eight.

'Got them all, sir. No problems. At least none we couldn't deal with. Families gave *them* a hard time rather than us. Wadsworth's and Armitage's wives went berserk. Screamed, "You promised never again!" Armitage is in bits. The two younger brothers are shitting themselves.

'We didn't have to look far for the cash, sir. Still in Wadsworth's jacket pocket. Hadn't even opened it. His wife saw us get it too. How much do you think?' He paused. 'Two thousand, sir.'

Porritt whistled. 'Wow, quite a stash. How long would it take to make that at the fishing game?'

'I know, sir. Somebody thought his services were worth it. Anyway, we'll check the envelope and notes for prints. We've impounded their boat. And we'll do a prints check on that too.'

'Great work, Dave. Sounds like Armitage might be the place to start. Keep us up to date. I need to know whether our man was on the way in or on the way out.'

Porritt hung up and smiled at Williams. 'Well. How about that? We got it right, huh?'

***

87

Kay cursed. He'd had to stop his agent training. Could think only about Brenner. *Where the hell was he?* As he pondered this, Elizabeth shouted through that Ted had just driven in. *Shit. What now?*

Ted shook hands and sat down at the table. Waited until Elizabeth left the room. 'You'll never guess what's happened.' Kay held his breath. 'My wife just heard from my mate's wife. The police lifted Bill the skipper and his crew early this morning. On charges of smuggling booze and fags.'

Kay leaned back in his chair and closed his eyes. 'Oh, shit. How stupid are these people?' He gritted his teeth. 'Is there anything that can come back to us?'

Ted shook his head. 'Don't think so, John. I've never used my real name with them. And made sure he memorised our phone numbers.'

'What about the cash? What if they find that?'

'The skipper's not daft. He'll have it well hidden. And even if they do find it, he won't talk. He knows he shouldn't upset us.'

Kay sat and thought. 'What about the crew? Will they talk?'

'Maybe. But they won't know anything about the business.' He paused. 'We should maybe be a bit more careful. But I don't think they can connect us.'

'Mmm. Hope you're right. But keep your ears open. If we need to, we can scarper quick time. And our chief will look after us very well.'

Ted rose. 'Will do. Are we still on for tonight?'

'As far as I know. Haven't heard from Brown yet. But I assume he's fixed the fence. I've arranged the diversions. So we're just waiting for Brenner to turn up.'

'Good. I'll check with you later.'

***

The medics had cleared Brenner to travel. So Porritt asked Andrews to bring him over from Skegness with a double police escort. He should arrive late morning. They'd take photos and settle him in. Then start the interviews after lunch.

Porritt thought back to his talk with Burnett last night. He'd said Brenner had been a bit too glib. An off-the-cuff remark he'd made without thinking. But he now realised that was right. It hadn't taken too much probing for Brenner to open up about a new aircraft engine. Almost as though Brenner *wanted* to tell him.

Senior staff knew Britain had built a new type of engine called a turbojet. It could transform an aircraft. They thought Germany had a similar engine. But less efficient. So Brenner's story was plausible.

Germany would be keen to know more about the British engine. But why tell him so easily? Was it a cover story to disguise the real purpose of his trip? He had to dig deeper.

Brenner also said he had been born and brought up in Munich. Porritt was sure, if he could check the staff records at Munich University, he would find a Professor Brenner. Maybe he'd been glib about *that* too.

Porritt had found over the years that people born and brought up in a city just knew details that strangers didn't know. Like what tram routes went where. What metro lines went to which suburb? Where department stores were located.

So he'd created a series of key questions for each of the major German cities. They had caught lots of people lying. He went to the filing cabinet and brought out the set for Munich.

He checked his schedule. Then booked an interview room for two-hour sessions at two o'clock and eight o'clock in the evening.

***

Porritt looked up as Williams rushed into the office just before eleven. 'I've got Dave on the phone, sir. He has a message for you. Think you'll like it.'

The phone rang, and Porritt picked it up. 'Yes, Dave, what've you got?'

'Your man was on the way out.'

'Wow. You sure?'

'Certain. Armitage has just coughed big style. Turns out his wife has kidney problems. Needs an operation. Which they can't afford. He's in bits now because he thinks he'll never see her alive again.

'Wadsworth offered him five hundred quid for what seemed a simple job. Use the motor boat to lift a lad from the beach at Mappleton. Take him to the fishing boat offshore. Then out to just beyond the twelve-mile limit. Transfer him to a U-boat. Then back to port and have his wife fixed up. Sounded dead easy.

'But on the way out, the motor boat hit some debris and sprung a leak. They were almost at the fishing boat. So Wadsworth swam on to get it. But by the time he got back, Armitage had lost hold of our man. And they couldn't find him.'

'So, Wadsworth was also in the boat?'

'Yes, according to him.'

'And were the two brothers on the fishing boat?'

'Yes. They looked after the boat while Wadsworth and Armitage went to the beach. He thinks they were getting a hundred each.'

'Does he know the paymasters?'

'No, he doesn't. Wadsworth dealt with all of that.'

'Well done, Dave. We need to close the loop though. We'll send a set of pics of our man up to you once he gets here. See if Armitage IDs him as the man in the boat. Keep him cooperating. There's an old phrase, "If you can't do the time, then don't do the crime." Wish to hell these people would remember it before they got themselves into trouble.'

'Agree, sir. Talk later.'

Porritt put his two fists in the air. 'Yes! Now we know where he was heading, I'm going to enjoy today.'

***

Kay's phone rang just after one o'clock.

'Hello, it's Brown here. Got some news for you. Your man Brenner is here. Arrived this morning. I'm on duty, so I settled him in. He's due for an interview this afternoon and this evening. I've told him we're going to spring him tonight, and he's happy.'

'That's good. He's a bright lad. And he's probably doing it already. But could you remind him to stick to the story he's on his way *in* to the country. Not on the way out. It's a better cover for having a German ID.'

'Will do. Are you okay for tonight?'

'Yes. Everything's set for nine.'

'Fine. All set this end too. See you later.'

Kay sat and thought. Now he knew where Brenner was, he could proceed with his plan. Fingers crossed.

***

Porritt sat beside Jane at the central table, with Brenner opposite. The German still had a small dressing on his temple. But other than that looked pretty fit. Williams switched on the recorder. 'Interview with Herr Karl Brenner. Seventh April, 1943, at Station 19. Led by Commander Porritt, with CS Williams and ST Thomson. Guards. Sergeant Brown. Corporal Henry. Time 14.07.'

Porritt began. 'Good day, Herr Brenner. Hope you're feeling better.'

Brenner seemed chirpy. He looked straight to Jane's eyes. 'It's good to see you again.' Porritt noticed she blushed as she translated.

'Herr Brenner, yesterday you told us you'd come here to have a meeting about a new aircraft engine. You had transferred from a U-boat onto a small motor boat that a man called Joe had brought out to you. He would land you and take you to the meeting. Is that correct?'

Brenner stared at the table. 'That's correct.'

'Fine. I'd just like to go through each stage of that journey. What was the name or number of the U-boat?'

'No idea. Didn't see any name or number.'

'So, what happened when the U-boat surfaced? How did you get off?'

'Just climbed down the tower and got into the boat.'

'And that was the motor boat with Joe in it?

'Yes.'

'Was there anyone else in the motor boat?'

Brenner paused. 'No.'

'You don't seem sure.'

'I'm sure.'

'Okay. Now, I'm an ex-navy man. I've also spent time in submarines. And I know the North Sea very well.

No one in their right mind would take a small motor boat out into the North Sea more than a mile or so. Say two kilometres. And no German U-boat captain in their right mind would come inside our twelve-mile limit. Because of the extra shipping traffic and patrols.

So you see, I have a problem with your story. Were you, in fact, transferred from the U-boat onto a fishing boat? Which then brought you closer to shore to transfer you into a small motor boat?'

Brenner sat still. Porritt reckoned he was working out what to say. After a couple of minutes, he shrugged. 'Well, it's clear. German U-boat captains are much more daring than British captains.' He looked direct at Porritt for the first time in the meeting.

'I'm sure you're right. But I know they're not *that* stupid.' Brenner seemed tense, but calm. 'So, you're saying the U-boat dropped you close inshore. And you then went into the small motor boat with Joe?'

'Yes.'

'And you said the boat hit something and sank?'

'That's correct.'

'And you lost the hold you had on Joe in the water?'

'Yes, I've already said that.'

'Now, you told us Joe was taking you to a meeting. How were you getting there?'

'By car.'

'And where was this meeting to be held?'

Brenner waved a hand. 'In England somewhere.'

'And who was it with?'

'Someone from the aircraft company.'

'Which company?'

'Gloster Aircraft.'

'And what was it you wanted to know?'

'How they designed their centrifugal compression. We were paying a lot of money for it.'

'How much money?'

'No idea. Joe dealt with that.'

'Now, you've made it clear your English is very poor. So who was going to translate for you?'

'Joe. He knows German.'

'Ah, I see. An all-round useful fellow, Joe.' Porritt paused for a moment. 'Can I just turn to something else? You said you were born and brought up in Munich. Is that correct?'

'That's correct.'

'Where did you live in Munich?'

'Oh, various places around the city.'

'Okay. Where was the last place you lived?'

'Vaterstetten.'

'What was your address there?'

'That's not relevant here.'

'And how far out is it from the city centre?'

Brenner shrugged. 'About twenty minutes by train.'

'So, where did the train drop you in the city centre?'

'At the main train station.'

'Did you ever visit your father at the university?'

'Sometimes.'

'And what's the best way to get there from the main train station?'

'By U-Bahn.'

'And does the U-Bahn run direct between the two, or do you have to change part way along?'

Brenner paused. 'It runs direct, I think. It's so long since I did it.'

Porritt felt Jane bump his leg. 'Can you remember the U-Bahn line number?'

94

'No. It's too long ago. Sorry.'

'That's okay. Why don't we have a short break now? We'll resume in a few minutes. Sergeant, can you arrange tea for Herr Brenner, please?' He turned to Jane. 'Let's go back to the office. Mike, you come too.'

Mike switched off the recorder, and the three of them left the room. Porritt shut his office door. 'Something you want to say, Jane?'

'Yes, sir. There are two points I'd like to make. First, I don't think he was born and brought up in Germany. He speaks very good German. But it's a bit formal in a way a German born person would not use.'

She paused. 'Let me try to give an example. Instead of saying "the three men went into a pub," he would say "the three gentlemen went into a pub." It's correct, but just a slightly wrong context sometimes in what he says.'

'And the second point?'

'Well, sir. He has a distinct way of saying the letter R. I've been trying to think where I've heard it before. And I've now got it. When I served in my father's shop, we had a customer who spoke the R in the exact same way. And he was Irish. I think Herr Brenner might be Irish, sir.'

Porritt glanced at Williams. 'Blimey. That does change things, Jane.' He sat back in his chair. 'Irish, huh?' He thought for a moment. 'Mike, remember the spy chap we lost in London about a week ago? Have we still got the artist's drawing here?'

Williams went to the filing cabinet and came back with the drawing Malcolm Craig had sent up. 'Doesn't look much like Brenner, sir.'

'No, it doesn't. But get the prints expert that Chris used to contact Malcolm and check against the partial he lifted in Hampstead. It's maybe not on file yet.

'Oh, and I assume we took our usual pics of Brenner when he arrived. Courier a set up to Dave, please?'

'Will do.' Williams picked up the phone.

Porritt stood. 'Let's get back and tackle this lad. He's lying through his teeth. Just dug a big hole for himself. And he's never born in Munich. He's far too vague on that.'

Porritt and Jane went back to the room and resumed their seats. Mike came in a few moments later and switched on the recorder.

'Right, Herr Brenner, let's start again. You've told us your story. But the fact is we found you knocked out on a beach near here, wearing a life jacket that had kept you afloat for about six hours.'

Porritt stopped, got up, and went over to Mike. He whispered, 'I didn't see a life jacket at the hospital. Call Chris and find out if they left it in the ambulance. We need to compare it to the ones our boat gang uses. Let's do that now, please.'

Mike left the room, and Porritt resumed his seat.

'Now, I've got a story for you, Herr Brenner. Early this morning we arrested the skipper and crew of a fishing boat for smuggling. And guess what we found? Lots of money. Much more than they'd ever get from smuggling alcohol and cigarettes. They got it from smuggling something far more valuable. And do you know what that was?'

Brenner stared at the table.

'That something was *you*, Herr Brenner. You see, it didn't take much for the crew to break down and admit what they'd done. And do you know what one of them said?' Porritt paused for effect. 'He said he was taking you out from a beach in Yorkshire in a small motor boat, when it hit something and sank. And he and you had to keep hold of each other until a third man swam on and brought a fishing boat back for you. But you lost your grip and floated away. They searched for hours but couldn't find you. Now don't you find that interesting, Herr Brenner?'

Brenner said nothing, but looked very serious.

'And you know what makes the story even better? That crewman's name was Joe. He described exactly the same as you said to us yesterday. Isn't that amazing? I certainly think so. Don't you, Herr Brenner?'

Porritt paused. Brenner sat still.

'Now, I have to break off to take a call. But we'll resume later. We have lots of time to get to the truth.' He looked up at the guards. 'Take him back to his room, Sergeant.'

Brown stood to attention. 'Yes, sir!' He got Brenner up from the table and took him out of the room.

Mike had only been out of the room for a minute and had caught up with Porritt's statement. He switched off the recorder. 'He's a cool customer, and no mistake.'

Porritt nodded. 'You know, some people think the best way to lie is to have as much of the truth in it as possible. So maybe the Gloster Aircraft story is true. And he's on the way out after completing it. Or maybe it's just a fancy cover story to hide what else he's done. Take your pick. Let's see what happens later.'

***

It was almost half past eight when they restarted. Porritt had endured a long call with senior Home Office staff on the operations at Bletchley Park and Station BX. He just got so annoyed with them. All talk and no action. Knew the cost of everything and the value of nothing. Useless ideas. A total pain in the arse.

Everyone was back in the same places as before. Williams switched on the recorder.

Porritt began, 'Well, now. What did you think of my story, Herr Brenner?'

Brenner shrugged. 'It wasn't me.'

'It wasn't you what?'

'It wasn't me in your story. It was someone else.'

Porritt paused. *Well, that was a new one.* This chap was saying, 'Stuff you. Prove it.' And he was right. Porritt had to prove it.

'Oh, but it *is* you. And all I have to do to prove it is bring that crew member down here. He'll pick you out as the man who floated away from him.'

Brenner shrugged again. 'You've got it wrong.'

'Oh no, I don't. You weren't coming here, Herr Brenner. You were leaving here. And I'd like to know what you were doing here.'

Brenner stretched his legs out under the table. 'No. You're wrong. It's not me.'

'Now maybe your story about Gloster Aircraft is true. But maybe it isn't. One thing is certain, though. You were on your way out. One way or another, we'll find out what you were doing here. And then you'll have twenty years in jail to think about it.'

Porritt paused to let that sink in. Brenner just shrugged again.

In the silence, Porritt heard a loud bang outside. Then another. He'd been around explosives long enough to know it wasn't a truck backfiring.

He jumped out of his seat. 'Sergeant, take him back to his room. Mike, you come with me!' Then dashed out of the room.

He and Williams ran through to reception. Porritt shouted to Alison, 'Is there a car here?'

'Yes. That's the driver over there,'

'Now! Take us down to the gatehouse.'

***

Jane lifted her bag and gas mask box, and put on her jacket. She didn't know why Porritt had left in such a hurry. So she'd just head back to the office. She smiled at Brown as she moved towards the door.

But Brenner spoke in English. 'Bring her.'

She turned back and stared at Brown and Henry. Now standing next to Brenner.

'Bring her!' Brenner barked again.

To her horror, Brown pulled his gun out and pointed it at her. 'Come on, you. Move!' He gestured that she should go with them through the door in the back wall.

Brenner had already hurried out. As she stumbled into the corridor with Brown, he came out of his room with his bag and coat. Henry had run on ahead and held a door open at the far end.

They all dashed through. She heard the door bang closed behind her. They ran across a rear courtyard towards the fence then moved down into the trees. Brenner held her while Brown and Henry worked at the fence. She shivered. Wasn't sure if it was shock, fear,

99

Brenner giving an order in English, or the cool night air. Maybe all of them. To her surprise, Brenner put his coat round her shoulders.

After about a minute, Brown shouted for them to move. They crouched down and crept through the tear in the fence held open by Brown and Henry. Then waited on the other side until they re-fastened it. Brown then led the way along a path through the woods, which came out into the open next to a steel fence.

They all piled into a car with its engine running. She sat shaking. Confused and afraid. In the middle of the back seat between Brown and Henry. The car took off along a rough road, and then on to a smooth road, and away from Station 19.

***

Porritt and Williams ran into the gatehouse. The fire alarm was ringing. 'What's going on?' Porritt shouted.

The security man looked dazed. 'There's been two explosions at the fence on the south side, sir. My mate's gone over there. I've set off the alarm to make sure staff get out.' Williams ran off towards the south end.

Porritt thought it wasn't the best course of action to set off the alarm. But too late now.

A few minutes later, Williams came running back. 'Two holes in the fence, sir. At the south end.'

Porritt yelled to the security man. 'Keep the gates closed. Don't let anyone leave the site. My orders.' They jumped into the car. 'Back up to the office, driver.' He turned to Williams. 'Someone's going to a lot of bother to create chaos. Why?'

'Anything to do with Brenner, sir?'

'That's a good question, Mike. Let's check.'

The outside lights had come on with the alarm, though they were still dim. Groups of staff gathered at the RV points. They ran through the interview room into the narrow corridor that had doors to the prisoner rooms along it. But there was no one there. They reached the closed emergency exit at the far end.

Porritt pushed the bar, and the door opened into a rear courtyard. It was pitch black outside, except for the dim light above the door. He stood in the dark, looking around. *Try to stay calm.* If the guards had taken Brenner out with the alarm, they'd have come out this way. Then gone down the side of the building to the RV point.

'Mike, go down there and check if they're at the RV point.' Williams went off into the dark.

On the other hand, if the guards were corrupt and had sprung Brenner, they'd also come out this way. With all the chaos focused on the other end of the site, they could have got through the fence here.

He walked along the fence. But it all looked intact in the dark. *Where the hell were they? Had they really breached his security to that extent?* The ringing stopped, and he went back inside.

He went into Brenner's room. Nothing there. No bags. No clothes. Nothing. If he had gone out with the alarm, some clothes would still be here. The empty room showed the bird had flown. *But how? And where?*

He went through to the interview room. The recorder still whirred. He stopped and rewound it. Then heard Brenner bark out his order, Brown telling Jane to move, and the scuffles as they all left.

He went to his office and found Alison. 'Get me CI Andrews at Lincolnshire Police, please.'

A few moments later, his phone rang. 'Can't get him, sir. He's out in a car. They're trying to patch him in. But it might take a few minutes.'

'Okay, thanks.' He laid a road map on the table, and opened it at the Lincoln page.

Williams came in. 'No sign of them, sir. No one's seen them.'

'No, they've flown, Mike. Brenner's room is empty. Everything gone. Looks like our guards were batting for the other side. And they've taken Jane too.'

'What? Why would they take her? To translate?'

'No, Mike. Go listen to the recorder. Brenner barks out orders in English to take her with them. So it's not that. Maybe she's some sort of hostage? Or did Brenner just fancy her? Want her as a playmate? He hardly took his eyes off her the entire time we were in there.'

The phone rang. 'CI Andrews, sir.'

'Chris, thanks for calling back. We've got chaos here. Brenner has escaped. We're not sure how yet. But he'll be in a car somewhere. Can you arrange some road blocks for us?'

'I'm sorry, sir. We've got our own chaos. Just had a bomb go off in a factory in Lincoln. Every car in the area is here. Not sure we can help.'

'Possibly linked, Chris. We've had a couple of explosions here too.'

'What? Then I'd say there's a definite link. Do you think they're diversions?'

'Could be.'

'Well, let's see what I can do to help. What are we looking for?'

'Three men and a girl. Plus a driver. Maybe heading for Liverpool or Stranraer if they're going to Ireland? Or south to the Channel?'

'Okay, I'll see what I can do. Get back to you.'

Porritt tried to stay calm. He asked Williams to have a guard take a torch and check the rear fence for a breach. Then have Kennedy, the captain of the guard, give him as much info as possible on Brown and Henry. Then call Dave Burnett to put roadblocks on Yorkshire ports in case they had a backup route there.

He then called Alison to come in. As she arrived, Williams shouted over, 'You'll never believe it. Most of the guards have food poisoning. Down with sickness and diarrhoea.'

Porritt closed his eyes and shook his head.

Alison asked, 'Can you say what's happening, sir?'

'The prisoner, Brenner, has escaped with the help of a couple of crooked guards. They've also taken Jane under duress. We're not sure why. The senior of the two guards is Sergeant Brown. Do you know him?'

She looked startled. 'Of course. He's always hanging around when he's off duty. And when he's on duty as well, to be honest.'

'Could he get access to staff records?'

She thought for a moment and shook her head. 'No, sir. We keep them in the safe. You need two keys, and I've got one of them. There's no chance he's seen these.'

'So what info on Jane *could* he get?'

'Well, there's the card index behind my desk. That has the main contact details for all staff.'

'Could you get me the card for Jane, please?'

'Yes, sir. Won't be a moment.' Within seconds, she was back with the card and passed it to Porritt.

Thomson, Jane. Date of Birth, 18 May 1918. Place of Birth, Prague, Czechoslovakia. Address, 811 Dalmarnock Road, Glasgow SE. Next of Kin, Thomas Thomson (Husband), Date of Birth, 14 March 1918, Married 26 September 1936. Contact Number, Home: Nil, Work: Rutherglen 2000 (Stewarts & Lloyds). Dependants, Stephen (Son), Date of Birth, 29 April 1937, George (Son), Date of Birth, 11 October 1938.

'So, this is the only info on Jane that Brown would have access to?'

'That's right, sir.'

'Could you do a couple of things for me, please? Get me three copies of the photos for Brenner, Jane, Brown, and Henry. And call the medics at Scampton. See if they can give our guards something to cure their sickness?'

'Yes, sir.' She got up and left the room.

He sat looking at the card. Not a lot the spies could leverage with. But they weren't daft. And the last thing they'd want is a reluctant young girl along as well. So, this chap Brenner must be key to them, if he could decide to take her with him, and they had to agree.

The phone rang. 'CI Andrews for you, sir.'

'Chris, what have you got?'

'Right, sir. Cambridgeshire Police have put a block on the A1 south at Sawtry. We've also blocked the A15 north at Scunthorpe. But it's a long shot, sir. There are lots of side roads they could use.

'And just to let you know the explosion here *was* a diversion. It was a derelict factory. No casualties. We're checking it out now.'

'They should come up here and have a look at our explosions. See if they're linked.'

'Good idea. I'll ask them to do that. Oh, is Mike with you, sir?'

'He's on the other phone. Can I take a message?'

'I've just heard from Jenkins, our prints man. He contacted Malcolm Craig. His partial print in Hampstead is a match for your man Brenner.'

'No doubts?'

'Not as far as I know, sir.'

'Thanks, Chris.'

Porritt closed his eyes and put his head down on to his pointed hands. '*Shit*. That's twice the bugger has slipped through our fingers. *Shit!*'

A minute later, Williams came off the phone. Porritt lifted his head and looked over at him. 'Now we know Brenner, Convery, and Emerald 3 are the same person. Dammit! He must have some vial info on him for them to make all this effort.

'And yet we found nothing when we searched his things. It must be *knowledge* he's carrying. Yet that doesn't make sense either. They could just send that over by radio signal. Feel like we've missed something here.

'And think of his last message. Return plan changed. Then he pops up in the north. Wonder if something went wrong with his usual exit route from the south.

'Check if there were any recent issues with fishing boats on the south coast. Did we impound a boat for example? Let's see if we can find an exit route down there that might also lead to the paymasters.'

Williams nodded and took notes.

Porritt pondered. 'So then he comes north and that exit route doesn't work either. What will they do now?

Might not have another fishing boat lined up. Get Dave to check whether that was the first time these boys had taken someone out.

'If that's the case, and he's so vital, they'll want to fly him out now. Not possible from Britain. But they could do it from Ireland. And that means going through Northern Ireland. Check the best options for doing that, Mike. And let's set up roadblocks on them.'

He paused, thinking about his next move. His thoughts flitted to Jane. He hoped Brenner wouldn't mistreat her. 'Right. I'll call Jim Stevenson in Glasgow. I think the crooks will have to get Jane to cooperate. And that's their weak link.

'Call Malcolm in London and Dave in Yorkshire. Ask them to review all their info on Emerald 3, aka Convery, aka Brenner. I'll talk to them in the morning. We're going to catch this chap, Mike. Even if I have to use all my three thousand staff.'

'Do you want to include Chris Andrews, sir?'

'No. Keep it within SB. Chiefs and seconds only.'

'Right, sir. Will do. By the way, our guard with the torch couldn't find any breach in the fence. We'll look again in the morning. And Dave has put some road blocks up in Yorkshire.

And a Doctor Kerslake sent Brown and Henry here as part of their recovery plan. He does that quite a lot. Both wounded abroad.'

'What were their injuries?'

'Not specified, sir. Just states medium to serious leg wounds. History shows they joined from Belfast at different times. Posted to various places before ending up here. That's all I've got for the moment, sir.'

Porritt asked Alison to get Jim Stevenson in Glasgow. He had a broad plan of action in his head. But now needed to get it started to thwart any plans Brenner may have.

He told Stevenson what had happened. Then went on, 'Jane's in a tough spot, Jim. But I think she's also a weak link for them. Like most innocent people taken by force, she'll resist where she can. If she does, Brenner might want some leverage. And that will have to come from Glasgow. The only info they have about her is this.' He read out the card.

'So, the only contact info they have is her address and the husband's work's number. But they know she's got a couple of kids. And that's where she's most open to pressure.

'Now, this lot are clever, Jim. They could ask an agent in Glasgow to get pictures of her kids to threaten her with. Our problem is we want them to get these pics if that's what they want. Because their other option would be to use brute force. And we don't want that.' He forced his mind to stay on track and not dwell on that thought.

'So, I'd like you and your team to figure out what that agent would do, from the info they've got, to get photos of the kids back to Brenner. I also want you to ID that agent and where he sends the pics. So we get to know more about them.'

He lowered his voice. 'But the crucial thing is, Jim. You need to do all of that and stay out of sight. You must not alert either her family or the agent. No matter what happens, the family must react as normal. I want to use this to bring down the whole bloody lot of them.

'But if any of the agents gets spooked, they'll throw an alert. And the big boys will escape. And we'll lose them. So, what do you think?'

'Phew. Not easy, sir. But we've done hard tasks before. Let me have a think about it.'

'Will you and your second call me in the morning at nine? I'd like you to run through your plans with us.'

'Okay, sir. We'll talk then. It's a big chance if we can pull it off.'

'That's the plan, Jim. Good to have you on board. Oh, and I'll send you up a set of pics of the crooks. Just in case they appear in your area.'

'Thank you, sir. We'll do our bit this end.'

Williams had hung up his phone. 'Stranraer to Larne is their only option to NI, sir. Liverpool to Belfast is out. Security too heavy there after the recent bomb blast. But I've alerted them anyway. And we don't think they'd use private boats with all the patrols in the Irish Sea.

'I've got road blocks on all routes into Stranraer. If they go straight there, they'd arrive around six in the morning. I've also got ID checks at Stranraer station for all arrivals by train. Just in case they go that way.

'I've also got someone checking on fishing boat arrests on the south coast over the last month. And Dave will get back to us tomorrow on the Scarborough crew.

'I've also fixed up calls with Dave and Malcolm for the morning, sir. Malcolm says he's just had a report in from one of his young detectives. He and Brian are going through it now. He reckons you'll want to see it. So he'll send a copy up by courier overnight.'

***

Jane sat in the back of the car, squeezed between Brown and Henry. Brenner sat in the front next to the driver. No one spoke. She could see the dashboard clock. It showed ten minutes past eleven. And still they travelled through the dark night.

During the drive, she'd calmed down and wondered why they'd taken her. Was it to translate for Brenner? Unlikely. Since she thought he was Irish. And had already barked out an order in English.

Maybe he just fancied her and wanted her with him. That would be really creepy. She now regretted holding his hand in the hospital. Maybe that's what started it? She reminded him of Liesl, he'd said.

She felt helpless. Brown was a nasty piece of work. It wouldn't take much for him to turn violent. Maybe even bump her off?

If Brenner *did* fancy her, then her best chance to survive was to go along with him. Be as nice as possible to him. That way, he would protect her against Brown. He must have influence in the group for them to bring her. Otherwise, it didn't make sense.

Finally, they stopped, and the driver got out to open a gate. They then drove into a garage, and piled out of the car. She stretched her legs and took deep breaths. Brenner had already walked across a garden towards a large house, as though he knew where to go.

She noticed the garage door still open. With a thrill of adrenaline, she waited until Brown let her arm go to pick up his bag. Then dashed towards the door.

Within a few steps, he caught her, and hissed in her ear. 'Listen, you. He wants you with him. Go along with it and you'll be fine. But don't give us any bother. Or you'll be in big trouble.'

He gripped her arm and walked her over to the house. A man held the door open in the darkness. Tall, with grey hair and glasses, she thought he looked like a pleasant grandfather. He stared at her as she entered. 'Who's she, Brown?'

'Ask yer man over there. He wanted to bring her.'

The man closed the door, drew the curtains and switched on the lights. Brenner had moved into another room, and the man hurried after him. She heard him say to Brenner, 'What the hell are you doing bringing her with you?' just before the door closed. The sound of their raised voices carried back to the kitchen.

A tall, elegant woman, who had been standing next to the table, came over. 'Welcome, my dear. I'm Elizabeth. And that was my husband, John. Can I take your coat? Would you like a cup of tea?'

Jane let her take Brenner's coat from her shoulders. 'That would be nice, thanks.'

The sound of arguing from next door continued. Everyone just stood in the kitchen while Elizabeth made tea. A few minutes later, the door opened and the tall man stood in the doorway. 'Jane? Can you come in here, please? Herr Brenner wants to talk to you.' He held the door open as she entered and then closed it behind her as he went back into the kitchen.

The room was a large garden room, with a semi-circular bay window covered by thick curtains, and with wicker chairs and tables. Brenner sat in an easy chair over by the window. 'Come in, Jane. Have a seat here,' he said in German, and waved to a seat beside him.

She walked over and sat down. There was a knock at the door from the kitchen, and Elizabeth carried in a tray with the tea things. She poured them each a cup and left.

Brenner leaned over and held her hand. 'How do you feel now?'

She shrugged and resisted the urge to withdraw her hand. 'I'm fine. Just wondering why I'm here.' She felt nervous, but tried not to show it. *Keep in with him.*

He smiled. 'I know. Let me explain.'

'Please do,' she said, trying to remain aloof.

They spoke in German, almost as though it was their own private language.

'I've thought about what to say at this moment a hundred times. And still don't know. So let me just say it. You're the most beautiful woman I've ever met. And I wish we could spend the rest of our lives together.'

She felt her face redden and looked straight at him. He was like a puppy dog waiting for a pat on the head. Well, she wouldn't encourage him. She sat silent.

'When I woke up in hospital and you held my hand, I thought you were Liesl. But you're even more beautiful. I just want to love you, and be with you.'

Now she knew why he had taken her, she felt angry. How dare he think she was just some sort of token he could take whenever he wanted. Yet she stayed calm and kept a clear head. She had to disguise her true feelings. Yet go along with him to stay safe. He was way over the top. Though it *was* nice to hear. No one else, least of all her husband, had ever said such things to her. But she had to bring him down to earth without riling him.

She put her other hand over his. 'Herr Brenner.'

'Call me Karl.'

'Okay, Karl. There are a few things in the way of doing that. First, I'm already married.' She waved her ring finger. 'Second, I already have two young sons who I love very much. Third, you know nothing about me.'

He smiled. 'I know all I need to know. I sense sadness in you sometimes. Maybe your marriage is not so happy. Why would you work so far away from your husband if your marriage was happy?'

She shrugged. 'It's happy enough. The war distorts everything.'

'But the war will be over soon. Some people say it'll be over by Christmas. Then we all need to get on with each other again. And I'd love the chance to help bring up your boys. I can offer you lots of love, security, and comfort. I'll be a regional commander after the war. So our life will be very rich. You would enjoy it so much. With a great social life among the right sort of people. It would be a great life for you. Nice house. Nice clothes. Everything you want.'

She gazed at him. He had it all worked out. But she couldn't just accept what he said. She had to push back. 'But what if the Germans *don't* win the war?'

He looked puzzled and shrugged. 'It doesn't look like it. But if that happened, I'd just go back to Ireland. I'm originally from County Wicklow, just south of Dublin. My family has a farm there. But I've lived in Germany since I was a small boy. I feel German now. But I could have a good life in Ireland if I had to. And it would be even better with you at my side. We could do great things together.'

He seemed smitten with her. She needed to keep that. But push back with some common sense. She had to play it very carefully.

'So, what's the plan from here on?'

'Well, I still have a job to do. And we need to wait here a couple of days to collect something. But I've told them I'm not going on unless you come too. And that's upset them. But they'll get over it. Then we'll go to Ireland and fly to Germany. It'll be great there. I've got some leave due. We could catch a train to Prague, your home city. You'd like that, I'm sure.'

'How do you know I'm from Prague?'

'Oh, Brown picked up some info at your workplace. So, what do you think? Will you join me on what could be a grand life?'

She studied him. *What if I say no?* She probably knew too much about them already. Even though she didn't know where they were. So they wouldn't let her walk away. And she probably couldn't escape from here either. But she might have a chance once they travelled again. Best to stick with the plan and keep in with him.

'Well, there's a lot I don't know about you. And there's a lot you don't know about me. But for the moment, let's see where it goes.'

His eyes lit up and he smiled. 'Oh, that's great. I agree. Let's get to know each other better. Thank you so much.' He got up, walked over to the door, and called, 'John, could you come in, please? We've got it all fixed.' He spoke in English with a soft Irish accent.

Kay came into the room with his wife. 'Okay. That's good. Elizabeth, would you take Jane up to her room, please? We've got a few things to talk about here.'

Elizabeth took Jane's hand. 'Come, my dear. We'll leave them to it.' She led Jane upstairs to a large bedroom with its own bathroom. 'I'm sorry, my dear, but we must lock you in at night. We don't want you to leave us. I've got you some toiletries and night wear. We'll sort out the rest in the morning.'

Chapter 9. Thursday

Porritt arrived in the office just before eight. Williams was already at his desk. 'Kept thinking about that bloody fence all night, Mike. There's no way these chaps would walk down to the south end where they blew the fence. It would take far too long. They must have got out at this top end. Let's go see.' Porritt led the way out through the interview room.

As they walked, Williams said, 'No word from Liverpool or Stranraer, sir. Nothing from road blocks either. We'll keep them going today. But it looks like they've gone to ground somewhere.'

'Yeah. They'll be in a safe house by now.'

They studied the fence. Porritt pointed to the right. 'It's wide open up that way. But the trees shield it down this way. Let's go down there.'

Porritt went a few yards into the trees and stopped. 'Look at this, Mike.' Down the centre of the fence, between two posts, they saw extra wire ties stuck to the fence. He tried to ease one off, but it was on too tight.

Williams went back to the office and got pliers and a screwdriver. He gripped a wire tie with the pliers. Then used the screwdriver to lever it off the fence. The wire tie fell to the ground, and the fence opened. He did the same with other ties until a large tear opened in the fence. They pulled the sides of the tear apart and crawled through into the woods.

114

They followed a path, and in less than fifty yards found themselves on open ground beside a fenced-off radio mast.

Porritt looked around. He admired the village down the hill to his left, nestling in the sun. On the ground, at the side of the fence, were new tyre marks. They faded out as the car had moved on to firmer ground and headed down the hill towards a distant road.

Porritt shook his head with a wry grin. 'That's how they did it. Simple when you know how.'

They went back through the fence and re-attached the wire ties. Once you had the knack, it was easy. They just clipped on with a bit of force. They stood looking at it once complete. 'Easy to miss in the dark, Mike. Can't blame the guard for that.'

Back in the office, Porritt called Kennedy. Told him about the tear in the fence, and asked him to get it fixed. He also asked about the sickness. Still weak, but the runs had stopped. He rang off and turned to Williams. 'Have we any info in the files on this Dr Kerslake?'

'Let me check.' Williams came back with a memo from the War Office, dated just before Station BX/19 opened. It referred to the shortage of security staff for the site. And stated that Dr Kerslake, an approved War Office doctor, had proposed the use of the new Station as a staging post in his recovery process for wounded staff. To get them ready for active duty again. He would assess them monthly. They had approved the proposal and applied it with immediate effect.

'I don't think I've ever seen this Dr Kerslake, Mike. Have you?'

'No, never met him, sir. But we've no reason to. The security lads don't report to us.'

'True. But still. Let's just check him out. Make sure he's not one of the spy group.' He pulled his papers towards him. 'Right, let's talk to Jim in Glasgow.'

***

Jane woke and stretched. It was a comfy bed. They had given her white fluffy travel slippers and a dressing gown. She got up, went to the bathroom, and then came back and opened the curtains. It was a bright morning. The room looked out over the back garden to the woods beyond. She noticed the gate in the back fence lay ajar. The house was silent.

Then she heard a key in the door. Elizabeth came in carrying a tray with orange juice, cereal bowl and a jug of milk, and put it on a side table. 'Good morning. Hope you slept well.'

She noticed Elizabeth hadn't closed the door. 'I did, thanks.' She walked over, her heart thudding. Elizabeth turned with a smile. Jane pushed her down into an armchair, ran to the door and down the stairs.

She heard Elizabeth screaming, 'Stop her! Stop her!'

At the foot of the stairs, Brown appeared holding a gun. 'That's not a good idea. Get back upstairs.'

She stopped and gathered her breath. Henry had appeared behind him. She turned and ambled back up the stairs. Brown and Henry followed.

Elizabeth stood at the top. Brenner appeared from a side room and watched her come up to the top landing.

'That wasn't very nice, Jane,' he said in German. 'We're here to look after you. We'll talk later.'

He turned to Elizabeth. 'Take her back to her room,' he said in English. 'I'll deal with it.'

Jane walked into her room, and Elizabeth followed. 'I know you may not like this, my dear. We don't like it much either. But just try to relax and go with the flow. You'll be all right if you do that.

'Now, why don't you take some breakfast? Once you're ready, knock on the door, and I'll come and take you downstairs. Maybe even get a chance to sit in the garden.' She left the room and locked the door.

Jane went over and sat at the side table. Maybe she had been a bit impulsive. But she wasn't willing to sit and wait just because that's what *they* wanted. At least now she had a clearer idea of where she stood. She'd wait and see what Brenner said later.

***

At nine o'clock, Porritt's phone rang. 'It's Jim Stevenson, sir. With Sandra Maxwell.'

'Good morning to you both. I've got Mike Williams with me. We'd like to discuss your plans for what we talked about last night, Jim.'

'We've got something we think will work, sir. We agree the spies would want photos of Jane's kids for leverage. But first, they have to find them. Now, Jane told us, when we first met her, that her in-laws have them outside the city. And that's not on the index card. The spies would have to dig deep to find that out.

'So we've tried to cover all the risk areas we can think of. We've set up covert teams at her home address, her husband's office, his parents' house, and at her parents' shop.

'At her home address, a flat in a Glasgow tenement, we're using the 'Gas Board' ploy in the backcourt. From there, we can film anyone at her door through the half landing window.

'At her husband's office, I know one of the Directors very well. He's agreed one of his senior staff will watch Tommy today, to see if he meets any strangers. We're also tapping his phone at the switchboard.

'For his parents' home, we've a 'Burglary Watch' team in the house across the street. They'll film anyone at the front door. We also have a team in the house at the rear to cover that side. We're also tapping their phone at the local exchange.

'Last, we've put a 'Shoplifting Watch' team in the rear of her parents' shop in case anyone goes there. We're tapping their phone as well.

'So, we'll stay under cover, sir. But, if a stranger appears at any of these, we'll have to break cover to find out what they said. We'll use the local crime watch excuse so we don't alarm them.'

Williams cut in. 'That's okay, if it's after the event.'

'Yeah. That's right, Mike.'

'So, what will you do if someone does turn up?'

'We'll use a technique that we've had lots of success with in the last few years. We call it "Following from the Front". Our team travels in front of the target and covers where he could go. Targets always check behind them. And use the "last on, last off" routine to slip their tails. They just don't see our team in front. We ID a lot more targets that way. And a have a higher arrest rate.'

'How does it work then?'

'You've got to wire up in advance, Mike. Each person has a mic on a wrist strap and an earpiece to hear everyone talk. It's bulky, with a heavy battery pack, and a limited range. You also need a car within range to carry the power links. But it works. Our team wears reversible coats to hide it and to change disguise.'

'Sounds great. Where did you get it?'

'From the US. A company called ARC, who make aircraft radio systems. They did a prototype for NYPD, I believe, and it went on from there. Other PDs bought it too. Our Chief bought a set after the RCMP showed it at the Empire Exhibition, here in Glasgow in '38. I think we got one of the last, though. They ditched them because of a pre-war surge in their aircraft side.'

Porritt cut in. 'Sounds good, Jim. Well done. Let us know how it goes.'

'Right, sir. Will do.' He rang off.

Porritt turned to Williams. 'That's a good team in Glasgow. But he does go on a bit. Now let's see how Dave's getting on in Yorkshire with his boatmen.'

Burnett rang in a few minutes later. 'Good morning, sir. We're still holding our crew for smuggling booze and fags. Which they deny. We've now told them other charges are pending, and they've all clammed up except Armitage.

'He says it's the first time they've done this. We've shown him the pics of Brenner you sent up, Mike. He confirms that's the man they picked up from the beach to take out to a U-boat. Got it all on record, sir. So, we've closed the loop on that one.'

Porritt nodded. 'That's great, Dave. Means we can bring in treason. And all the rules go up in the air. They need to know they're looking at ten years at least.'

'Right, sir. We did a prints check on the envelope with the money. It's only got the skipper's prints. The cash has lots of prints, but no matches so far.

'We checked the life jacket you sent up, Mike. It's the same as the ones the crew use. But it's a common brand. We'll check it for prints as well.

'We're trying to get our Joe to tell us about the paymasters. He's says the skipper had a private meeting with a man Joe thought was local. So maybe Yorkshire still has more secrets to give up. That's it, sir.'

Porritt rang off and looked over at Williams. 'Happy with that?'

'Yes. He's doing fine.'

'Right, ten minutes before Malcolm rings in. Let's have a cup of tea.'

Craig rang in at ten. Porritt took notes. 'Okay, Malcolm, what do you have from London?'

'First, fishing boats on the south coast. We checked with South region. Three weeks ago, they impounded a boat for smuggling brandy. The owners, two brothers, seemed to live very well. We've asked them to check for prints against our partials from Hampstead. And send accountants in to follow the money trail.

'Turning now to Convery, sir. The man in the top flat said he'd seen him with two girls in the pub. Well, they turned up again there last weekend. He told a policeman I wanted to talk to them. We saw them on Monday night. They're two sisters from the West Midlands doing a course in London.

'They couldn't tell us much about him, though. Said he was a pleasant Irish chap, who had treated them to a meal in another pub. But he didn't talk about himself much. They all went back to their flat, listened to music, and had a few drinks. One thing led to another. He and one of the sisters got very friendly. The other went to bed and left them to it.

'The sister with him said they kissed and petted. He'd moved his hand inside her blouse. Then suddenly stopped, jumped up, and said he had to go. He dashed out of the flat as though scalded. It upset her at the time because she thought they were getting on great.'

'So, what happened?'

'I asked her what she wore under her blouse. She has a necklace with a gold Star of David. Turns out they're Jewish and enjoy their Saturday nights in London. But we think that's what turned our man off.'

Porritt sighed. *Bit of a dead end.*

Craig went on. 'The next thing I want to talk about is the phone call that made him scarper. Now, we all know it's hard to trace a call from a public phone box. Because of the manual links needed to connect it. So we didn't hold out much hope.

'We gave the job to a young DC called Edwards. He'd just joined us from Merthyr, and it was his first day in London. He didn't know things are hard to do here, and applied his usual gritty Welsh approach.

'He started with the Hampstead number and went to see the relevant GPO people. They told him in central London, they'd tested a new semi-automatic system to prepare for direct dialling after the war.'

'What does that mean, then?'

'Well, in the old way, an operator physically made the link to the end number. The new way holds the call in the exchange. Then the operator just redirects it to the end number. Because of the new single link, they can now trace the caller number from a receiving number. So, when they checked their records for the Hampstead number, they found the caller's number. A public phone box in Trafalgar Square.

'Edwards then got a list of the calls from the phone box that morning and spotted the one to the Hampstead number at 09.27.'

Porritt listened with mounting interest.

'He then went to Trafalgar Square and found the phone box. The left-hand one of a bank of four in the south-east corner. He then saw a group of men with a tower wagon fixing something high on a wall on the south side. They had just replaced the film in a camera used by Westminster Council to study peak traffic flows as part of their post-war planning.

'So he then went off to meet the traffic engineers. Asked to see the film of the square on the morning of the call. He found that a man entered the phone box at 09.21 and emerged at 09.29. When he checked against the list of numbers called, the man had made a call at 09.22, another at 09.25, and a third at 09.27. He then went back to his GPO contacts and got the names and addresses of the first two numbers the man called.'

'Do we have pics of this man?' Porritt asked.

'Yes, sir. He has blown up photos of the man going in and out the box. We don't know him. Or how to identify him without blowing our cover. So we're a bit stuck at this point.

'Edwards wrote the whole thing up in a report. We got it last night. I sent a copy to you overnight, sir. Have you seen it yet?'

Porritt raised an eyebrow at Williams, who left the room. 'Haven't seen it, Malcolm. Just hold on and we'll check where it is. I think young Edwards has done a first-class piece of work. Please pass on my congrats for a job well done.'

'Will do, sir. I'm sure he'll appreciate that.'

Williams came back with a large envelope. 'Alison didn't want to disturb us.'

Porritt opened it and pulled out the report. 'Right, I've got it here now, Malcolm.'

'The photos are right at the back, sir.'

Porritt stared at them in silence. His mind went into turmoil. He felt tears in his eyes. He slammed his fist down on the table. 'Bastard!' He paused. Then brought both fists banging down on the table. 'Bastard!' he shouted through gritted teeth.

Total silence. No one spoke or even coughed.

When he spoke, his voice trembled. 'I'm sorry, guys. You'll gather I know this man. And it's a blow. I need to take a break and think what to do next. Ring me back in ten minutes please, Malcolm.' He rang off.

Porritt looked over at Williams. 'Can't talk, Mike. Need some air.' He left the room and stood in the fresh air outside the building. Now he knew the Whitehall mole. Churchill had been right. But before he could go back to the PM, he needed a rock-solid case. How could he achieve that?

***

Porritt had perked up by the time Craig called back. 'Right, Malcolm. We need to talk about this report. And about the man in the photos. First, the report. Get every copy of it, together with the films and backup info, and put the lot in your safe. Access only to you and Brian. I'm sure Edwards is proud of his report. And rightly so. But we need to keep it well hidden. Can you do that today, please?'

'Yes, sir.'

'Now, what were the first and second numbers the man called?'

'They're listed on page six, sir. The first was to a small shop called Lyall Shoes in central London. They make and sell handmade shoes. The second was to the home of Mr and Mrs Roger Lyall in West Hampstead. The owners of Lyall Shoes.'

Porritt grimaced. 'Dammit. It was the shoes, Mike. When we checked Brenner's things at the hospital, he had a pair of Lyall shoes. They must have hidden the secret info inside them. Never even thought. No wonder he was so damn cocky. Dammit!'

Williams shook his head. 'I'm sorry, sir. Should have picked up on that. We just focused on the bag.'

'Oh, no use crying over spilt milk. And a hundred other phrases that cover it. We are where we are, Mike. So let's get on with it.'

'Yes, sir.'

'Okay, Malcolm, let's talk about the man in the photos. He's Sir James Dunsmore. Senior MI5 chap. Member of the Strategy Review Committee we followed a few months ago. And nothing showed up then. But I'll bet if we check our notes, we'll find he visited that shoe shop. That's how they passed the info. He's probably the covert Aquila 2 we've been searching for. So much now becomes clear to me.'

'Wow. Didn't expect that, sir.'

'Now, I know Dunsmore. Always thought him overrated. He's an admin type. Not an operations man. He couldn't organise his way out of a paper bag. So, I think this Lyall fellow must be one of his top operators. Maybe Aquila 3 or 4. These are the men that make it happen in the field.

124

'And if you took a pic of Mrs Lyall to your landlady in Hampstead, I'll bet she'd nail her as Convery's aunt who booked his room.

'Put a tail on Dunsmore. Twenty-four seven. I need to know where he goes. Who he sees. All about him. Cover all exits wherever he goes. And I'm sure I don't have to tell you to stay well out of sight, Malcolm.'

'Understood, sir.'

'And put a tap on his home phone. No point doing it with his office phone. He won't use it for this stuff. He'll use public phone boxes to make these calls.

'Do the same for Lyall. I need to get more evidence to break this group. And this is our chance. We need your best people on it, Malcolm.'

'Going to take a lot of resource, sir.'

'I don't care. This is top priority. Bring in people from other forces. Use my authority if you need to. But be very quiet. Give it a code name. Don't talk outside our group. Dunsmore will have links everywhere. And if either of these chaps looks like heading out the country, pull him in. We can't lose them now.'

'Yes, sir.'

***

Jane knocked on her bedroom door. She thought about Elizabeth's comment, 'We don't like it much either.' So Brenner had forced her on them. She just had to keep close to him. No matter how much she hated it.

Elizabeth unlocked the door, and took her down to the garden room. Brenner looked up and smiled. 'Jane. Here, have a seat.' He spoke in German and waved to an armchair beside him.

She sat and smiled back. 'Good morning again,' she replied in German. She looked around. 'Nice room. Nice garden.' She noticed the back gate now closed and probably locked.

He leaned over and touched her hand. 'I'm upset with you, Jane. I thought we'd sorted it all last night.'

'Well, we had. But I just don't like to feel trapped. And locked in. Makes me think you don't trust me.'

He raised an eyebrow and nodded. 'Fair point. Though it's not so much me. It's more the others. They need to keep a low profile. So they're nervous about having you here.'

She thought she could push it further. 'I can see that. But if you want me to give up my life for you, then we have to be open with each other. I admit I don't have much of a marriage. You're right there. And what you say sounds exciting. But only if we're partners. I don't want to become a doormat to yet another man. That's no life for me. So I'm sorry for my actions this morning. But I hope you now understand.'

He smiled. 'Of course I do. But I need to keep in with the others. Tell you what. Why don't we have a wander round the garden in the fresh air?'

'Sure.' She hoped her words would help him relax and support her against the others. She took his pleas at face value. And hoped he took hers the same way. That would give her the best chance to survive this.

They went out into the garden. A fine morning. Sunny and bright. Birds sang in the trees beyond the rear fence. But spoiled when Brown stood at the back gate and Henry at the side gate. As they walked, she put her head on Brenner's shoulder to make him feel better about her.

126

He was a fine figure of a man. And she still savoured his words last night. No one had ever called her beautiful before. Genuine or not, she liked it. But did he see her as just a brief stand-in for Liesl? Or did he really feel something deeper?

As they strolled, he talked about the new life they'd have. Mixing with the right people. Spending his wealth. She just let him talk. They stopped next to a large oak tree in the far corner. He pulled her close. 'You're so beautiful,' he whispered. His mouth close against her cheek. She held her breath. Her heart thumped. It just seemed right to turn and let him kiss her. She thrilled at the contact. Then they strolled on.

He held her hand. 'Oh, by the way, we need new travel papers. And they want to change our looks. Elizabeth will get you a couple of casual outfits so you can change out of your uniform. Give her the sizes and what suits you. Is that all right with you?'

She nodded. Maybe Elizabeth was right when she said just go with the flow. That's just what she would do. For the moment.

***

Stevenson paced the room. Lunchtime, and nothing at any site. No callers at the home address. No phone calls to Tommy's work. A couple of phone calls to the in-laws house. But nothing dodgy. And nothing odd at the shop in Byres Road. He looked over at Maxwell and shook his head. 'Something should have happened by now, Sandra. Let's grab a quick lunch and go out to Cambuslang. What do you say?'

'Great idea, sir. By the way, that's my old stomping ground. Brownside Road. Grew up there. Know it well.'

'Mmm. Could be useful.'

In the car, she turned to him. 'You know the phone call mum in-law got this morning? From the Malmaison. A free meal in exchange for feedback? Do you think that's for real?'

'Yeah. All these top restaurants are struggling. We had the same call last week from the Grosvenor. They got our name from a previous visit. They're all at it. They need people back through their door again. The war's gone on too long already.'

'Wow. Nice if you can get it.'

'I'll let you know how it goes.'

'Oh, thank you, sir.'

The car dropped them a couple of streets away. They then strolled up the hill and along Brownside Road to number 18. As they entered the gate, they glanced across to number 11, the in-laws house. All quiet.

They showed their warrant cards to the woman at number 18. 'To join our colleagues.'

She stood aside to let them in. 'Of course. It's the door facing you at the top of the stairs.'

Sam and Jill stood as they entered the room. Sam smiled. 'Good to see you, sir, ma'am. Not changed since we last spoke. No visitors. No phone calls.'

Stevenson pursed his lips. 'It's all too quiet, Sam. They should have done something by now. Let me call Don and Tina at the rear.'

He and Maxwell had put on their comms gear before they left the office. He pressed his mic button. 'Don, Tina? Stevenson here. Just popped in to number 18. All okay with you?'

His earpiece crackled, 'Yes, sir. All quiet here.'

'Yeah. Sometimes it's like that. Just be patient.'

The four of them stood in the shadow of the curtains and looked across at number 11. Stevenson worked out the front of the house faced south. So the back garden faced north. That was the wrong way round for him. He loved his south-facing back garden at home. It was a nice house, though.

The street was quiet, apart from an occasional car. He thought it looked a well-off area. Detached houses. Gardens well-tended. Good place to live.

'Here's our next visitor,' Jill said. A man worked his way from house to house along the other side of the road coming down from the left. Put flyers through each letter-box. He did number 11. Then number 9, and each house to the end of the road. Then crossed to their side, and worked his way back up. Nothing suspicious there.

'And here's the next one,' she said. And again pointed up to the left. A little old lady entered the gate of a house up the road. She carried a handful of flyers.

Stevenson watched as she rang the doorbell and waited. No reply. She pushed a flyer through the letter-box, came out and went in the next gate. He couldn't get a clear view because of trees as she talked with someone at the door.

A couple of minutes later she emerged and went through the next gate. Then worked her way down from house to house. She had grey hair, glasses, and wore a grey coat and hat, black shoes, and carried a large black handbag. She had a jerky walk. Every step she took with her left foot seemed to lift her body slightly. She talked to the woman at number 13, gave her a flyer, and then moved to number 11.

She approached the house and rang the bell. Mrs Thomson came to the door, with two boys trailing behind her. They looked up at the visitor.

The two women talked for several minutes. Mrs Thomson smiled and nodded to the old woman. Sam started the film camera behind them. Stevenson wished he could hear what they said.

On another case, a few months ago, he had recorded two men talking. But it had taken him hours to set up. They had hidden the large mic in a vase on a sideboard. And covered the wire that linked it to a recorder in the next room. He just couldn't do that here.

At one point, the old lady held up her bag and rummaged inside it. She found two sweets and gave them to the boys.

The women smiled and parted. Mrs Thomson guided the boys back into the house. The old woman turned towards him up the driveway, moved on to number 9, and talked to the woman there.

He murmured, 'What do you think?'

Sam shrugged. 'Looked okay to me. Maybe a free offer or something?'

'Yeah. Everyone's giving free gifts these days.'

Maxwell still watched the old woman as she emerged from number 9. 'Hold it. There's something wrong. She's glanced back, missed number 7 and rushed away.' She pressed her mic button. 'Tina, get your car. There's an old woman just leaving Brownside Road. Going into Greenlees Road. Grey coat and hat. Big black handbag. Kind of jerky walk. Her body lifts with each left footstep. I need to know which way she goes. Down the hill to Main Street. Or up the hill to Kirkhill Station. Fast as you can, please.

'And Don. Get round here now and take over the obs. We're going to follow that old woman. Go over to Mrs Thomson. Use the local crime watch excuse we talked about. Find out what the woman said to her.'

'Will do, ma'am.'

Stevenson felt the sudden rush that came from finding a target. He ordered his car round. And told Sam and Jill to get their car too. They all needed to get ahead of the target to 'follow her from the front'.

Tina came on the line. 'The woman is walking down towards Cambuslang Main Street. I'll pass her and park to see where she goes.'

Maxwell said, 'If she crosses over, she'll catch a bus going east to Hamilton. If she stays on this side, she'll get a tram or bus into Glasgow.'

'She's turned left, ma'am. At the tram stop now. Looks like she's going into Glasgow.'

Stevenson cut in. 'We're just turning into Main Street. Passing target at tram stop and parking. Tina, could you go on to the next stop and get on the tram when it comes. So we can keep our eyes on her.'

'Will do, sir.'

Maxwell then cut in. 'Shit. Don, have you seen Mrs Thomson yet?' Stevenson turned to her in a panic.

'Yes, ma'am. Just left her. The woman's from the David Livingstone Centre in Blantyre. They've just put in a new children's swing park and café. If you present the flyer she left, you get a free tea and biscuit. Mrs Thomson said she was a very pleasant lady.'

'Yes, I'm sure she is. But I need you to go back to her. Think up an excuse and get the sweets the woman gave the kids. They might have poison. Get the lab to check them later.'

131

'Yes, ma'am. Will do.'

Stevenson was on the edge of his seat. He loved these chases. 'The tram's coming up to the stop. It's a number seventeen to Whiteinch. Target not moving. Still at the stop. Now she's moving out. Okay, she's doing the last on, last off ploy. So, she's a professional. Hold on, that's the tram just passed us. Target on the lower deck about halfway along on this side. What's the next major junction down the line, Sandra?'

Maxwell paused for a moment. 'Farme Cross. About two miles. She could go left on a tram to Rutherglen and Burnside, or a bus to Croftfoot. Or an SMT bus to East Kilbride. Lots of choices there. Or she could stay on the tram and go right towards Glasgow.'

Stevenson pressed his mic button. 'Okay. Sam and Jill. Can you go on and cover if she goes left? We'll cover if she goes right.'

Tina cut in, almost a whisper. 'On tram. Just inside lower deck. Target rummaging in her bag.'

Maxwell grunted. 'I'll bet there's a camera in there. When she held it up to look for a sweetie, she took pictures. Wow, she's good. Her cover story's totally credible. If she hadn't rushed past the last few houses, she'd have got away with it.'

Sam asked, 'So the David Livingstone thing is just a dodge, then?'

'Yeah. She'll just go into a large hotel, pick up some flyers, and spin a story. She's good at it, though.'

'Wow. She fooled me.'

Stevenson worried about tracking targets through major junctions. 'We're just coming up to Farme Cross. We'll wait in a side street here. Sam and Jill, are you in position?'

'Yes, sir.'

Stevenson watched the tram approach the junction. 'Okay, tram here. Target still on board. Tram held by points policeman. Target has just got off the tram. She's off the tram. Target strolling towards the cross. Now crossing over towards the Tennent's pub. Now waiting at the tram stop.'

Maxwell cut in. 'She's going to Rutherglen. Tina, can you get off and catch the next twenty-six tram coming from Dalmarnock Bridge?'

Stevenson asked, 'Where do Sam and Jill go now?'

Maxwell said, 'Sam and Jill, you go on up Farmeloan Road to Rutherglen Cross. It's about half a mile. That's the next major junction. She could get an eighteen tram from there.'

'Okay, will do, ma'am.'

Tina cut in. 'Have crossed the road. Number twenty-six tram to Burnside approaching.'

Stevenson watched the little old lady at the tram stop. How the hell did a woman like this become a spy? 'Target doing the same thing again. Holding back to be last on.' He watched the tram cross the junction and head up the hill towards Rutherglen. 'Like the glasses and headscarf, Tina. They suit you.' His driver moved the car out to follow the tram.

Sam cut in. 'Am at Rutherglen Cross, opposite the tram stop.'

Jill said. 'Have crossed Rutherglen Main Street. Now looking in window of Boots the Chemist. Can get a clear view in reflection.'

Sam came on the line, his voice low. 'Twenty-six tram just arrived. Target still on board. Now, she's off the tram. Waiting to cross Main Street. Now heading straight for you, Jill.'

'Yeah, I've got her. Looks like she's coming here. I'll stroll into the shop in front of her.'

Sam said, 'Target has entered Boots the Chemist.'

Tina came on the line. 'Now off the tram. Walking down Stonelaw Road towards Main Street.'

Jill spoke very quietly. 'Can see target on the other side of shop. Looking at lipsticks. But really looking at the door. Now moving to the back of the shop. To the photos counter. I'll see if I can get into a better position. Handing over film from her bag. Getting receipt. Paying with two half-crowns. No change. She's taking the special one-hour service. Now turning and leaving the shop back into Main Street.'

Stevenson got his people into position. 'Sandra, can you go west along the north side of Main Street? Tina, can you turn left and walk along the south side? Sam, can you just hang back and see which way the target goes? I'll go into Boots and see if I can get a copy of the film she's left. Jill, can you find out how we contact the shop manager, please? And then join me.'

Sam asked, 'Why would a spy use Boots?'

Maxwell said, 'Chemicals are so scarce now, Sam. Only businesses can get them. Boots try to maintain a full service. Their West End branch did our family snapshots last month.'

'Oh, I see. Makes sense, then. Target waiting to cross Main Street to the north side. Now crossing and walking about twenty yards behind you, ma'am.'

'Thanks, Sam. I'm coming up to an alley that runs north off Main Street. Lots of people using it. I'm going into the alley. Can you come across Tina and pick her up if she goes straight along Main Street?'

'Will do, ma'am.'

'Alley takes me into King Street. Turning right towards a school.'

Sam stated, 'Target turning into alley, ma'am.'

'Okay, Sam. Will do a quick change and see where she goes at this end.'

Tina cut in. 'You should see her in a sec, ma'am.'

'Yes, got her. Target crossing King Street and . . . hold it . . . then walking across a gap site towards the back close of a building backing on to us here. Okay, she's entering the back close and climbing the stairs. Going into a flat one floor up to the right as I look at it. And there's a man at the kitchen window. Grey hair, glasses. He turned as she entered. Also, a telephone line runs to the flat from a pole in the backcourt. Tina, can you come through to the street behind King Street?'

'Will do, ma'am. In a side street now and then into Victoria Street.'

'It's the third close from the east end of that building, Tina. If it's the right one, I'll see you through the landing window.'

'Entering number 25 and going up the stairs. Can you see me?'

'Yes, Tina. I see you. What's the name on the door on the first floor right as I look at it?'

'Pointing to the door. Is that the right one?'

'Yes, that's it.'

'Name on the door is Brady. B-R-A-D-Y.'

'Okay, sir. That's it. Brady, 25 Victoria Street.'

135

Stevenson punched the air. 'Great stuff, people. We're getting a copy of the film she left under the guise of a quality check. Which they do every so often, anyway. Gives us a copy without alerting the operator.'

Maxwell said, 'I've got to move from here, sir, I'm too obvious. Now walking west on King Street.'

He thought for a moment. 'Let's assume she goes back to Boots in an hour. Tina, get your car round to Victoria Street and cover the close at number 25. Sandra, get our car round to King Street so you can see her if she comes that way. Wait, the manager's just come back.'

There was a brief silence.

'Okay. You were right, Sandra. The film contains pictures of the Thomson kids. Let's think. Once the target gets them, she'll want to send them somewhere. Sam, can you get to your car and call the office? Within the next fifteen minutes, I need to meet the person responsible for post box collections here in Rutherglen. Can you also get them to put a tap on the Brady phone line? My authority.'

'Will do, sir.'

'Jill, could you change and stay here in Boots to watch the target when she comes back, please?'

There was a delay while everyone got into position.

Sam came on the line. 'Right, sir. The person for postal collections here is Jack Millar. Go to the post office on Main Street. To the counter window on the far right. And ask for him. He'll come and get you.'

'Thanks, Sam. Can you go back to Main Street and watch the alley?'

Stevenson found the post office, went to the right-hand window, and asked for Jack Millar.

Within a minute, a young man in a white shirt, who walked with a stick, came through from the back. 'CS Stevenson?'

Stevenson showed his warrant card. Millar opened a door and guided him through to a quiet area behind the counters. 'I need a favour, Mr Millar.'

'I'll do what I can, of course.'

'I've got a team watching a person of great interest to us. But we don't want the person alerted in any way. Now, we think the person will post a letter in about twenty minutes. Once the person has done that and moved away, we'd like to have the box opened so we can see the address on the letter. Then put it back in the box to go on its way as normal. Can we do that?'

'Yes, shouldn't be a problem. I'll get one of my lads to open it for you.'

'Great. Now, where are the local post boxes?'

'Well, there's one on the back wall of the post office here. There's also one outside on the pavement. The next nearest is on this side at Rutherglen Cross. And there's one the other way, outside the Odeon Cinema.'

'Okay, I'll stay here with you. My team will alert me by radio which box the person goes to. You can then get your man to open that box?'

'Fine. We'll just empty it as usual. We do it around this time, anyway. But we'll hold the top three inches in a separate bag. Then it's just looks like a normal collection. He'll bring them in here for us to look at. Is that okay?'

'Sounds good. We just have to wait now.'

'Right. I'll bring a lad in here. And set up a chap in a van round the corner. He can then get to any of the street boxes in a few seconds. Back in a minute.'

A few minutes later, Stevenson's earpiece crackled.

Maxwell said, 'Target on the move. Crossing King Street into alley through to Main Street.'

Sam spoke quietly, 'Okay. Am looking in shop window. Right, got her. Target walking towards the Cross. Am ten yards ahead of her.'

Stevenson felt that excitement in his stomach again. 'Jill, ready in Boots?'

'Yes, sir. Inside watching the doors.'

Sam said, 'Target stopped. Waiting to cross. Target now moving across towards Boots.'

Stevenson thought what the target might do with the pics. She probably wouldn't put them in an envelope in Boots. She'd do that at home. Or maybe in the post office. He pressed his mic button. 'Sam, change and get back here to the post office. There's a post box on the back wall. And a writing shelf beside it. Stand at the shelf near the post box and look busy. Fill in a form or something. I need to know the size of envelope and anything you can see of the address the target writes. Sandra, come in to the post office. Mingle with the crowd and keep an eye on the target if she comes here?'

'Will do, sir.'

Millar came back with another man carrying a couple of bags. They nodded to Stevenson.

Stevenson whispered, 'Jill, I need to know if target leaves the shop and goes to the post box at the cross.'

'Right, sir. Target in shop. Watching the doors. Now moving to back of shop. Presents receipt at photo counter. Gets folder of pictures. Glances at them. Puts them in her bag. Now heading out of shop. Waiting to cross Main Street. Now crossing and walking west towards Town Hall. Not near post box.'

'Okay, Jill. Keep obs from south side of street. Tina, I need to know if she uses the post box outside the post office, just next to the Town Hall.'

'Right, sir.'

Jill interrupted. 'Target still walking along Main Street. Passes alley. Heading towards the post office. Now entering post office. Over to Sam and Sandra.'

'Got her,' said Maxwell, quietly. 'Target going to writing shelf on back wall. One person between her and Sam. Don't talk, Sam. Target watching the door. Now into bag. Pulls out folder of pictures and envelope. Am too far away to see address. Puts pictures in an envelope. Seals it. Back into bag. Bites off a piece of sticky tape and fastens to back of envelope. Packs her bag. Picks up envelope. Walking out and drops it into post box on back wall.'

Stevenson turned to Millar. 'Right, the person has just dropped an envelope into the postbox on the back wall. Can we get it now, please?'

Millar gave his man the nod, and he went through the door into the post office.

Stevenson said, 'Tina and Jill, can you just make sure target goes back home, please?'

Tina answered. 'Target in public phone box outside post office. Making a call. Putting in more than three pence. So a long distance call.'

He grimaced. *Dammit. Should have thought of that. But we couldn't trace the call anyway*. 'Sandra, Sam, can you come to the right-hand window, please?' He turned to Millar. 'Can you let them through, please?'

Millar opened the door and Sandra and Sam came in to the back area. The postman followed with the two bags and put them on a table.

'Have you got any fine gloves?'

Millar shook his head. 'Not handy, I'm afraid.'

'Not to worry. Just you handle the letters, then.'

The postman emptied the small bag of letters onto the table and spread them out. 'This is the top three inches or so.'

Sam said. 'It's an ordinary-sized envelope. The top line of the address is only three letters. And there are four lines on the address. Couldn't see the detail, though. There's sticky tape on the back at the flap.'

The postman ruffled through the letters. 'There's this one. It's the only one that matches.'

They looked at the letter. Stevenson noted the address. 'SMC, Albemarle House, Pickering, Yorkshire. Do you think it has photographs?'

The postman felt it. 'Could be.'

Sandra bent down and sniffed. 'Can you turn it over?' The postman did so. She sniffed again. 'That's got a dab of perfume on the back. They're using perfume to verify it. Very clever.'

Stevenson nodded. 'Have we got everything?'

'Think so, sir.'

Stevenson turned to Millar and the postman. 'Thank you. That was important for us. Can you make sure the letter gets back into the system for delivery, please?'

'No problem,' said Millar, and the postman put the letters in the bag and carried them out to the collection office. 'It'll be delivered in the morning.'

'Great. Thanks again.' Stevenson led the way back to the post office.

Tina's voice came over the radio. 'Target finished call. Walking back along Main Street. Turns into alley. Over to you, Jill.'

140

'Okay. Got her crossing King Street. Going straight through the gap site back to house in Victoria Street.'

Maxwell asked, 'Do we need obs on her, sir?'

He shook his head. 'No, she's done her job for today. Let's all get back to the office. We'll meet at four for a debrief.'

Back in the car, Stevenson called the office. 'Gillian, can you patch me in to Commander Porritt, please?'

'Yes, sir. One moment.'

'Porritt,' said the familiar voice.

'Jim Stevenson, sir. Got some info for you. We've tracked a person who took photos of the Thomson kids. She's posted them to the following address.' He read out the address. 'Sounds like it's in Dave's area.'

***

Porritt hung up the phone and smiled at Williams. 'Sounds like another brick in the wall, Mike.' He picked up the phone again and asked Alison to get him CS Burnett in York. 'Dave? Jonathan Porritt here. Got some news for you.'

'Yes, sir?'

'One of Jim Stevenson's ops has paid off. He tracked someone who took photos of the Thomson kids and sent them to the following address.' He read out the address. 'Right in your area, Dave.'

'Pickering, huh? Don't know the house, but we'll find out about it, sir.'

'Quiet as you can, please. It could be where they're holding Jane. Do a quick recce and let me know what it looks like.'

'Will do. It'll be an hour or more before I get back to you.'

Porritt hung up. 'Let's see the map, Mike. Where's Pickering?'

Williams opened the map, and they pored over it. 'There it is, sir. Pretty close to Scarborough. That could be our local link to the fishermen.'

'Right. How far from here, do you think?'

'Mmm. Maybe eighty or ninety miles.' Williams used his fingers to measure the distance. 'A three-hour drive?'

'Too far to nip up and have a look. Let's wait and see what Dave comes back with.'

***

Jane watched in the mirror as Rosie worked with her hair. When had she ever had her hair styled like this? Maybe the day she got married? But this girl had flair. 'Make you just like Rita Hayworth,' she said. Jane just let her get on with it. Rosie had also brought two sets of tops, skirts, and underwear, with a coat, hat and a pair of shoes in the sizes Jane had given Elizabeth earlier.

The girl had already changed Brenner. She had darkened his hair and cut it into a wavy style. Once she got the colour match, she pressed on a moustache. She also aged him with lines around the eyes and on the forehead. He had now moved into the other room for Elizabeth to take his photo.

Jane would do the same once Rosie had finished. She tried to keep her mind blank, and just go with the flow. But she wondered if Porritt and his team would ever find her. *Just be patient.*

142

***

Stevenson sat in the centre of a long side of the table. Sandra Maxwell sat opposite. The rest of the team spread around it.

He passed on Porritt's thanks for a job well done. For some it had been a bit of a wasted day. But that's the way it went sometimes.

Andy said it had been a normal day at the shop. Mr Wiseman had left just before one to visit a long-time customer, Dr Mair, at the university. He was back in less than an hour. Just a routine visit.

Stevenson had called the meeting to discuss how the woman with the flyers knew the kids were at Brownside Road, when there had been no calls to the home address or to their father's work number. He passed round copies of Jane's data from the card index. 'That's all the info she had. How did she do it? What are we missing?'

No one spoke. They all studied the data. But looked blank. After a minute Maxwell broke the silence. 'Can I ask a daft question? When you get married, you get a certificate. Right?'

Stevenson and several others nodded.

'Does that give addresses for the bride and groom?'

They all looked blank again.

Stevenson picked up the phone and asked for his home number. A moment later he said, 'Janice, it's me. Can you look out our marriage certificate, please?' He laughed. 'No, no. Nothing like that. I just want some info. I'll wait.' A couple of minutes later, he said, 'Right, what does it say?' He took notes. 'That's brilliant, Janice. Thanks, love. See you later.'

He hung up. 'It does give the addresses of the bride and groom.' He looked over at Sandra. 'So, what now?'

'There must be a central place that holds a copy. Is it possible for anyone to see it?'

'Good question. Let's find out.' He picked up the phone. 'Gillian, can you get me the Glasgow Registry Office, please?' He handed the phone to Sandra.

'Good afternoon. This is Inspector Maxwell of the City of Glasgow Police. Is it possible to talk to someone about whether a member of the public could check a marriage certificate?' She paused. 'Yes, I'll hold on.'

She waited. They all sat silent. A Mr Maitland came on the line. She asked him whether someone could come in to his office, with the name of a bride and groom and the date they married, and see a copy of the certificate.

He confirmed it was possible, if the marriage took place within the City of Glasgow. She then asked him if he could check whether anyone had asked to see Jane's certificate, and gave him the details.

A few moments later, he confirmed a young woman, who showed the ID of Shona Robinson, had asked for the certificate that morning. He didn't have an address for her, but she carried a University of Glasgow bag.

Sandra thanked him and hung up. 'That's how they got Tommy's address as 11 Brownside Road. All they had to do then was call and check if the kids were there. And I'll bet that's the call from the Malmaison. What was the guy's name?'

Sam checked his notes. 'Mr Bertram. Or maybe Bertram's his first name.'

'Let's listen to that call again.'

Sam played the recording.

'Good morning, Mrs Thomson. My name's Bertram and I'm calling from the Malmaison restaurant at the Central Hotel. Do you know us at all?'

144

'Oh yes. We attended a business dinner there last year. It was very good.'

'Oh, that's good to hear. May I have just a moment of your time, please, Mrs Thomson?'

'Yes, of course.'

'Thank you so much. Each year, we invite five couples to come in and sample our new summer menu free of charge. In return for a detailed feedback. Now, one of our contacts passed your name to us as people who enjoy food and would give us a fair report.

'Would you like to take part in this? If so, you'd have to take the meal on Monday to Thursday within the next three weeks. What do you think, Mrs Thomson?'

'Well, yes, of course. Thank you.'

'Good. Oh, is that children I hear?'

'Yes. My grandchildren.' There was a brief pause. 'Shush, George. I'm on the phone.'

'Sound like a handful. How old are they?'

'Five and four.'

'Well, they're just too young to try our new family menu. But we'll keep your details on file for the future if you like.'

'That would be fine.'

'Right, Mrs Thomson. I'll post the voucher out to you for our summer menu tasting. Once you get it, just phone us, give the voucher number and arrange for your free meal. Okay?'

'Yes. Thank you so much.' She sounded pleased.

The recording ended. Sandra looked round the group. 'That's a foreign accent. And the kids only get a mention almost in passing. But he confirms it's them by asking their ages. Very clever, huh? Let's just check.'

145

She picked up the phone. 'Gillian, can you get me the Malmaison at the Central Hotel, please?'

It soon became clear there was no Mr Bertram or anyone called Bertram there. And they had no summer menu. It had been a trick call. But with a purpose.

Sandra clapped her hands. 'There you go. All very plausible. Another perfect cover story. Just like the old woman. So, let's complete the picture, shall we?'

She called Glasgow University. Got through to someone who gave her the address of a student called Shona Robinson, a second-year student in Applied Chemistry. She then asked about the staff member called Dr Mair. He taught Applied Chemistry. Had come over from Vienna six years ago to do his PhD and stayed on. Became British, and changed his name from Meier to Mair. His wife was a nurse at Gartnavel.

Stevenson smiled. 'Sounds like a result. So, Mair sends the girl for the address info. Then calls Mrs Thomson as Bertram to confirm where the kids are. Passes that info on to Mrs Brady. And has Wiseman visit him as well? Maybe take some sneaky pics while he's there? Smart, eh? Sam, would you get a tap on the Mair's home phone, please? My authority. And check if there's anything on the Brady's phone. And Don, check the lab on these sweets, please.'

He looked round the group. 'We've done well today. A great result. And a chance to take out some nasties when the time is right. Let's leave it at that for the day. Have a good evening. And remember. Very quiet about this one. Sandra, could you stay behind, please?'

The others all left, and within a few seconds, they were on their own again. 'Big lesson on getting the address info. I'll never forget that one.'

Sandra nodded. 'Yeah. Always another angle.'

There was a knock, and Don popped his head round the door. 'The sweets are fine. No poison.'

'Thanks, Don. Better safe than sorry.'

Then another knock. Sam came in with a recording. 'Think you should hear this, sir. From the tap on Brady's phone.'

He set it up and pressed the play button.

'Hello?' A woman's voice.

'Hello, Mary, Aquila 4 here. Sorry I missed you earlier. All go okay?'

Stevenson felt a chill go down his back.

'Yes, fine. Have sent pics of the wee birds.'

'Oh good. Thanks. See any owls in your travels?'

'No. None at all. All quiet.'

'That's good. Give Brady my regards. Hope he gets well soon. The fee's already on its way.'

'Okay. Talk soon. Bye.'

The line went dead.

Stevenson sat silent for a moment. 'Well, well, well. We've got him on record. And we've stayed hidden too. What accent is that, do you think?'

'I've heard that accent before from a lad I met at the rugby. I think he might be South African, sir.'

'We'd better let the boss hear it.' Stevenson lifted the phone. 'Gillian, get me the boss, please.'

After a moment, the familiar voice. 'Porritt.'

'Hello, sir. Jim Stevenson here. We put a tap on the phone of the woman we tracked today. Thought you'd like to hear this.'

Sam played the recording.

'Oh, great stuff, Jim. Now we know Aquila 4 is the man in Pickering. Which means the shoe man in London is Aquila 3. Well done, Glasgow. Exactly what we were looking for. Can you and Sandra call me again tomorrow at nine, please?'

'Yes, sir. We'll do that.'

Stevenson hung up. 'Think he's happy with that. He'll move fast now. So let's put a twenty-four-hour tail on both Brady and Mair. Let's make sure we can pull them in when he gives the word. Oh, and put a twenty-four-hour watch on the Thomson kids until this whole thing's over.'

Sandra took notes. 'Yes, sir. Will do.'

'Great. Time to head home. See you in the morning.'

Sandra and Sam left. He sat alone and thought about the day's events. They had been bloody lucky to catch the Brady woman. If they'd been half an hour later, they'd have missed her.

Thank God for Sandra. Of the four officers in that bedroom, she was the only one who sniffed something wasn't quite right with the old woman. She was probably the best natural police officer he had ever worked with. She had superb clarity of thought. That's why he'd pushed through her CI for next month. A rare honour for a woman. But she was worth it.

She was no doubt his successor. He didn't really know much about her private life. Lived in a big house in Hyndland with her mother. He heard she'd once had a boyfriend. The love of her life. Killed in an RAF plane crash. But she never talked about it. And he never asked.

Crime fighting was getting tougher. It had moved on from one thug bashing another. Now, with more soft crime, they needed a fresh approach. Even if they had missed the Brady woman, a study of the Bertram call and the Mair visit would have given them leads.

But it would have been much harder to trace them. These clever crooks succeeded because they were so plausible. He needed to think how he was going to train his bright young team to cope. But for now, it was time to go home.

***

Jane liked her new look. Even though the hairstyle and make-up made her look ten years older.

Elizabeth took her into another room and sat her in front of a plain sheet. She took several photos. In a few minutes, Jane was free to move around again.

Brown was never very far away. Since he had a gun, she was very wary of him. She went through to the garden room where Brenner sat reading.

He looked up as she approached. 'Wow! You look so different.'

'So do you.'

He laughed. 'We look like an old married couple. That's what we'll be for our journey.'

'When will that be? Do you know yet?' She tried to keep her voice casual. As a wife might ask a husband.

Brenner shook his head. 'Might be tomorrow. But we're still waiting on word. Tell you what. Do you want some fresh air?'

She nodded, and they went out into the garden. While they strolled, she took his arm and raised her face to savour the sun. She'd learnt her lesson about escaping earlier. He prattled on about their life together in Germany and how good it would be. She just let him talk. Her moment would come. At some point.

Brown and Henry had appeared and taken up the same positions at the gates. She and Brenner strolled past them and stopped next to the large oak tree. Behind it, the guards couldn't see them. But she couldn't see any escape routes.

Brenner pulled her to him. 'You look and smell gorgeous. Love you.' He kissed her again, and she felt his hand coming up onto her breast. She pushed it away. But they remained close, whispering sweet nothings. Despite herself, she felt a flush rise in her cheeks, and her tummy did small flips. When had a man last told her he loved her? She couldn't remember.

Brenner tried to feel her breast again. But she pushed his hand away. 'No. Not yet.'

They walked back to the house and resumed their seats in the garden room.

***

Porritt picked up the phone, eager to hear how Burnett had fared in Pickering.

'Right, sir. Albemarle House is a large detached house, surrounded by woodland. About a mile east of Pickering on the road to Scarborough. It's got a long drive, and not easy to observe quietly.

'Owners listed as Mr John Kay and Mrs Elizabeth Kay. In their fifties. He's a mining consultant. Runs a business called SMC. Local cops say they moved here from South West Africa before the war. Well thought of in the area. Quite wealthy. Not known to us.'

Porritt scribbled notes as he listened.

'Kay owns two cars. A small Morris and a large Austin. Uses a local man as a driver. A chap called Ted

Richmond. He may have black market links. Always seems to have cash to splash. But not known to us.

'We're doing the 'Electricity Board' ploy. We've set up a couple of digs along the main road to watch from.

'About an hour ago, Kay drove into Pickering. He went for a pint in the White Swan pub. But also used the public phone box at the back of the lounge bar. It was a long-distance call. So the pattern fits. We'll put a tap on that phone, sir. And once it's dark, we'll do some scouting around the house.'

'Okay, Dave. Thanks. By the way, we've now had it confirmed from one of the Glasgow taps that your man there is Aquila 4.'

'Oh, wow. That's great.'

'You say there's woodland around the house. Any other way into it? I'm bloody paranoid about that now since the escape here.'

'Haven't seen any, sir. But we'll check tonight.'

Porritt thought for a moment. 'Can you call me at 09.30 in the morning, Dave? Oh, and if this chap Kay makes a run as though he's leaving the country, lift him. I don't want to lose him at this stage.'

'Okay, sir. Will do.'

'Good. Talk again then. Bye for now.'

'Goodbye, sir.' He rang off.

Porritt looked at Williams. 'We're getting closer to them, Mike. Just keep your fingers crossed no one makes a mistake and blows it all. Get Malcolm to call me at ten in the morning, please.'

'Will do, sir.'

***

Jane had to go back to her room before dinner. Elizabeth brought her meal up on a tray. Jane assumed the others ate together downstairs.

Her windows were open. And after eating, she lay on her bed to read. She then heard raised voices from below. Got up and glanced out the window. The open roof windows in the garden room let the voices carry up to her. She hid behind the curtains and listened.

Elizabeth's voice carried clearly. And got louder as she went on. 'I don't care if it's the love match of the century. You're not getting the key. I'm not having you do any hanky-panky stuff with her in my house. So you can forget it right now. Is that clear?'

Jane heard the murmur of Brenner speaking. But couldn't make out what he said.

After a moment, Elizabeth started again. 'You're not hearing what I'm saying. Listen to me. I don't care if you've got to make love to her to keep her in line. That's just rape. And you're not doing it in my house. What do you not understand about that? You can do what you damn well like once you're out of here. But while you're in my house, you'll behave as I tell you to behave. Do you understand?'

Brenner murmured something in reply.

Elizabeth shouted, 'For Chrissake, will you listen to what I'm saying? You've dragged that poor girl along with you just because you think you're God Almighty. I know your type. I've seen it all before. You have your way with her, and then you ditch her and move on to the next one. Your type always does. You even tried it on with me the last time you were here. Well, you're not doing it in my house. So you can bloody well forget it.'

John told her to calm down. And Jane could hear Brenner's low voice, although she still couldn't make out the words.

Elizabeth shouted even louder. 'Don't you dare tell me to calm down in my own house, John. You should tell this bloody *idiot* to shut up. And while you're at it, get on the radio and get him and his bloody circus out of here. I'm fed up listening to this shit-head telling us all why he's so important. Well, you're not important to me. So, I don't want to hear another word out of you while you're here. Is that clear? I've had enough of you. Just shut up.' A door slammed.

Jane could hear the men muttering to each other again. She went back and lay on the bed. Was Elizabeth right? Had Brenner just dragged her along as a transient plaything? He seemed sincere enough when he was with her. But she realised she didn't have much experience with men. In fact, she only knew one in that sense. And that hadn't worked out too well. She needed to be even more cautious with Brenner. She would still play up to him as she had been doing. But she must also be more alert to his real purpose.

***

After dinner, Kay drove into Pickering and stopped at a phone box on the Malton Road. He asked for a long distance number.

'Hello?'

'Hello Three. This is Four here. How are you?'

'Fine. Yourself?'

'Could be better. I need your help. I need to get this lad on his way. He's driving us all nuts. What's with the new info we're waiting for?'

'Just got it now. So ready to go.'

'Can you get it up here fast, please?'

'Okay. I'll courier it up by motorbike overnight.'

'That would be great.'

'No problem.'

'Thanks very much. Really appreciate it. Bye.'

Chapter 10. Friday

Porritt was a morning man. Always woke clear-headed and refreshed. He got into the office early to plan how he could wipe out the Aquila group. And pulled out a pad to sketch his thoughts.

The picture had become clearer. They seemed to have three top men. Sir James Dunsmore was Aquila 2. The shoe man, Lyall, Aquila 3. And Kay, Aquila 4. Lyall and Kay ran agents around the UK. And helped couriers such as Brenner to get secret info from Dunsmore back to Germany.

Porritt had three problems. The first was Dunsmore. He was a very big fish. And a wily one too. He was the mole Churchill wanted. But Porritt didn't have a rock-solid case yet. If there was any wiggle room, Dunsmore would take it. So, he needed hard evidence to lift him. And that had to be in the info Brenner carried.

On the other hand, if he lifted Kay and Lyall, where he *did* have proof, would that let Dunsmore escape? He hated that thought.

His second problem was that Aquila used clever ways of working that were better than his. The ham radio pick-up in Hampstead was just one example. His teams should have caught those signals.

He had to assume they could alert everyone if he picked up one of them. That would mean, for example, if he stopped Brenner and his pals in a car, they could press a panic button. And they'd all then scarper.

He had to either lift them all at the same time, or lift Brenner at a point when he couldn't contact anyone. And that had to be when he was on a boat. After the shambles with the U-boat pick-up, Porritt was sure they'd want to fly Brenner out from Ireland.

That meant travel via Northern Ireland, and a ferry trip. The checks at Liverpool and Stranraer had thrown up nothing. But the news from Glasgow about the house in Pickering could mean Brenner was still there today.

And that brought Porritt to his third problem. He had to assume Lyall and Kay were well organised. They'd have lots of data on their agents. But in a form they could get rid of at a moment's notice if they had to.

He was also sure they'd have a panic button close to their bed or desk. And booby traps as well. So, his people would have to stop them within five seconds say, to take control.

His plan to get them all was now forming. Malcolm Craig had called last night with a message from a phone tap. Lyall was sending new info up to Kay overnight. Brenner could well move out today. Porritt thought they should put their plan into action that night.

They'd lift Brenner when he was on a ferry. Then lift the three top men at say, two in the morning, They'd then have four hours to gather intel on the agents. Then lift all the agents at six.

Alison would act as a clearing house for the agent info. She'd pass on their names and addresses to the relevant SB heads. He'd now check all this with his key people and get them to come back with detailed plans.

Williams arrived, and Porritt ran through his outline plan. They discussed lifting Brenner on a ferry, and Williams agreed it was their best chance.

He said they had moved car ferries off the Stranraer route. They now used Clyde steamers instead. So the Brenner party would have to leave their car and travel on foot. They couldn't carry an aerial big enough to send a panic signal from the ferry. They'd be out of contact during that time.

Williams also made a couple of other useful points. He proposed they include Alan McGowan, the head of SB in Northern Ireland, in their discussions. He would have to take control of Brenner and his pals when they arrived in Larne. He also thought Kay and Lyall might hold their agents' info in coded form. Should have codebreakers as part of the raid teams.

Porritt agreed. 'Let's talk it through with the lads when they call in.'

***

It was after half-past eight when Jane heard the key in her door. It opened and Brown came in with the breakfast tray. She raised her eyebrows. 'Morning. What's happened to Elizabeth?'

'Not too good today. Asked me to bring it up.'

'Well, thank you very much.' She glanced over at the wide open door.

'Don't even think about it.'

'Think about what?'

'Running off again.' He grabbed her forearm, pulled her towards him, and snarled, 'We need you to do what he says. Give us that, and you'll be okay. But if you don't, we'll hurt people. Like these.' He threw three photos on the table.

Her mouth opened in horror as she stared down at them. The first photo was her father. The other two her lovely boys. She stood still. Tears welled in her eyes, and she began to sob.

'Just keep that in mind.' He left the room, and locked the door.

She went over to the bed, ruffled the pillows, and lay against them, looking at the photos through her tears. Her precious father, still working so hard. And her two precious sons, smiling up above the camera. When would she ever see them again? What had she got herself into? And how was she going to get out of it?

Her father had his tape around his neck like most days. But he was not in the shop. And yet she knew where he was. She had been there before years ago. To a customer. She couldn't think who. But she recognised the room. It was at the university. So, this group had someone at Glasgow University? Part of their gang? Her head dropped, and she sobbed again.

They had taken the boys' photos at her mother-in-law's front door. Was it the same person? Couldn't be. Must be someone else. And neither her father nor her boys knew they had photos taken.

For the first time, she realised how much trouble she was in. She now knew too much about them. *They had no scruples. They'd stop at nothing.*

What did this mean for how she dealt with Brenner? She just had to stay in with him. It was her only option.

She kissed the pictures. 'Oh, my darlings. If I ever get back to you, I'll never leave you again,' she whispered, as tears coursed down her face.

***

Porritt took the call from Stevenson and Maxwell at nine. They updated him on the agents Brady and Mair. 'Got round the clock watch on them, sir. Just waiting for the word to lift them.'

Porritt outlined his plan. They agreed to lift both agents within the five-second target at six the next morning.

He told them Brenner, with Jane and the two guards, might catch a ferry from Stranraer later in the day. If they left Pickering at one, they could catch a ferry about midnight. Stevenson agreed to lift Brenner and the group on the ferry before it docked at Larne. 'We'll come back to you with a plan, sir.'

Dave Burnett called in at nine thirty. His team were now watching Kay around the clock. He had gone out last evening, but used a different phone box. So they had no details on the call. They also had a look round the house last night. And timed a power cut while they were there. Just in case.

'The house has an alarm, but the outhouses don't. We also found the big Austin car in a garage at the back. It seems to use an access road off the main road about fifty yards beyond the drive. So, you were right about another access, sir. We're now in a waiting game until you give the word.'

Porritt updated him on Malcolm's call last night and Brenner's possible travel. Burnett agreed to have a car tail them. He also agreed to work up a plan for his own team to raid Kay's house at two the next morning. And capture them within five seconds. 'We'll also pick up Ted the driver, wherever he is at that time.'

Porritt was happy with that.

Malcolm Craig called in at ten. Porritt went through his plan. Asked him if he was okay raiding Dunsmore, Lyall, and the Lyall shop at the same time.

'I'll pull a team together and work out a plan, sir. Our big problem will be Dunsmore. He lives in rural Surrey, and has a dog. So we'll have a tricky approach. The other two should be easy enough. By the way, sir, if we pick up agents' bank account numbers, do we have a means of getting their addresses?'

'Yes. Alison holds contact numbers for the on-call people at all banks. She'll get them for you.'

'Great. I take it we're lifting them for treason, sir?'

'That's right. Emergency Powers. Treachery Act 1940. We're covered by these and my authority.'

By the time he hung up, Porritt was happy his teams knew what he wanted, and would come back with plans that would work. He'd asked each of them to ring back in four hours.

***

Jane rubbed the red mark on her forearm where Brown had grabbed her. She'd stopped crying, though her gaze kept flitting to the photos. She took some breakfast, but now felt so alone with her thoughts. There was very little she could do to help herself. She was really at the mercy of these people.

The others in the house would also have seen the pics. But Brown, the nasty one, had brought her the message. He was more or less just a thug. And no stranger to violence.

Henry was much the same, except he didn't talk as much. But they were the enforcers of the group. Would squash anyone stepping out of line.

The Kays seemed more caring about her position. And she was grateful for the stand taken by Elizabeth last night. The last thing she wanted was to have Brenner make love to her. That was way beyond what she could cope with. And would make her even more at risk.

She didn't like sex much anyway. It was smelly, sweaty, and messy. She was willing to admit that men, or at least the one man she knew in that context, seemed to get some brief pleasure from the act. But it always left her feeling used.

What would Brenner say now he knew there were other real people in her life? He was so self-centred. She wondered why he hadn't probed about her family. Or how and when she'd come from Prague. He'd just brushed off her question.

He seemed smitten with her. Though she didn't really know why. She seemed to remind him of his lost love, Liesl. And he wanted to go much further with her. Which she didn't want. But she still needed to keep in with him for protection. And not upset him.

She'd have to hide the supposed Jewish background in her family. It meant nothing to her. But she knew the Nazis hated that. And Brenner would too. She just had to be so careful in how she handled him.

There was a gentle knock on the door. Kay said, 'Jane. May I come in, please?'

She got off the bed, put the pics in her bag, and straightened her skirt. 'Yes, come in.'

The key turned in the lock and Kay stepped inside. 'How are you feeling?'

161

She shrugged and didn't reply.

'We need you to come down now and get ready for your journey. We've got Rosie here to help.'

She pursed her lips and moved towards him at the door. They went down and entered the lounge. Rosie stood next to the chair in front of the mirror, just as the day before. Jane went over and sat down. There was no sign of anyone else. She sat back and let Rosie tidy her hair and do her make-up.

Kay then took her through to the garden room. Brenner jumped up when he saw her and came over. Kay left the room without a word.

Brenner took her hand and looked concerned. 'I'm so sorry about this morning,' he said in German. 'Brown was out of line. He shouldn't have done that. He can be a bit brutal at times. I hate the thought we upset you. Come on, sit here.'

He leaned over to her. 'We need to travel soon. Are you all right with that?'

She had no alternatives. 'Yes,' she murmured.

'Good.' He reached to the table beside him. 'Here are your new travel papers.' He handed over a passport and an identity card.

She opened the passport. It was a British passport in the name Ingrid Gallagher, with the picture of her taken yesterday, showing her looking much older. It stated her place of birth as Glasgow, and her date of birth ten years earlier. The ID card in the same name carried her real address.

He smiled at her. 'We'll travel as a couple. I'm Daniel Gallagher.' He opened the passport. His picture also showed his older appearance. It also stated his place of birth as Glasgow.

162

'Do you have your own passport and identity card?'

She reached into her handbag. 'My passport is back in my room at Station BX. I always just left it there until I travelled. Here's my identity card.' She handed it over. And felt a sudden pang at losing that identity. He put it in his pocket.

'Tell you what, we've got time before we need to be ready. Why don't we have some tea and relax, huh?'

He went to the door and called through to Kay for tea. Then came back and sat beside her again and smiled. She thought he was trying to be kind. 'I hope you don't mind we changed your place of birth on the passport. Just made it easier. Prague might have raised all sorts of questions.'

She nodded. 'Okay.'

'When did you come over from Prague?'

This is it, she thought. *Here it comes*. She hesitated for a moment and tried to keep calm. 'A long time ago. In mid-1935. Seems a lifetime away now. I was just a young girl.'

'Did your father just decide to bring the whole family over then?'

She nodded again. 'Yes. Being a tailor in Prague was tough at that time. He had a friend who'd come over to England in '34 and did very well. Made twice the money he'd been making in Prague. My father thought that sounded like a good move. So we upped sticks and came over. We settled in Glasgow. And it's worked out very well. He's probably making three times what he did in Prague. And life's more pleasant in Glasgow.'

Brenner thought for a moment. 'So, that was it? Just to make more money? No other reason?'

She feigned puzzlement. 'What other reason?'

He seemed flustered. 'No, no. I'm sorry. I didn't mean anything in particular. But I know lots of people went to England then for religious reasons.'

'Well, we didn't,' she snapped, trying to keep her voice level. 'My mother was a lapsed Catholic. And my father thought all religion was nonsense. That man created God. Not the other way round. We never got involved in it.'

Brenner seemed to calm down. 'Interesting. I didn't realise you'd make such money in Glasgow.'

She shrugged. 'Well, the opportunities were far greater. In fact, it made a huge difference to our lives. My brother attended a great school. We had a far better standard of living in Glasgow.'

'Oh. What does he do? Is he a tailor too?'

She shook her head. 'No, he's in the RAF. He's a bomb aimer.'

Shit. As soon as she said it, she knew she'd made a mistake. A big mistake. Brenner's face changed. There was no smile any more. He stared at the floor and didn't look at her as he wrestled with his emotions.

He stood. 'Please excuse me,' and left the room.

She sat and waited, her heart beating faster. It had been a stupid thing to say. She knew that now. She could be in big trouble, and didn't know how to make it better.

Kay came in with the tea tray. 'We need to be away no later than one o'clock. Is that all right?'

'Yes, should be fine.' She poured some tea and picked up a magazine. But she couldn't read it. Her mind struggled to think what to do. She took the magazine and walked through to the kitchen, where Brown was standing near the back door. 'May I go out to the garden? Get some fresh air?'

He nodded and opened the door. Then followed her out and sauntered to the back gate. Like magic, Henry appeared at the side gate.

She sat on the garden seat and opened the magazine on her lap. But her mind still swirled with thoughts. She wished Brenner would come back and sit beside her and talk about what she'd said. Then she heard raised voices from somewhere in the house. It was Brenner and Kay arguing. Though she couldn't make out what they were saying. *Oh my God. She had blown it. What would happen now?*

***

Porritt wrapped up his plans with Williams. 'Contact the SB heads, Mike. Give them the background. If there are any agents found in their area, I want them lifted at six on the dot. Okay?'

'Will do, sir.' Williams left the room.

Porritt sat and thought about his people. At the start of the war, after he had helped set up Bletchley Park to decode German signals, it became clear that follow-up action was sometimes weak. In particular, where local police forces controlled SB operations.

Churchill demanded changes, and brought in Porritt to combine SB across the UK. Then link it to Bletchley Park, MI5, and the War Office. As part of that, Porritt created eighteen SB regions, each headed up by a senior officer he selected to meet his high standards.

There had been the usual carping from those that lost their local fiefdoms. But after he fired a few, it calmed down and became an effective operation. He knew his regional heads would carry out his orders to the letter.

He asked Alison to get him Hugh at Bletchley Park. When the familiar cultured voice answered, Porritt said, 'Hugh, I'm looking for a small favour from you. Well, maybe a big favour.'

'Aha. A big favour. Must be very key then.'

'It is. Remember about ten days ago you helped my chap in London decode a German signal? Well, it's the same case. Heading for a finale. Hope to nail the whole bloody Aquila group.'

'That sounds worth doing. How can we help?'

'We've got three raids early in the morning. One in Yorkshire. Two in London. To nail the heads. We hope to find lists of agents they're using across the UK. But we think these lists might be in code. So we'd like a codebreaker on hand to get us the data. We want to lift these agents as well a few hours later. I'm on to see if you could help with three chaps tonight?'

There was silence for a moment. 'Well, I have a couple of lads in Leeds right now. One of them could help with the Yorkshire raid. Though missing his Friday night out will piss him off. But I daresay you can make up for it in some way? For the two in London, I'll get a couple from BP to fit the bill. On a similar package.'

Porritt chuckled. 'Not a problem, Hugh. What if I pick up a meal for two for each of them at the best restaurant in their town? Would that work?'

'Yes, I think that would work fine.'

Porritt always enjoyed talking with the team at BP. They were just such an amazing bunch doing fantastic work that the great British public would never hear of. But which was moving the war in our favour. They were so modest too, given their talent. Some of their exploits often left him open-mouthed.

He then asked Alison to get him Alan McGowan in Belfast. He'd put him in charge there just over a year ago. Now he was one of his best leaders. A big, heavy-built man with an even bigger smile. Handled the tough nuts over there with great skill. Within moments, he heard the warm Belfast accent.

'Alan, I need your help with a job tonight. Have you got a few minutes?'

'Yes, sir. Just wait a second till I close my door. Right, sir. How can I help?'

Porritt gave him the background. Jim Stevenson and his team from Glasgow would arrest a bunch of spies on a ferry from Stranraer later that night. So, he needed help from McGowan in four areas. First, to lock up the spy gang until morning. Second, to lift the driver of the car waiting to take them to the border without letting him alert anyone else. Third, to provide lab support to find the secret info the spy carried. And fourth, to lift any agents in NI at six o'clock.

They discussed the tasks, and McGowan agreed he'd plan to meet all four. 'Oh, and one last thing, Alan. The two guards are from Belfast. Could you check them out, please? Might save time later. One is Robert John Brown. Late thirties. Round face. Dark hair. Heavy build. Bit of a bruiser I'd say. Must have a record somewhere. The other is a Patrick Henry. Maybe younger? Again dark hair. More of a narrow face. He could also have a record. I've got photos of them here. And their staff records. I'll radio telegraph them over to you. So, let's talk again in four hours.'

***

Kay came out into the garden with a small blue bag and told Jane it was time to pack. As they went upstairs, she asked him if Brenner was all right. Kay shrugged. 'He got a bit upset earlier. A British bomb killed his girl, and you brought it all back. But he's calmed down now.'

'Oh, I'm so sorry.' She felt sad for Brenner. 'This war's hellish. If you see him, tell him I'm sorry for his loss. It wasn't my brother, though. He's only just joined the RAF.' That wasn't quite true. But she thought it her best option to ease the situation.

Kay nodded and locked the door behind her. She stood and stared at her room. Her coat and hat now lay on the bed. Someone had been in the room while she was downstairs. She looked around to see if anything else had moved. But it was all as she had left it.

She laid her bag down, lifted her coat and hat, and stopped still. A shiny black and silver object about four inches long lay on the bed. She put her hat and coat on a chair and lifted the object. It was heavy in her palm.

She didn't know what it was. It had a button on the side, which she pressed, then tried to move back towards her arm. But nothing happened. She tried to move it forward. There was a click, and a blade appeared out the front. It took her a few seconds to realise it was a knife. The blade was about four inches long and very sharp on both sides. It came to a point at the tip.

She moved the button back. The blade disappeared into the handle. She flicked the button a few times to get the feel of it. A serious weapon. And left for her.

But who and why? Her stomach knotted. It *had* to be Elizabeth. And it must be a warning that she, Jane, was in danger. The knife was an attempt to offer her some defence.

She put the knife in her coat pocket, and packed her few toiletries and clothes. Her heart raced. She knew something had changed when she was downstairs. There had been a tension in the air. Had her appeal to Brenner now run its course? If he wanted to ditch her, the Kays would not want her left with them. He had brought her with him. He'd have to deal with the problem. She felt now in great danger.

There was a knock at the door. 'Are you ready, Jane?' Kay asked.

She put on her hat and coat. 'Yes, ready.'

Kay opened the door, stood aside to let her pass, and they went down to join the others in the hall. Brown and Henry had bags similar to hers, but different colours. Brenner had a larger grey bag, and held a small brown leather case. That must be what they'd been waiting for.

They all walked outside to the car. The driver had the boot lid open and they put their bags in. Jane held on to her handbag, and Brenner kept the case. He didn't say anything or look at her.

As she turned to get into the car, Elizabeth came out the front door. Jane gave her a wry smile, and Elizabeth nodded and smiled in return. Then Elizabeth's eyes filled with tears and she turned and went inside.

Jane got into the rear seat between Brown and Henry. In the same positions as before. She wrapped her coat around her so the knife would not bump Henry on her right. No one spoke. They didn't even wave goodbye

She sat silent, her head full of thoughts. Elizabeth had clearly been upset. She remembered how Elizabeth had shouted at Brenner the previous night. Elizabeth had protected her then. But now they were away from the house, she was on her own.

How was she supposed to use a knife? She'd never ever hit anybody. Not even her brother in fun. She tried to think through what she'd do if she had to use it. Pull it out, flip the button to get the blade out, and then stick it into . . . where? The chest between the ribs? Or the neck? Or the back?

If she *did* have to use it, she'd have to be quick. These men were much stronger. So she'd have to take them by surprise. On the other hand, maybe they'd just dump her at the side of the road with a warning not to talk to anybody. There was no reason to kill her, was there? Why would they do that? Because she already knew too much? She'd just have to stay alert.

As the car passed through towns and villages, she was amazed to see life as normal for everyone else. People were queuing at shops, talking with friends, pushing babies in their prams, looking after their children. She wanted to scream she was in danger. But that was not possible. She'd just have to sit quiet. And behave as they wanted. For now.

***

Stevenson rang in from Glasgow at one, and went through his plans with Porritt and Williams. His team would catch the same ferry the spy group caught. There would be eight of them. All dressed as a hiking party so they could mix on board and find the target group. Two of the lads would carry arms. Just in case.

He'd aim to lift the spy group just before docking. They'd then least expect it. Porritt told him McGowan's team would help take the group into Belfast. And that he should bring them last off the ferry.

His biggest worry was to find the right group on board. He'd met the girl in Glasgow and had photos of the others. But they might change their looks for the journey. 'Can I get a report from the tailing car, please?'

Williams scribbled on his pad. 'We'll cover that in the next call in four hours, Jim.'

Dave Burnett called in from Yorkshire at one thirty. He told Porritt and Williams the spy group was now on the move west from Pickering. He thought they'd use the A1 north, then the A66 across the country, then the A6 north, and the A75 west to Stranraer.

'If the route changes, I'll let you know. I've got a car tailing them. But I'd like if police along the route could report in as they pass.' He gave the reg number of the spies' car.

Williams asked Burnett to get his people to give a description of the group if they got a chance. Burnett agreed. The latest was there were five people in the car. With the girl in the middle of the rear seat.

For the raid on the Kays' home, Burnett planned to use fifteen people. They'd cut the power, phone line, and the link to the large radio aerial at the back of the house. Disable the alarm. Then go in using the 'silent burglar' approach. They'd cut the glass out of two windows, one on each side. They aimed to get into the Kays' bedroom and capture them within the five-second target.

The big unknown was the number of people in the house. One of their team had walked a dog up the path through the woods and seen a middle-aged couple in the garden. They weren't the Kays. And didn't match the photos of the spy group. So they'd prepared for other people staying there as well.

Burnett asked, 'What about intel on the agents? Kay seems to use public phones a lot to keep in touch. If we pick up agents' numbers, can the GPO give us their names and addresses?'

Williams took a note again. Then told Burnett he'd have a codebreaker as part of his team.

Malcolm Craig called in from London at two. His plans to raid the Lyall house in West Hampstead were much the same as Burnett's for the Kays' house. They were going in with thirteen people. He said they'd meet the five-second target.

'The shop is open today as usual. It has an alarm, but we'll cut it when we go in. We'll also alert the local police. We'll dig out what info we can on the shoes.'

They had also worked out a way to get into the Dunsmore house. And meet the target time. They'd use fifteen people there.

Williams told him he'd also have two codebreakers to assist. One for each house raid.

Porritt called McGowan in Belfast. His plans were also now in place for his four tasks. But he had to know the travel names of the spy party so he could pick up the right driver. Also, he could find no record of the two guards in Belfast. So they might be using false IDs.

Porritt and Williams planned to fly over to Belfast later that evening. 'Can you pick us up from the airport, please?' And gave him details.

'Consider it done, sir.'

All in all, Porritt was happy with his teams' plans.

***

Jane woke up from a doze and realised her head was resting on Brown's shoulder. She jerked it up. 'Sorry.'

Brown just shrugged. 'No problem.'

She still had the problem of how to use the knife running round her head. Her big advantage would be surprise. Which meant she had to make the first thrust count. Then follow up with a second. She thought she should go for the neck first. And pictured how she'd do it. The more she went over it in her mind, the more sure she became to use the knife and save herself.

Of course, she still had the problem that her boys were under threat. She therefore could only use the knife when the police could rescue her. And then make sure her family were safe.

The journey seemed endless. She didn't know where she was. Or where she was going. There were no signs on the route. Between towns and villages there was little traffic. And the towns all looked the same. She just waited for her moment.

After some hours, the driver spoke. 'Right, lady and gentlemen. We're stopping at a café in the next few minutes for food and a toilet stop. We've got about forty minutes here. May I just point out there are single toilet cubicles for men and women with no outside exits? And if I may say to the young lady. It would be best for you not to contact anyone or make a scene. Thank you.'

They pulled up in the café car park, got out and stretched, and then went inside. She behaved as required. There was no talk. Brenner said nothing. Before long, they were back in the car and on their way.

***

By nine, Porritt had made a last check round his teams.
Burnett confirmed police had clocked the spy group on
the A75. They should arrive at Stranraer around 22.30.
The police had lifted the roadblock. So the group now
had a clear run.

The tailing car had called in a description of the spy
group from a café stop. Porritt paused while writing.
'Are you sure that's right? One female. Five foot six.
Dark hair. High cheekbones. Glasses. Late thirties. Grey
hat and coat, with a brown handbag?'

Burnett confirmed that's what they'd said. Wow, he
thought, they've really changed her looks. She was never
in her late thirties or needed glasses.

Alison passed the descriptions to Stevenson. He was
due to arrive at Stranraer around the same time as the
spy group.

In his call to Craig, Porritt stressed he should keep
Dunsmore separate once he had lifted him. And hold
him under a false name. It was vital his real name did
not leak out. Porritt knew he'd have a problem with him.
So let's keep him cut off from contact for at least a day.

McGowan asked if the aircraft could wait at the
airport till morning. His team had discussed what agents
they might have to lift in NI. They thought at least one
would come from the nationalist side in the Falls Road.
But it was such a sensitive area. Things could blow up so
fast there. He thought it would help calm the situation if
they could fly that agent out to England. Porritt agreed,
and told him to plan it with Williams.

Porritt sat back and stretched his legs under the desk.
His plan was now in play.

Chapter 11. Saturday

By the time the ship sailed from Stranraer just after midnight, Jim Stevenson realised he'd made a mistake. He thought the night-time run would be quiet. But it wasn't. It seemed the full load of 1,918 passengers had crammed inside on a cool night. The ship was jam packed. Most of them soldiers.

His team of eight had squeezed into a space next to a bulkhead, near the doors to the main bar. Each dressed as a hiker with a rucksack marked 'Clyde Valley Hiking Club'. He and Sandra Maxwell led the group. With three pairs. Sam and Jill, and Don and Tina, who had worked on the spy trail that week. And Tom and Bill, both armed. Which they now couldn't use in that crowd.

And he still had to find the spy group. He hadn't seen them at the harbour. The crowd crammed the booking hall. Then spilled out onto the open pier. In darkness because of the blackout.

Three pairs left Tom and Bill with the bags that held their day clothes and searched separate lounges to find the spy group. Because of the mass of people, if the group had seats, they'd only see them if they were right on top of them. And they couldn't see them.

Twenty minutes later, they met back at base. Sandra said, 'Why don't we try and find the girl? I mean, how many women did you see on your way round? Very few. And most of them looked like the local hookers.

'Even though they've changed Jane's looks, we should still recognise her.'

Stevenson nodded. 'Let's go round again.'

The three pairs went off again in different directions. They tried to get round as far as they could, but the large lounges were all packed with people. They returned with no result.

Don and Tina had searched around the deck. 'Few people out there. Too cool, with a gusty wind. But it doesn't seem to stop some couples finding dark corners to enjoy themselves.'

We've got to think differently about this, Stevenson thought. Just then, two soldiers squeezed past him wearing Military Police armbands. He went after them, and asked if they had a commanding officer on board.

'We do, sir.' They turned back and pointed. 'Captain Allen, sir. The tall man with the cropped fair hair and moustache.' Then one of them called, 'Captain Allen, sir? This gentleman would like a word with you.'

Allen turned towards him and he felt daunted. *Wow, he's a tough nut.*

Stevenson explained who he was and showed his warrant card. He then asked Allen if his officers could help find a group of German spies on board and gave him their descriptions. Allen agreed.

'The girl is one of ours held against her will. It's the three males we're after. If your lads find anybody who matches, let us know. We're just out here in this area.'

Allen nodded. 'Fine, sir. Leave it with me. I'll get back to you as soon as I can.'

***

Brown had used this route dozens of times and knew the ropes. He'd got on board early, grabbed a few beers, and four seats round a small table in a corner of the lower lounge. He and Henry sat with their backs to a blacked-out window. Brenner and the girl sat opposite with their backs to the crowd.

As people swarmed around and stood over them, Brenner became more edgy. Brown knew he hated boats, and would now feel queasy as the ship rolled on its way to Larne.

Brenner leaned over to him. 'I need to get some fresh air. We're going outside for a few minutes. Can you keep our seats?'

'We'll try,' he said, and put bags on them.

Brenner lifted the brown case, took Jane by the hand, and squeezed through the crowd towards the exit.

'I'd better go with them,' Henry said.

Brown shook his head. 'Forget it. They're not going anywhere. It's cold out there. They'll be back in a few minutes. The Belfast whores have already taken all the cosy corners. They do a return trip at night and make their week's money. Shit-head just wants to go out there and feel her tits. I'll be glad when we're shot of him. What a pain in the arse.'

'So, is he about to do the dirty deed then?'

'What dirty deed?'

'I thought he was going to ditch her. Over the side.'

Brown shook his head again. 'No, that was shit-head's idea. But he's bloody stupid. He asked me to do it. But I told him no way. They don't pay me to do his dirty work. No. Kay talked him out of that idea. He's got sense. We'll ditch her in Ireland. Brenner gets on the plane. She doesn't.

'We get back in the car and leave her there. Stuck in the middle of Ireland. By the time she sorts herself out, we're back over the border. She knows nothing about us. Hasn't seen the car number. There's no trace back to us.'

'That makes sense. What happened to the world's greatest romance, then?'

'Oh, that's bloody shit-head for you. When he saw the father's picture, he thought he looked Jewish. Stupid. What does Jewish look like? He wasn't like Fagin. Just an ordinary bloke.

'But shit-head started to think he was Jewish. And that *he* would be a laughing stock, or worse, if he took her back to Germany.

'And then when he thought her brother had killed his girlfriend, he decided to ditch her. And that's why he's gone out. To try and get *some* pleasure from dragging her along. Bloody idiot.'

***

Jane held Brenner's hand as he slowly pushed his way through the crowd. Her coat hung open. She put her hand in her pocket to make sure the knife was still there.

This was it, she thought. The first time they'd been on their own. Away from the guards. What would he do? Strangle her? Throw her over the side? She ran her fingers over the knife. She'd use it if she had to.

As they pushed out of the lounge into a packed open area, she saw a group beside a pile of rucksacks marked 'Clyde Valley Hiking Club'. *God, people are still living normal lives. In the middle of all this madness. How can they do that?* She wanted to scream. But knew she had to keep herself calm.

She looked at the group and caught her breath. One of the women looked like Sandra. The police girl she'd met in Glasgow. Was it her? She wasn't sure. And the woman hadn't seen her. She tried to mentally cry out to her. *It's me. It's me.*

Just as she was past the group and heading towards the exit, she glanced back. The woman stared at her. Recognised her? Then she was outside on deck in the fresh air and darkness. There was some light spray. But it didn't matter. She now felt a lot better. *Time to go with the flow. But take action.*

***

Sandra Maxwell gaped at the crowd. They'd just missed this in their planning. Stevenson had gone off with a couple of MPs. Which was a good move. They needed all the help they could get.

A middle-aged couple squeezed their way out from the lounge. Sandra's glance took in the woman top to toe. Not Jane. But hang on. Slim waist and rib cage. Full breasts. A bell rang in her head. She'd seen that figure before. She checked the face again as the woman passed. High cheekbones. *It must be Jane*. But she looked so different. Would never have recognised her. Even though she knew her looks had changed. As the woman moved towards the exit door, she glanced back. It was definitely her. Definitely!

She grabbed Sam. 'Get your jacket. We need to move. Jill, tell the boss I've seen Jane. She's just gone out on deck. We'll follow her and find the others.'

***

The weather was gusty, and the ship rolled and yawed as it headed across the Irish Sea. Jane snuggled into Brenner and listened as he murmured in German. She felt his arm round her as they leaned against the rail. 'I'm sorry about this morning, Jane. I just got a bit of a shock. And it wasn't fair on you. It's not your fault. It's just this damn war. I need to be with you, Jane. Are you still okay about your journey with me?'

She glanced up at him and nodded. 'Yes, I'm fine.' *Just keep calm but alert.*

He took her hand. 'What about your family?'

'I just have to deal with it.'

'Is that a problem for you?'

'Not really. To be honest, I don't have much of a marriage. With me and the kids away, he's living like a single man again. We had a big row the last time I was home. The place was a heap. Dirty dishes. Dirty clothes all over. Just a total mess. I hate that. And he didn't seem to care. It wasn't very pleasant.'

'Oh, Jane, I don't want you to feel like that. I want you to be happy. To have a great life. Lots of fun and laughter. Even if we've to settle in Ireland. It's a grand country, you know. Good people. Good craic.'

'What's craic?'

'It's fun. Laughter. Having a drink with friends. Cosy and happy.'

'Mmm. Sounds good.' She looked out across the water. She needed to keep him calm and rested her head on his shoulder. 'Might be nice to start again.'

He held her tight. Maybe too tight, she thought. There were very few people on deck.

He coughed. 'I hate to break the spell, but I'm not feeling too good. Bloody boats. I hate them.'

She leaned back. 'Are you going to be sick? If you are, don't be sick into the wind.'

He half-smiled. 'Let's go down this way then.'

They strolled towards the stern and stood at the rail next to a lifeboat hanging on its support structure above them. The white wake stretched out in the black sea. The lifeboat hid them from the rest of the deck. His grip grew ever tighter around her as he tried to push her against the rail. Her hand tightened on the knife in her pocket.

'Oh, I think I'm going to be sick.'

He dropped the case and gripped the top rail with both hands. Then stepped up onto the bottom rail, gulped twice, leaned forward and threw up. He leaned over further and retched again, several times.

She took her chance, bent down, and grabbed the case. Brenner glanced down at her and frowned. Then kicked out at her. She thrust her arm up to defend herself, hit his outstretched leg, and he unbalanced and toppled over the top rail. His shout carried away in the wind. There was a soft splash as he entered the water.

Jane stood still for a second. Shocked at what had happened. Her heart raced. Hadn't done it on purpose. Or had she? She really didn't know.

She gripped the case and her handbag against her chest and ran round the lifeboat structure along the deck towards the front of the ship.

A stair led to the upper deck, and she dashed up it. Then another set of stairs going up further to the top deck. She headed for the bridge as fast as she could.

Further along there was a barrier with a 'No Access' sign. She pushed, but it didn't open. She threw the case and her handbag over the barrier and used the rail at the side to climb over.

She picked up the case and handbag, and ran on towards the bridge. The passage was dark, with the bridge outlined against the night sky.

At last, she got to the steps leading up to the bridge. She saw people inside a cabin lit with a blue light, opened the door and ran in. All three men on the bridge turned in surprise. A young man in a heavy sweater held a steering wheel. An older man in uniform stood at a large table, talking with another man.

She sobbed when she saw them. 'Help me. Help me, please. I've just escaped from a kidnapper. I work with British Intelligence. There are spies on board. And I need to talk to a police woman on board too. Oh, please help me.'

The older man dashed to her side and held her. 'Come on, sit down here,' he said in a broad Scottish accent and guided her towards a high stool. 'I'm Captain Ferguson. Now, just take a moment to get your breath back. Then tell me who you are and what happened.'

***

Sandra stood close to Sam. About ten yards from the couple. She hoped Stevenson had got the message. But they had to stay with the targets for the moment.

The couple moved towards the stern. She and Sam followed, keeping well in the shadows. They wore dark clothes in a black night, so blended in okay.

They watched as the couple went down the side of the lifeboat structure. The deck curved at that point, and she told Sam to go round the inboard side of the structure and try to watch them from the other side.

She couldn't quite see the couple now. They were in the darkest shadow of the lifeboat and hidden from her view by the support stanchions.

Suddenly, she heard a shout that seemed to come from the other side of the lifeboat. Then the sound of someone running along the deck. She thought the shout sounded like Sam and tried to look underneath the lifeboat. But it was too dark.

She slowly moved towards the stern and realised the couple had now gone. But where? She peered further down the side of the lifeboat. But they weren't there. She followed the curve of the deck round until she was on the other side of the structure.

She heard moaning. From a figure lying on the deck. Bent down to help, and found it was Sam.

'What happened?' she asked.

He sat up and rubbed his face. 'Thumped by a soldier. Accused me of sneaky-peeking him and his girl in that corner.'

'Did you see where the couple went?'

'What couple?'

'The couple we were following.'

'Oh,' He shook his head. 'No idea. Sorry, ma'am.'

'That's all right. Come on. Let's get you back on your feet.' She helped him to stand as he rubbed his jaw. 'Let's get you back inside.'

***

Jane had her breath back. Though her heart still thumped from her dash from the stern and the shock of what had happened. Her words came out in a rush.

183

'My name is Jane Thomson. I'm a translator with British Intelligence at Lincoln. A few days ago, a German spy escaped with the help of two corrupt guards. And they took me with them as a hostage. I need to talk to a police woman on board the ship.'

The captain lifted a notepad. 'What's her name?'

'Sandra. She's with Glasgow Police.'

'Sandra what?'

She wracked her brains. 'I can't remember. Oh, no. But she's on board with a group of . . . what do you call people who go walking over the hills?'

The two officers looked at each other. 'Ramblers?'

She shook her head. 'No. They walk in the country with sticks and backpacks. Oh, what do you call them?'

'Hikers?' the captain suggested.

'That's it. The police woman is with a group of hikers just outside the lounge on the lower deck. Called the Clyde Hikers Club or something like that.'

The captain picked up a phone. 'Barry, have you seen a crowd of hikers on board tonight? Just outside the lounge on the lower deck? Right, go and find them and see if there's a police woman called Sandra with them. We've got a distressed woman on the bridge here who needs to talk to her. As soon as you can please.'

'Thank you,' said Jane. And sighed.

'Now, tell me what happened to you. Who was the kidnapper? And how did you escape?'

She was still shaking with shock. Her voice came out in a sob. 'We were on deck. He was going to push me overboard. And then he started to be sick.'

He butt in. 'Who was on deck with you?'

'The German spy. Brenner. He kidnapped me.'

'So what happened then?'

184

'He leaned over the rail to vomit, and . . . and I . . .' *Careful what you say.* The thought leapt into her brain from somewhere. '. . . and he just fell overboard. I grabbed his case and ran. It's got a secret in it, I think.'

The captain's mouth fell open in horror. 'What? How long ago was this?'

She shook her head. 'I don't know. How long does it take to run here from the back of the ship?'

The captain turned and shouted to the other officer. 'First. How long has she been here?'

'I'd say five minutes, sir.'

'And how long to run here from the stern?'

'Maybe a minute?'

'Work out our position six minutes ago. As fast as you can please, First.'

'Yes, sir.' The officer turned away to the other side of the table and brought out a chart.

'Shall we turn back, sir?' the helmsman asked.

The captain paused. 'What are his chances in that sea tonight without a life vest? Maybe five minutes? It would take us seven minutes at least to get back there. He'd then be in the water for thirteen minutes.' He was silent for a moment. 'Dark night. Can't use search lights. No chance of finding him. Just press on to Larne.'

'Yes, sir.'

The captain turned to her. 'Right, just tell me again what happened. You thought he was going to push you over. Is that right?'

Jane nodded. 'That's right.' She was still tearful.

'And then he started to be sick?'

'He had his hands on the top rail. Then leaned over and vomited. And then leaned over further and vomited again. And then just . . . just toppled over. '

'Didn't you hold on to him?'

'No,' she snapped in anger.

'But couldn't you have held on to him to prevent him going over?'

'Of course I could. But he was trying to kill me.' She burst into tears again.

The captain let out a huge sigh.

'Here's the coordinates, sir.' The first officer handed him a piece of paper.

'Thanks. I'll need to get them to the office.'

There was a knock on the door. It opened, and in came another officer, followed by Jim Stevenson.

She looked up, saw him, and relief flooded her body. She ran over to him and held on, shaking, sobbing into his chest. 'Oh, sir. I'm so sorry.'

He held her back from him. 'Jane. It's all right. You're safe now. We'll look after you.'

'But sir, they'll go after my kids!' She burst into tears again.

'No, they won't. We're watching your kids. They're quite safe, believe me.'

'Oh, thank you, sir,' she said through her tears.

'Now, do you want to tell me what happened?' He turned to the captain. 'Oh, by the way. I'm CS Jim Stevenson of the Special Branch. I've a team on board. Your man asked for Sandra. But she's out on deck. We're trailing a bunch of German spies who had kidnapped this girl. So, sorry for the turmoil, Captain, but we plan to arrest the spies soon.'

'So her story's true?' asked the first officer. 'She really *has* been kidnapped?'

'Oh yes, it's true.'

'Bloody hell. That's a first.'

There was another knock at the door, and in came another crewman followed by Sandra. 'Inspector Maxwell, sir,' he said, and left again.

Jane rushed over to Sandra and sobbed again. Sandra held her close. 'You're okay now, Jane. You're okay.' She looked over. 'I was told to follow you up here, sir.'

'Yes, thanks, Sandra. We were just about to find out what happened.'

The captain spoke up. 'I'm Captain Ferguson. The girl's in shock. Let me tell you what she's told me.'

The captain repeated Jane's story on how the spy fell overboard. 'After it happened, she grabbed the man's case and ran up here.' He picked up the case and passed it to Stevenson. 'She says there's a secret in it.

'And here are the coordinates of our position when the incident happened. There's no point in going back. He wouldn't have survived. That's as far as I've got.'

'That's very helpful, Captain, thanks.' Stevenson put the paper in his pocket. 'Jane, why do you think he was trying to kill you?'

She eased herself away from Sandra. 'It was the very first time we'd been alone. I mean without the guards. They never left us alone before. And the woman at the house we stayed in knew something bad would happen to me. She gave me this for my protection.' She pulled the knife out of her pocket and pressed the button to release the blade. Stevenson stared wide-eyed at it.

He asked her to close the knife and drop it into an evidence bag he took from his pocket. He wrote on the label. 'Thanks, Jane. Now we need to arrest these two guards. Can you identify them for us? Are you all right with that?'

She nodded. 'Yes, I'll try.'

Stevenson turned to Maxwell. 'Sandra, go down and see if Jill has any disguise with her. Like a headscarf or reversible coat, or both. We need to get Jane into the lounge to point these men out for us.'

***

Henry glanced at his watch. 'They've been away a while now. Wonder where they've got to.'

Brown snorted. 'Don't worry. Shit-head will have her tits out somewhere. Or maybe even screwing her. He'll have a stupid grin on when he gets back.'

'Mmm. Think I'll just have a wander round.' He got up and squeezed out through the crowd.

Ten minutes later, he was back. 'No sign of them.'

Brown scoffed. His words slurred with the beer. 'Forget it. They're in a dark corner somewhere. He'll be back any minute. Have another beer.'

'We're supposed to get him to Ireland.'

'Calm down. We'll get him to bloody Ireland.'

The bunch of soldiers next to Brown had become more and more raucous as time went on and the beers went down. They were now shouting and arguing with each other. Brown moved his head away as they swayed above him.

Very quickly, two MPs were on the scene. 'Right, lads. Keep it down. Don't want to hear you.'

The group calmed down and muttered.

Thank God they had MPs on the ferries now, thought Brown. *Stopped the rabble. Cut the trouble. Made a hell of a difference.*

***

Stevenson looked up with relief as Jill and Sandra returned to the bridge with Barry, the ship's purser. Jill had a rucksack and pulled out a headscarf. She took Jane's hat off, put the headscarf on, and tied it round her chin. 'Do you need these glasses?'

Jane shook her head. 'No, they're false.'

Jill took the glasses off and ruffled Jane's hair under the headscarf to bring tufts down onto her forehead. She then pulled out a reversible coat and helped Jane put it on. She turned to him. 'What do you think, sir? Is that different enough?'

'Yes, that should work.' He worried about Jane, though. 'Now, are you okay with this, Jane? If you're not happy about it, just let us know.'

Jane nodded, but said nothing.

'Do you know if Brown and Henry are armed?'

'They are, sir. Brown already pulled a gun on me.'

Stevenson bit his lip. 'I think I'll get Captain Allen to help us. These guys are trained military. Could be too much for Bill and Tom to deal with.'

Barry led the way down an internal stair that brought them out near the purser's office. Stevenson asked them to wait there while he talked to Captain Allen.

He came back with Allen a few minutes later. 'Let's go, Jane. We want to go into the lounge at the opposite side to the spy group.'

Jane led them slowly through the crowd. But there were so many people standing in the way. Then she turned. 'There they are, sir. The two men with glasses below the "Fire Exit" sign.'

He turned to Sandra. 'Keep her here.' Then he and Allen, together with Tom and Bill, and Don, Tina and Jill, moved closer to the men.

They waited while Allen went off to talk to his men. When he came back, he said, 'We're all set. We've got cuffs for arms and legs, gags, and ether with us to keep them quiet. Just give us a minute to start a fight. My men will get them down. It's up to you to disarm them and read them their rights.' He disappeared into the crowd.

Stevenson nodded. Allen sure was a tough nut.

They waited for a moment. Then a couple of soldiers standing next to Brown started singing.

'Follow, follow, we will follow Rangers.
Everywhere, anywhere, we will follow on.
Follow, follow, we will follow Rangers.
If they go to Dublin, we will follow on.'

'Shut up, ya proddy bastards!' shouted a couple of other soldiers in the same group.

'There's not a team like the Glasgow Rangers. No,
not one. No, not one. There's not a team like the
Glasgow Rangers. No, not one. No, not one!'

'Shut up!' shouted the other soldiers, and started pushing towards them.

'Away, ya Fenian bastards, back to Ireland. The famine's over!'

Within seconds, there was a huge melee in that corner. A few moments later, loud whistles pierced the air, and a bunch of MPs arrived with batons drawn. But instead of going to the fighting soldiers, they rounded on Brown and Henry. In a matter of seconds, the pair had their arms behind their backs, hands and ankles cuffed, and gags in their mouths. Brown was powerful and kept kicking out. But Allen stepped into the middle of the melee, knelt on Brown's back, held his head up, and pressed an ether pad against his face. Brown stopped kicking, and Stevenson's team moved in.

Tom took Brown and Bill took Henry. They arrested both of them under the Treachery Act 1940, and gave them their rights. The team searched them. Brown had a handgun and a stiletto knife. Henry also had a gun. The team found their IDs and emptied their pockets. Jill and Tina bagged it all.

Once the team was clear, Stevenson gave the nod, and the MPs lifted the pair on to their feet. The girls gathered up all the bags, and the group set out to push through the crowd towards the purser's office. To a side room that could hold the men.

One of the soldiers in the fight asked him, 'Are they really German spies, sir?'

'Yes, they really are. And thanks for your help.'

Suddenly the group of fight soldiers began to sing to the tune of the Colonel Bogey March.

'Hitler has only got one ball. Goering has two, but very small. Himmler has something sim'lar, but poor old Goebbels has no balls at all.'

Everyone there took up the refrain. Stevenson and his team, together with the MPs and the prisoners, exited the lounge to that song voiced by hundreds of soldiers.

'HITLER HAS ONLY GOT ONE BALL. GOERING HAS TWO, BUT VERY SMALL. HIMMLER HAS SOMETHING SIM'LAR, BUT POOR OLD GOEBBELS HAS NO BALLS AT ALL!'

Stevenson shook from the tension as they dumped Brown and Henry on the floor in the purser's side office. He turned to Allen. 'Thanks for your help. We couldn't have handled that on our own.'

Allen gave a wry smile. 'That was a good cop. Glad to help.' He and his MPs all left the small room. The team began to examine the material they'd gathered.

Sandra brought Jane into the room, and asked her to formally identify that the two men were Brown and Henry, who had kidnapped her from Lincoln. Stevenson held his breath.

Jane nodded. 'That's them.'

Brown looked up at her, his eyes deadpan.

Jane turned away. 'He just scares me so much.'

Sandra turned to Barry, the purser. 'How long till we arrive in Larne?'

He glanced at his watch. 'About forty minutes.'

'Do you have a staff rest area on board? You know, a sort of quiet place away from the crowds?'

'We do. At the back of the servery in the tea room.'

'Could some of our team take Jane down there to get her a cup of tea and help her relax? She's been through a tough time of it.'

'No problem. Come on, I'll take you down.'

Sandra turned to Jill and Sam. 'Could you take Jane for a cup of tea? Make sure no one talks to her, please.'

'Yes, ma'am. Shall we bring our bags in here?'

Barry nodded. 'Yes. Go ahead.'

Stevenson turned as Sandra murmured to him, 'Can I have a word, sir?' and indicated they move out of the office. They went out on deck to find a quiet spot.

'Got a problem, Sandra?'

'I've got two problems, sir. But first let me tell you what happened when Sam and I followed Jane and the spy out here. Let's walk down to the lifeboat.'

As they walked towards the stern, she went through the experience step by step. He listened and looked at the scene as she spoke.

When she finished, he asked, 'Okay. So what are your two problems, Sandra?'

They stood at the rail where Sandra had last seen the couple. 'Well, my first problem is the spy looked well-built and fit. But fit men get sea sick, of course. Anyone can. But imagine you're standing here and going to be sick. What would you do?'

Stevenson gripped the top rail and bent forward as though he was being sick.

'No, you're going to be more sick than that. Really sick. Really retching. You need to get it out further.'

He stepped onto the bottom rail to give himself more height. To get his body out further. Still holding on to the top rail.

'Right, sir. Now, how likely are you to overbalance from that position?'

'Well, the top rail is right at my waist. I might lose my balance if the ship heaved at the same moment.'

'Right. Now, the spy was a couple of inches shorter than you, sir. Would that make a difference?'

Stevenson moved himself down a couple of inches. 'Yeah. Maybe less likely to overbalance from there.'

'Now, Jane said she didn't try to grab him to stop him going over. Even though she could have done. So, there's no crime there. We can't charge her with not saving someone. So, on that point, she's in the clear.'

'That's because she *thought* he was going to kill her. And there's some evidence that's true.'

'Exactly. But what if Jane *did* push the spy over while he was being sick? She thought he was going to kill her. And so she took the chance to kill him first. Is that a crime?'

He thought for a moment. 'She would argue self-defence. And it would be hard to prove she did it unless there was a witness. And you said no one saw it.'

'That's right. And that brings my second problem.'
He stepped back on to the deck.

'What if she didn't push him over? What if he didn't go over at all? What if this is all a charade? And he's still on the ship? And changed into a soldier's uniform?

'We'd never find him among all these soldiers. They don't check IDs on leaving the ship. So if he *was* still on board, he could just walk off and head over the border.

'The two of them were *very* lovey-dovey out on the deck. Very close and hugged each other. They were just like a couple of lovers. And they were also travelling as a married couple.

'I spoke to her in the lounge. Her ID is for Ingrid Gallagher. And the spy was Daniel Gallagher. Husband and wife. Same address. I think we've got to at least wonder if he's still on board. Unless we have proof he really did go over the side.'

He looked over the rail. But it was too dark to see anything. 'So what do you think we should do, Sandra?'

'Well, I think we ought to have someone go over the side here and see if there are any signs of blood or skin to indicate that Brenner *did* go over. And if we can't find anything, we check the IDs of everyone going off to see if there's a Daniel Gallagher among them.'

'Of course, he could have another ID.'

'That's true. But remember, he only had a German ID when we picked him up. And it's not that easy to get new IDs. But if it *is* the case, then we would at least have done everything we could to catch him.'

He looked over again. 'It wouldn't be easy to go over the side to search for clues.'

'The easy way, sir, would be to lower the lifeboat. Which is right here. And inspect the ship from there.'

194

He looked at her with a wry smile. 'You know, Sandra. Sometimes you're brilliant. And sometimes you're bloody brilliant.'

She laughed. 'Thank you, sir.'

'Right. Let's get this organised.'

'Can I just check, sir? If we *do* prove he went over, what about Jane?'

'Well, if she sticks to her story that he fell over, and she didn't try to grab him, there's not a damn thing we can do about it. Even if she did push him. Without a witness, there's no case to answer.'

They went back along the deck.

***

By the time they got back to the group, the team had finished their search and had laid everything out on the floor. Brown carried two IDs. A passport, ID card, and British Army papers in the name Robert John Brown. And a passport and ID card sewn into his coat in the name Charles Coyle. All of them listed his addresses and place of birth as Belfast.

Henry was the same. A passport and ID with British Army papers in the name Patrick Henry. And another sewn into his coat in the name Patrick Doyle. Again, all addresses and place of birth were Belfast.

That reminded Stevenson. He asked Don, 'Could you get the purser to send a message to our Belfast team that the spy's travel name is Gallagher. They want to pick up his driver at Larne.'

He then got Barry to take him and Sandra down to the tea room to see Jane. They found her, still a bit tearful, sitting with Jill and Sam.

'How do you feel now, Jane?'

'Better now, sir. Away from the crowds.'

He turned to Sam. 'And how are you? Sandra's just told me about your thumping. Would you recognise the soldier who punched you?'

Sam shrugged. 'I'm fine, sir. My pride's hurt more than my head. I just didn't see it coming. And wouldn't know him again. A big Glasgow lad. But there must be dozens like him on board.'

'Glad you're not any worse. Just to let you know, Jane. Commander Porritt will meet the ship at Larne. He'll be glad to see you again.'

Jane looked up at him and burst into tears again. 'Thank you, sir.'

'Right, must get on. Leave you to it for now.'

As he and Sandra walked out, she said, 'I still think her reactions aren't quite right, sir. Through all the tears, I still feel she's hiding something. And it's one of my two theories. Either she pushed him over and won't admit it. Or she's complicit in his escape.'

'Let's go see the captain. Hope he'll go along with our idea and get it all organised.'

Captain Ferguson agreed to lower the lifeboat to see the side of the ship. But they'd have to do it with the ship stopped in Larne harbour before docking. Tom and Bill, and two ship's officers, would search the ship's side. They could use torches for a few minutes as an emergency. The captain agreed to announce they had to check a technical problem with the ship.

***

Porritt and Williams sat in the back of the car, parked well back from the dockside at Larne. It was now three minutes after two. Porritt wondered how the raids around the country had gone.

He had met up with Alan McGowan in Belfast. Then called Burnett and Craig to review their plans one last time. He was happy with them. Of course things could go wrong. And often did. But he could do nothing about them now. He had to be patient and wait to hear from each of them.

He watched the ship arrive in the harbour. And then it stopped about thirty yards out from the dock. Why would they do that? After a few minutes, McGowan came from the car in front. 'The captain's announced a delay in docking, sir. Because of a technical problem. They say it'll only be a few minutes.'

'Thanks, Alan.' What technical problem could stop the ship docking? He couldn't think of any. *What the hell was going on out there?*

***

As the deck officer lowered the lifeboat, Tom and Bill studied the side of the ship with torches. They saw signs of sick below the deck line. Then halfway down, they came to a huge buffer strip. About two feet wide and the same deep. It ran the full length of the ship. 'Stop,' said Tom, and looked closer at the top of it. 'Bill, have a look at this. What do you think?'

Bill moved over beside him and peered at the surface. 'Looks like blood. Let's get a sample.'

197

He got a small evidence bag and a pocket-knife, and scraped off some red material. 'I think there's some skin there as well, Tom.'

He put the material in the bag. Then scraped more off and held the knife to his nose. 'Yes. It's blood,' and passed the knife to him.

Tom sniffed it and nodded. 'Okay, we've got enough. Let's get back on deck.'

They stepped out of the lifeboat on to the deck. And the ship's officers put the lifeboat back into its cradle.

Stevenson came over. 'Did you find anything?'

Tom smiled. 'Yes, sir. Human blood and skin on the buffer strip just below here. All the signs someone smashed into it on the way down. We've got a sample.'

'Okay. Let's get everyone off the ship.'

The deck officer headed for the bridge. A few minutes later, the engine speed increased, and the ship moved slowly towards the dock. A huge cheer rose from the crowd waiting to get off.

***

Porritt waited until the mass of people had cleared. Then he and Williams left their car and walked over to the ship. They showed their warrant cards at the gangway. Then walked up it to find Jim Stevenson and Sandra waiting for them on deck. They all shook hands.

'Well, how did it go?'

'We lost the spy Brenner, sir. He fell overboard.'

'What? How the hell did that happen?'

'He was at the rail with Jane and began to be sick. He leaned over to vomit. Then leaned over again too far and overbalanced.'

198

'Well, couldn't she have caught him? Stopped him going over?'

'She could've, sir. But didn't. She thought he was trying to push *her* overboard to kill her. So she just let him fall over. Didn't try to catch him.'

'Bloody hell. Any witnesses?'

'None, sir. Sandra and Sam from my team were ten yards away. But lost sight of them in the dark. When Brenner fell, Jane grabbed his case and ran to the bridge. She says there's a secret in it.' He handed it over.

'Well, at least that's something.' Porritt thought for a moment. 'Do we know the ship's position when the spy went over?'

'We do, sir. The coordinates are here.' Stevenson handed over the paper with the figures.

'So, who *have* you got, then?'

'We've got the two guards gagged and bagged. And Jane is with our team down in the staff tea room.'

'What about your team? Are they staying over?'

'If it's all right with you, sir, I think my team would prefer to go back to Scotland. Sandra and I will stay. I've got teams set to lift the two Glasgow agents at six. And any others we don't know yet. But I can manage that from this end. It's probably easier to debrief us while we're all here.'

'That's fine. Mike, could you dig out Alan. Tell him only two of the Glasgow team will stay overnight. Also, give him these coordinates. I want a sea search launched at daybreak to find Brenner's body. Make sure he has someone who knows the currents around that area. Oh, and can he get two cars for the prisoners and a car for Jim and Sandra round to the gangway?'

'Right, sir.' Williams left the ship.

Porritt followed Stevenson to the purser's office and into the side room, where the two guards still sat on the floor. 'Well, well, well. Mr Brown and Mr Henry. Good to see you again. We'll now look after you for a *very* long time. Right, let's go see Jane.'

As they walked towards the tea room, he said, 'You've got them well trussed up, Jim. Did you have a problem with them?'

'Well. They're armed men with military training, sir. So I got help from some Military Police on board. They subdued the two of them in two seconds flat.'

'Yeah. MPs are good at that..'

They went down the side of the servery into the staff area at the back. Jane looked up as he approached and began to weep. He had to look twice to recognise her. To his surprise, she rushed over and hugged him. 'Oh, sir. It's so good to see you. I'm so sorry about all this.'

'Well, let me make it clear, Jane. It's not your fault.' He helped her back to the table and sat opposite her. 'Brenner took a shine to you and decided to take you with him. Were you treated okay?'

She nodded, still with tears in her eyes. 'I was, sir. The lady in the house protected me. Brenner wanted to rape me. But she stopped him. Just before I left, she gave me a knife to protect myself. She knew something bad was going to happen to me.' She burst into tears again. 'I'm so sorry, sir! Brenner fell overboard. We lost him.'

Porritt patted her hand. 'Don't worry about that, Jane. We'll pick him up in the morning. This is the important thing.' He held up the brown case. 'This could make a huge difference. Thank you for getting it for us. We really appreciate it.'

She tried to smile. 'Oh, thank you, sir.'

'Now, we want to get you to a hotel. We'll get a doctor to check you out, and give you a pill to help you sleep. We'll then meet again in the morning.'

Jane fumbled around for her handbag. 'Oh, my other bag has my things in it. I don't know where it is.'

Sandra leaned over. 'We've got it with the others, Jane. We'll give you it upstairs. What colour was it?'

'Blue.'

'We'll find it.'

Sandra helped Jane to her feet, and she and Jane left the tea room. Porritt touched Stevenson's arm and held him back. 'What do you think, Jim? Did he fall or was he pushed?'

Stevenson shrugged. 'She says he fell, sir. And we've no evidence that points to anything else. We can't charge her with not trying to save him, if she thought he was going to kill her.'

'Did she really have a knife?'

'Yes, sir. We've got it. A bloody fierce stiletto.'

Porritt raised his eyebrows. 'Maybe she's right.'

'I hadn't heard about the rape, sir. But it sounds plausible. And that would be hellish for her. So thanks to the woman at the house.'

'Yeah. Brenner was delusional and very sly, Jim. For us, her freedom from oppression must take priority. Let's give her the benefit of the doubt, huh? We'll check it out in the morning.'

'Yes, sir. I can live with that.'

'Not sure she can, though.'

They left to catch up with the others.

***

Porritt helped Jane into the back of his car. Then watched while McGowan's team got Brown and Henry into separate cars off to Belfast Police HQ. As Porritt walked round to get in the other side, a car drove up and McGowan get out.

'Well, we got the driver, sir. It couldn't have been easier. Jim's team had given us the spy's travel name. And he was standing beside his car with a sign. But it's given me a bit of a headache.'

'Oh? Why's that?'

'We know the driver, sir. Declan Flynn. He's the youngest son of one of the biggest gangsters in the Falls Road. Charlie Flynn. We asked him where he was going and he said "Armagh". Which means the border.

'We're assuming he'd go straight there. So would be out of contact for a few hours. We've taken him and his car to a safe police station up in County Antrim under a false name. Charlie Flynn's a dangerous man. And if he's involved in this, it's bad news, sir.'

Porritt paused 'Or it could be good news.'

'How do you mean?'

'Well, keep in mind they caught Al Capone for tax evasion. If Flynn is an agent of the Germans, you'll get him put away for a long time. But would he risk that?'

'He'd do anything for money, sir. Bloody greedy. And doubtless well paid for this. Got politicians, lawyers, maybe even some police in his pocket. He's a big "businessman". And we've never been able to pin anything on him. So, you're right, sir. Maybe it *is* a chance. But if Charlie Flynn is one of our agents, it'll cause a riot in the area when we lift him.'

'Would people still support him if they knew he'd worked for the Germans?'

'Well, there's a big group on that side who see Britain as their enemy. They take the view that anyone fighting their enemy is their friend. So they'd be sympathetic to the Germans. Most of them wouldn't mind if he *is* working for the Germans.

'There would be others, of course, that would hate him for it. But I think the safest thing would be to get him out to England as fast as we can, like we talked about. Take the heat out of the situation.'

'Right, let's do that. See you back at base. Oh, and Alan? Can you have the police doctor check Jane? To make sure she's okay, and give her a sleeping pill. She's had a rough time tonight.'

***

Malcolm Craig and his team gathered outside the big house in Surrey. Dressed in black, with balaclavas, they blended in to the darkness. At five minutes to two, they snaked through the gate and around the garden to the back of the house. Then they separated into two groups that crept down each side. They pressed themselves against the wall to make sure they kept out of sight of the doors and windows.

The dog had started barking as they moved down the sides. Craig watched as John, their amateur dramatist, walked up to the front door. He wore a dinner suit, with a black bow tie and white scarf, a top hat at a jaunty angle, and appeared to be tipsy, but not drunk. He rang the bell and stood back from the door. The dog barked even louder. He rang the bell again and stepped back into the driveway.

A window above the front door opened, and a man appeared. 'What are you doing here?' he shouted in a very pukka accent. 'Get off with you!'

John looked up. 'Oh, sorry to bother you, sir. But the bally car's broken down just at your gate. Any chance of using your phone?'

'No! Bugger off, or I'll call the police.'

'Well, actually, sir. I *am* the police.' John went into his pocket and showed his warrant card. 'Name's Hoxton. Assistant chief at Guildford.'

A young woman in a full-length ball gown with a fox fur round her shoulders appeared in the driveway. Her cue had been any mention of the police. 'John? John! Any joy, John? It's getting cold out here.'

'Sorry, sir. My wife.'

'Oh, hold on then.' The man closed the window.

Craig and his team stood ready. A few moments later, they heard the man unlock the front door. John and the girl walked forward towards it, and John kept talking to distract the man. 'Got one of these new radio phone thingies in the car, but the electrics have all gone. The damn thing's useless. Really appreciate your help.'

As they entered the vestibule, the man stood aside to let them enter the house. Suddenly, the two groups of police ran round and in the front door. Cries of 'Armed police!' rang out, and officers grabbed the man, pushed him to the floor face down in an armlock, and cuffed him. Craig knelt on his back as his team spread through the house. 'Sir James Dunsmore. I'm CS Craig from Special Branch. You are under arrest for breaches of the Treachery Act, 1940. You have the right to remain silent, but anything you do say will be taken down and may be used in evidence. Do you understand?'

Dunsmore struggled, face down, and kicked out behind him. 'You bloody cretin! Don't you know who I am? What do you think you're doing?'

The dog had stopped barking and the house was now quiet. Craig continued to kneel on Dunsmore's back while he squirmed, and searched his dressing gown and pyjama pockets. 'Can you cuff his legs, please, John?'

'Yes, sir.'

'Are you bloody Porritt's people?'

'Yes, sir,' Craig said, as he found a handgun in the dressing gown pocket. 'Can you bag this for me, please, Sally?' He handed the gun to the girl in the ball gown, and then found a bunch of keys in the other pocket.

'You tell Porritt I'll have his balls for this!' Dunsmore shouted.

'Yes, sir. I'm sure he'll be interested to hear that. Do either of you have a gag handy?' Craig asked.

'Yes, sir. I've got one here.' Sally went into her bag, pulled out a gag, and fastened it on to Dunsmore's head.

'Can you look after him while I check with the rest of the team?' Craig stood up, took out his notebook, and recorded Dunsmore's comments. He thought they might be useful later.

He remembered the layout of the house from the briefing. The large lounge/drawing room was on the right. The dining room ran along the back, with picture windows over the gardens, and the kitchen was on the left. He went into the lounge.

The team had spread out, searching through tables, furniture, and a large desk in the far corner. 'Got this, sir,' said one of them, pointing to a wall safe.

Their expert safecracker worked at it, and Craig watched as his fingers flew across its surface. There was a satisfying click, and the safecracker said, 'Got it,' and swung the door open. The team pulled out papers and documents and laid them in a pile on the desk. One of Craig's senior team members, together with the codebreaker, studied the papers.

'I've got a bunch of keys here if you need them, lads,' Craig said, and headed upstairs to Dunsmore's bedroom, which ran across the front of the house. A large bed opposite the door dominated the room.

'No sign of a panic button, sir,' said Rob, one of his senior team.

Craig looked around. His team members were all intent on their search. Some of them were searching built-in wardrobes on one side of the door, and others were in the en-suite bathroom and dressing room on the other side. Again, he mentioned he had a set of keys if they needed them.

'This one's locked, sir,' said one of his team at the wardrobes, indicating the left-hand section.

Craig pulled out the bunch of keys. He tried the ones that might fit, but none of them worked. 'Hm. That's strange. Any other locked sections here?'

One of the team at a writing bureau said, 'We've got a locked drawer here, sir.'

Craig went across and tried the keys. One of them unlocked the drawer. He opened it, and inside lay four ladies' rings – two wedding and two engagement – and four Rolex watches – two men's and two women's.

'Family heirlooms. Worth a pretty penny, I'd say. Let's bag 'em and keep them safe.'

The locked wardrobe still intrigued him, and he went over to it again. The wardrobes were about fifteen feet wide, divided into five sections, each about three feet wide. Four of them had open shelves and hanging space for shirts and ties, shoes and socks, underwear, and casual sweaters and cardigans. Lots of clothes. But the section furthest from the window had a locked door.

He pulled out the bunch of keys again and tried them in turn. Then he remembered the Benjamin Franklin definition of insanity – doing the same thing over and over and expecting a different result.

He knew that if he really wanted in, he could jemmy the door open. But anyone could do that, and he was concerned there might be a booby trap. This was more of a puzzle, and there had to be a key for that lock somewhere in the room. He looked around again. It *had* to be in the writing bureau with all its little drawers.

Craig got the safecracker and explained the problem. Could he help find out whether there was a secret section in the bureau that held the key?

The safecracker examined the bureau. Craig watched as he gently pulled out the bottom set of drawers containing writing paper and notelets. He then measured the depth of a drawer front to back and checked that against the side of the bureau cabinet. Then he pulled out the second row of drawers, which came out as far as the first row. He then pulled out the third row, and this time they only came out part way. They were about five inches shorter coming out than the second row.

The safecracker put his hand in the middle drawer of the third row and smiled at Craig. 'Think I've got it,' he murmured. He kept his hand in the middle drawer of the third row and closed the second row, then closed the bottom row. There was a click, and the third row of drawers came out the extra five inches. Running the full length of the bureau behind the three drawers was a single compartment.

Craig peered inside and saw it contained a series of pocket diaries. From a brief glance, it looked like they went back several years. There was also a key ring with a single key on it. The safecracker said, 'It only opens if you've got all three drawers in the third row open and all the other drawers closed.'

Craig nodded. 'That's brilliant. Really appreciate it.'

'No problem.'

Craig took the newly revealed key over to the locked wardrobe and put it in the lock. It was the right key. He opened the door. There were a series of shelves down one half of the unit and hanging pegs down the other half. On the shelves were a series of very hard-core pornographic magazines. Craig, like most policemen, had come across pornography before, but this was at a different level. The magazines were German and featured gross pictures of active homosexuality. Most of them were so far out they would certainly be illegal in Britain. Hanging on the pegs at the side were various whips and harnesses made of leather and rubber, some of which featured in the magazines. Now he knew why Dunsmore lived alone. He called Rob over. 'Let's box all this stuff, Rob. Keep it separate from everything else, and don't let anyone else see it.'

'Yes, sir.' Rob headed out of the room. He came back in a couple of moments with three cardboard boxes, and he and Craig put the magazines and harness equipment in and sealed them.

Craig locked the internal wardrobe door, and put the single key on the ring with the other bunch of keys. Then he walked back to the bureau and pulled out the pocket diaries. There were eleven of them, going back to 1932. He riffled through the pages. The entries looked like they were in code. He went off to find the codebreaker.

He found him studying the papers that had come out of the wall safe. 'Anything of interest?'

The codebreaker shook his head. 'Looks like financial and bank statements. I think you'll need an accountant to interpret them.'

'That's a good idea. Let's put them in a separate box. Mark them 'SJD Financials Confidential' and I'll get an accountant to look at them later.'

The codebreaker got a box from an adjacent pile, marked it, and sealed it.

Craig asked, 'Now, could you come upstairs with me for a moment? I need your help.'

They went back up to the bedroom, and Craig went to the bureau. He opened the three drawers, put his hand in the centre, and pressed the button. The three drawers extended out to their maximum. 'Can you check these diaries, please? The entries seem to be in code.'

The codebreaker picked up a diary and started studying it, and Craig left him to it. He went into the bathroom. It was a long room, about fifteen feet by nine feet wide, with all the facilities, and beautifully tiled.

He then went into the adjacent dressing room, which was the same length as the bathroom, and about six feet wide with rails of suits, jackets and coats down one side. Nothing of interest there.

Finally, he came out into the hall. Everyone was bustling around him. 'Cleared' notices already appeared on doors. He glanced at his watch. It was only 2.23, but he felt like he had already been there for hours. He wondered how his assistants, Brian and Graham, were getting on at the Lyall house and shop.

As he pondered this, he stood at the top of the stairs just outside Dunsmore's bedroom and looked up at the ceiling. There was a glass dome above the centre of the hall, which let light in during the day. After staring at it for a few seconds, he realised there must be a roof space. He needed to check that too.

The house was symmetrical, with doors opposite each other along the gallery on each side. He went into the first bedroom on the left. A nice big room with fitted wardrobes on the wall behind the door, and very well decorated. He wandered down the hall and checked the other rooms.

He then came back along the other side of the gallery, looking in each room. All decorated to a very high standard. For someone who lived alone, Dunsmore kept the house immaculate. The last bedroom on that side was identical to the first room he had seen opposite. He came out and closed the door and saw one of his senior lads walking past. 'How's it going, Jack?'

'Pretty good, sir. Just as we planned it. That's the upstairs clear except for the main bedroom.'

'Good. Could you make sure you check the roof space? I don't think we had that on our list.'

'Will do, sir.'

Craig stood at the top of the stairs again. It had all gone very well. But he had found no evidence that linked Dunsmore with the spy organisation, and that was a worry. And the wardrobes in the main bedroom niggled at him. He went back into the bedroom and looked at them. The team had cleared everything out now, with all the stuff in boxes and marked.

He stood facing the door. There was something wrong with the room, but what was it? He looked to the left-hand side at the bathroom and adjacent dressing room, and then to the right-hand side at the wardrobes. Then it hit him. The house was symmetrical. The two bedrooms behind the main bedroom were in identical positions. But on one side, the bathroom and dressing room used up about fifteen feet of space. The wardrobes on the other side used only three feet of space. There must be twelve feet of space behind the wardrobes.

He went over to the wardrobes and examined them, then took out the single key and unlocked the internal door of the section on the left. They were just ordinary wardrobes, custom made, with beautiful dark wood. He knocked on the back wall of the wardrobes, but they sounded solid.

He needed help again and went off to find the safecracker. He brought him back up to the bedroom again and explained his problem. 'There's got to be something like twelve feet of space behind these wardrobes. How do I get into it?'

The safecracker ran his expert fingers around the back of the wardrobes from one end to the other. Nothing. He stood studying them. 'If what you say is correct, sir, then one of these back panels must move.' He examined them all again and shook his head. 'The only section that's different is this one with the internal door. The panel between it and the next one is twice as thick. Is that because of the door?'

He pulled the door open again and examined the inside of it. 'Its hinges are bigger than the outside doors. Why would that be?' He pulled out a magnifying glass and examined the lock on the internal door. 'Wonder why they did that?' he muttered. 'Can I have the key a minute, sir?'

Craig passed him the key. The safecracker put it in the lock and turned it as though locking the door. The rectangular lock bolt sprang out. He turned the key the other way and the lock bolt sprung back into the door. He then turned it again as though unlocking, and there was another click. 'It's a very clever double lock. So what's just unlocked?' He pushed on the shelves and the whole section moved backwards smoothly and silently. They looked at each other and smiled. 'Let's see where this goes,' the safecracker said. He pushed it all the way through until it cleared the back panel and opened up another hidden room.

Craig laughed. 'Brilliant.'

They pushed the section all the way back, which allowed them to enter the hidden room. Inside, there was a desk and chair, with wall shelves, cupboards, and a filing cabinet. On a side table sat a short-wave radio set. The aerial was just visible around the window. On another table sat photographic equipment. The room also seemed to double as a darkroom.

Craig opened drawers and saw books and papers with words and numbers all written in code. 'Bingo. We've got the bastard now.' He opened the drawers in the filing cabinet and rummaged through a series of files, each one tabbed with a name in code, filled with papers.

He went back out to the bedroom and got the codebreaker, who was still writing out entries from the diaries. 'Could you come through here a minute, please? Have you cracked the code?'

The codebreaker nodded. 'It's the same word-based progressive code we did for you a couple of weeks back. They seem to use it everywhere.'

They entered the hidden room. Craig showed the codebreaker the books, papers and files. He examined them. 'Yep. It's the same code. Have you got a name you would expect to see here?'

'How about Lyall? L-Y-A-L-L.'

'Okay. That would translate as M-A-D-P-Q. Do you see that anywhere?'

Craig looked at the first page in one of the books. 'There it is! Just as you say. Brilliant. These books seem to contain names, addresses, phone numbers and bank account details. What a find. Could you concentrate on these first and give us a list of who they are, please?'

'Sure. No problem, sir.'

Craig smiled. It was all so worthwhile, and he realised what a brilliant team he had. He went downstairs and found his car out front, picked up the radio telephone and contacted Alison.

'Tell the boss we've found masses of stuff at Dunsmore's place in a hidden part of the house. All in detail and coded. Tell him I don't think he'll have any problems getting evidence against Dunsmore.'

***

Burnett and his team had decided to enter the Pickering house in two ways – through the French windows leading on to the garden, and through a bedroom window on the other side, which they could access via an outhouse roof. In each case, they would have a glasscutter take out the glass to give them clear access.

At five minutes to two, the team assembled in their groups on each side of the house, dressed in black, and invisible in the darkness. Burnett had to keep his usual active attitude still in these last few moments.

At one minute to two, a toot from a car on the main road indicated they had cut the power to the house. The team at the house then cut the telephone wires and radio aerial, and muffled the alarm with heavy goo. Then the glasscutters moved in.

Right on two o'clock, Burnett led his group through the French windows, then the lounge and up the stair. He stopped outside the front bedroom door to let everyone catch up. Then he opened the door, and they all switched on powerful torches.

'Armed police, armed police!'

The officers rushed to the bed, pulled back the covers, turned the occupants over, cuffed their arms behind their backs and shackled their ankles. All within the five second target.

'What the hell?' said the male occupant.

Burnett knelt on Kay's back. 'Mr John Kay and Mrs Elizabeth Kay. I'm CS Burnett from Special Branch. You are hereby arrested under the Treachery Act, 1940. You have the right to remain silent, but anything you do say will be taken down and may be used in evidence. Do you understand?'

He searched Kay and a female officer searched Mrs Kay. 'All clear, sir,' she said.

'Search the side tables.' They found a handgun on his side, and a stiletto knife on her's. Burnett pocketed a bunch of keys lying on his side table.

'I need to go to the bathroom,' Kay said.

'You're not going anywhere right now.'

'But I need to go, urgently!'

'You're not going. Pee the bed if you have to.'
Burnett saw an internal hall light come on. 'Right, lads,
let's get the lights on.'

The lights came on in the bedroom and throughout
the house, and Burnett began to relax. His team had
spread out around the house to assess the other rooms.
'Upstairs clear, sir,' said a voice. A few moments later,
'Downstairs clear, sir.'

Burnett searched for a panic button. He pulled out
the bedside table. Nothing there. He searched under the
bed and saw a wire coming down from one side of the
bed frame into a metal box. There were no wires on the
other side of the bed.

'Take these two off the bed on that other side, lads.
Sit them down on the floor against the wall. Put a sheet
over each of them.' He heard Kay murmur something to
his wife. 'And gag them. Make sure they don't move an
inch unless I say so.'

Burnett looked under the bed again. The box,
plugged into a socket on the floor, had a small red light
showing. He pulled out the plug and the light went off.
He lifted the mattress off the bed and examined the bed
frame. There was a brown button on the inside of the
frame about halfway along, just about at hand level if
you were lying on the bed. Had Kay touched it before
they cuffed him? Unlikely, he thought. They had cuffed
him very fast.

But could he have pressed the button with his knee?
He *had* been squirming under Burnett, but the button
was down the side of the frame. He wouldn't have been
able to get to it with his knee because of the mattress.
And they had cut off the power and the radio aerial. So

the chances were, even if he *had* pressed the button, it wouldn't have sent a signal. However, he wanted to be sure, and asked one of his team to find the comms man.

A few moments later, he appeared. Burnett explained the problem. 'I don't think Kay hit the button, but if he did, even with the power off, would the unit still have sent a panic signal?'

The comms man knelt beside Burnett and checked its operation. Then disconnected everything, took off the box cover, and examined the innards.

After a few minutes, he said, 'I'll need to take it back to the lab to be sure, sir, but I don't think it has operated. It has a battery, so the button would have worked with the power off. But it would need a repeater station to amplify the signal, and the radio aerial to send it. I'll give you a definite answer once I've checked everything, but my initial thoughts are, without power and an aerial, even if pushed, it wouldn't send a signal.'

Burnett smiled in relief. 'Good. Thanks very much.' He stood up and looked for the bathroom. Had Kay really needed the bathroom, or was there something there he wanted to flush away?

Just then, one of the team stopped him. 'We're clear upstairs except for a locked room at the end of the hall, sir. I believe you've got some keys?'

'I have.' Burnett pulled out the bunch of keys from the bedside table. 'Let's go see.' He turned to one of his senior team members in the room. 'Tony, don't let anyone go into the bathroom until I get back here, especially not the man there.'

Burnett walked with the lad along the hallway to the locked door. There were two locks on it. He hesitated. 'Have we found a safe anywhere?'

'Not to my knowledge, sir. You want me to check downstairs first?'

'Yes, please. Let's do that. And if you see the safecracker and our codebreaker, ask them to come up here please?'

The lad went off downstairs, and Burnett looked at the door. There was also an adjacent table lamp on a small stand, plugged into a wall socket. Why have a double lock on an inside door? And why have a table lamp here? Even in the middle of the night, there was plenty of light in the hall.

He walked back to the bedroom and caught the comms man just before he left. 'Can you come and have a look at this for me please, Jeff?'

They got to the locked door, just as the lad returned with the safecracker and the codebreaker. 'There's a locked section in the desk, sir, but no safe so far.'

'Thanks, Andy.' Burnett turned to the three others. 'I think we might have a booby trap here, lads. A double lock on an internal door? A table lamp that's not really necessary? This might be a three-way switch you need to get right to open the door, otherwise . . .'

'What? You think it blows out on you?' the safecracker asked.

'Well, maybe not that. But it might destroy something inside. Like secret papers. So, we're the best we've got. How do we solve the puzzle?'

They all studied the door and the table lamp.

'Let me get this,' the safecracker said. 'You think to open the door, you need to put the table lamp on, and open the locks in the right order? Is that right?'

Burnett nodded. 'It could be. Obviously, I don't know. But it just feels like that.'

217

'So,' the codebreaker cut in, 'we need to get into the room without opening the door. Why don't we take one of these panels out and go in that way?'

They all looked at each other. 'Any better suggestions?' Burnett asked. They all shook their heads.

'Let's look at these doors,' the safecracker said.

They all moved up the hall and examined the door of the next bedroom. It was a heavy wooden door, with two panels – a large panel on top and a smaller one underneath. The safecracker knocked on the door with his knuckles. 'Pretty solid. Let me get my tools.' The others returned to the locked door.

The safecracker put a drill bit in the chuck of a hand brace. They all watched as he drilled a hole in one corner of the bottom panel. He then drilled holes in the other three corners. Then he pulled out a mini handsaw and started sawing through the door from the top left hole towards the top right hole.

Burnett went back to the bedroom and found Tony and his team tidying up. 'Tony, take the prisoners down stairs. Let them pick out the clothes they want to wear. Have a couple of our girls look after the lady. Always have two of you with each of them at all times. Never leave them alone, even when they're in the toilet or dressing. Our safety is more important than their dignity.

'And could you find the master switch for the power? I may need to switch it off for a few minutes. I also need four of these powerful torches, please.'

Burnett went back to the locked door. He checked his watch. It was only 2.22. He watched as the safecracker stuck a sucker on to the panel before he cut through the last edge. He then pulled the panel from the door, placed it against the wall, and peered inside. The others crowded down to look as well. The torches arrived, and the safecracker lifted one and shone it around the room. Opposite the door there was a large floor-mounted safe, about three feet square.

'What about these door locks?' Burnett asked.

The safecracker turned onto his back, put his head through the panel gap, and looked up at the locks. 'We have cables from each lock into a box mounted on the wall. There's also a cable from the skirting, maybe from the table lamp. And there's a cable from the box to the top of the safe. So, what's that all about?'

Burnett nodded. 'That's our booby trap.'

'So, the two locks and the table lamp give a possible six different sequences to set an access code, done within the box. If you get the sequence right, you can open the door and nothing happens. But if you get it wrong and open the door, power goes across to the safe and operates . . . what?' The safecracker thought for a moment. 'You know, I heard about something like this years ago. A safe fitted with heating elements in its roof, so if you didn't get the right access code, they heated up and burned all the papers in the safe within two or three minutes. I'll bet you that's what this is.'

Burnett nodded again. 'Sounds reasonable. These people have a lot to hide, and a lot to lose if we get their papers. So what do we do?'

'Well, I think we've bypassed the booby trap by coming in through the panel. So the system will stay dormant. Once I get the safe open and the papers out, we can then figure out the sequence to open the room door safely. But I think I should open the safe with the power off, just to be on the safe side, no pun intended.'

'Are you able to open the safe?'

'Burg safe? Yes, I've opened them before. Maybe take me ten minutes or so, sir. Do you have the keys?'

'Yes, here they are.'

'Right, I'll go in on my own. You wait out here until I give you a shout.' The safecracker went through the panel into the room and took his case with him. 'Let's have the power off.'

'Can we have the power off now, Tony?' Burnett shouted down the hall. 'Tell everyone it'll be off for about ten or fifteen minutes. And keep close to these bloody prisoners. Don't let them move an inch.'

A moment later, the power went off and the house plunged into darkness. Most of the team had torches, and within seconds, torch lights were everywhere.

Burnett left them to it and went out to his car, now parked at the front door. He called Alison.

'Could you get a message to Malcolm Craig and Brian Walker please? Tell them two things. First, that we found the panic button here hidden in the bed frame in the master bedroom. It connected with a box under the bed. Our box plugged into a socket on the floor. We've unplugged it and think it's safe. But it has a battery and will still work with the power off. So don't let anyone near that bed frame. And make sure they cut off the radio aerial.

'The second thing is we found a sort of operations room inside the house. It has two locks on the door and there's a table lamp outside the door in the hallway. We think you need to unlock the two locks and switch on the table lamp in a particular sequence, otherwise power goes to the safe in the room and burns all the papers in it within two or three minutes.

'We've bypassed the booby trap by taking out a panel in the door and going in that way. We're also opening the safe with all the power off, just in case. If they've got a similar set up and want any more details, get them to phone me. Someone will find me.'

He went back upstairs and into the en-suite bathroom off the master bedroom. He'd done enough raids in his time to know crooks often flushed stuff down the toilet. If Kay wanted to flush something away, it would have to be easily accessible, and not too light or too heavy. It would have to be about a couple of inches long and an inch in diameter. He shone the torch across the shelves. Nothing obvious.

Down the side of the toilet seat was a black-handled toilet brush in a holder. He pulled it up and examined it, then looked in the holder. Nothing. As he put the brush back in the holder, he noticed the end of the handle reflected the harsh torch light slightly differently from the rest of it. He took it in both hands and tried to pull off the end. It came off, and was about three inches long and an inch diameter. Just what he was looking for.

He studied the end piece. Was that a faint line round it? He tried to twist it, and the top screwed off. He gave it a shake, and a key dropped out. 'Bingo.' Someone sitting on the toilet could have easily flushed away the top end, and no one would notice as the brush handle still looked normal. Bloody clever.

He heard a shout. 'CS Burnett!'

'In here. In the bathroom.' He put the key in his pocket, screwed the end piece together, and bagged it.

'Sir, we have Superintendent Walker on the radio phone for you.'

He went to his car and picked up the phone.

Walker said, 'Thanks a lot for your message, Dave. We have a similar situation here at the Lyall house. We found the same panic button set-up, and we've also got a secure room with two locks and a table lamp. But we've only got one of the door lock keys, and can't find the other. So we were just going to force the door open. But you've made us think twice. Could you tell me again how you got into the room?'

Burnett explained how the safecracker had drilled out the door panel. 'That keeps the booby trap intact, but you can then crawl into the room through the hole.

'We think the safe in the room has heating elements built into its roof, and so if you try to unlock the door with the wrong sequence, or break in, it sends power to these elements and burns the papers inside. You should open the safe with the power off, just in case.

'Oh, and Brian, I've just discovered the end of the toilet brush in the master bathroom has a secret hiding place for a key. It just pulls off and then screws off. Check if you've got the same. I'll bet it's the other key for that internal door.'

He hung up, went back into the house, and found Tony. 'Where are we now?'

'All rooms clear, sir, except the en-suite and the locked room. We've still got a locked section in the desk downstairs, but we've boxed everything else.'

'Good. You can now go into the en-suite. I've found what I was looking for there.' He held up the bag with the end of the toilet brush in it. 'This is what Kay wanted to flush away. Had a key in it. I'm guessing it's for one of the safe room door locks. If he had flushed that away, we'd have had to break in, and that would have burned all the papers in the safe. Clever, huh?'

Someone else shouted, 'CS Burnett, sir!' This time it was his driver. 'Phone call from CI Hardcastle, sir. Says to let you know they've now got Ted Richmond, the spy's driver, in custody. Says he's in bits about it.'

Burnett had forgotten about Ted. They had heard he left Stranraer after dropping off the spy gang around 23.00 and estimated he would be on the A66 by two o'clock. So they had arranged for a road block caused by 'an accident'. He wondered about Ted's reaction. But hey, you never really knew how a person would react when arrested.

Someone shouted for him again from upstairs. It was the comms man this time. 'We're in,' he said with a smile as Burnett reached him.

He bent down and peered into the room. The safecracker sat against the wall beside the open safe. 'Come in and have a look at this, sir.'

Burnett crawled through the hole. 'Can we get the lights on now?'

The safecracker nodded. 'Sure. The safe's empty.'

'Put the power on, Tony.' The lights came on in the hall, and he switched them on in the room.

The safecracker indicated two piles on the floor. 'This is from the top shelf. It's all books and papers. And there's a card index too. All in code. This pile here is from the bottom shelf. It's all blank passports and ID cards. Looks like they had a forgery racket as well.'

'Wow. Brilliant job,' Burnett peered into the safe at the lines in the roof. 'Are these the heating elements you talked about?'

'Yes, sir. That's them.'

'So you were right? Good thinking.'

223

The codebreaker crawled into the room. Burnett showed him the pile of books with coded notes. Some of them looked like names, addresses, phone numbers and bank accounts. 'Could you decode these first, please?'

The codebreaker took the books to a desk. 'Looks like a simple word-based progressive code that's quite common. Do you have names you'd expect to see?'

Burnett thought for a moment. Jim Stevenson had passed him the names of the two agents he had in Glasgow. He checked his notebook. 'Brady and Mair.'

The codebreaker wrote them down. 'If I'm right, we should see them coded as C-T-D-H-D and N-C-L-V. Do you see them in the books?'

Burnett looked at the letters and turned the pages of a book. The codebreaker did the same. 'Here's one of them,' he said, showing it to Burnett. 'And here's the other. I think that works. I'll get busy decoding.'

'Very impressive. We really appreciate your help.'

Burnett looked round the room. Aside from the safe and the desk and chair, there was a filing cabinet. He found the right key and opened it. There were pages of financial transactions with various clients, all in code. They would have to wait till later.

Burnett called over to the comms man. 'Can we get the room door open to make it easier for us?'

'What about the safe, sir? We need to use the right access code, otherwise the safe will heat up. Could have a pretty fierce heat in here. And if we get it wrong, how do we reset it?'

The safecracker thought for a moment. 'There must be a way. How about if we're wrong, we reverse the sequence, then put the power off and on again? That should reset it.'

Burnett nodded. 'Let's give it a try.' He went to the door. 'Tony! When we call down, can you switch off the power, count to ten, and switch it on again?'

'Right, sir. Will do.'

Burnett turned to the safecracker. 'You first. What sequence will you try?'

'Unlock top. Unlock bottom. Switch on lamp.'

The comms man set up his measuring instrument where the cable from the wall box connected with the safe. He held the two prongs in place. 'Right, try that.'

Burnett went out into the hall. One of the keys in the bunch fitted the bottom lock, but he needed the key from the toilet brush to fit the top lock. 'Right. Unlock top. Unlock bottom. Switch on lamp. Open the door.' He looked through the hole for the comms man to react.

'No, that's not it. I've got a current.' He placed his hand inside the safe. 'Yep, that's the plates heating up.'

'Right. Close the door. Lamp off. Lock bottom. Lock top.' He shouted, 'Tony, power off, please.'

The power went off. Ten seconds later it came back on. Burnett asked the comms man. 'Still got a current?'

He looked at his instrument. 'No, there's no current.'

'Your turn now,' Burnett said to the comms man.

They repeated the exercise with a different sequence, but that didn't work either.

'Your turn now, sir,' said the comms man.

'Okay. Let's try this. Unlock bottom. Unlock top. Switch on lamp. Open door.'

'That's it! No current. Well done, sir.'

'That's why he's the boss,' the safecracker said, and everybody laughed.

At the far end of the safe room, a door led into the next room towards the back of the house. Burnett wandered through it and found a series of benches and desks used for preparing printed documents. There were copying and printing machines over on a side table. That must be where they created their forgeries.

A door in the far wall led to the next room, which had a couple of tables, with a desk and drawers. On one of the tables sat a short-wave radio set. The aerial ran round the window. He went back into the first room and got the comms man. 'Come and see this, Jeff,' he said, and they walked back through to the third room.

Jeff studied the radio set. 'Pretty powerful unit, sir. Could reach Germany with that.'

'What do you want to do? Take it to your lab, or can you test it here?'

'I'll test it here first, sir.'

'Fine. I'll leave you to it.' He took the keys downstairs to the lad working at the desk in the lounge. 'Here's a key for the locked section. Sorry it took so long to get to you.'

The lad took the keys and found the one that fitted. There were five folders inside marked 'Aquila 2', 'Aquila 3', 'Boat', 'Emerald 3', 'Agents General'. He gave them to Burnett.

Each folder contained handwritten notes and typed letters relating to the subject. Burnett opened the 'Boat' folder, and read the notes on Kay's meetings with Bill Wadsworth, the skipper of the fishing boat from Scarborough. The notes were very detailed. Got to hand it to the Germans, he thought. Always well organised. This stuff would be dynamite for building a case against Kay and the gang.

'Let's bag this and keep it separate for my attention only,' he said to the lad.

'Yes, sir. Will do.'

Burnett smiled and nodded. It had gone well. Now he needed to get all the stuff back to York and start building the case.

***

DI Graham Fox led Craig's third team into the Lyall shoe shop at two o'clock. They cut off the burglar alarm.

Porritt had asked them to find a list of clients and check they were all genuine. He also wanted to know who made the shoes with secret spaces.

Fox found lots of locked drawers and cupboards. They kept the safecracker busy. It would just take time to go through all these records to get Porritt his info.

***

Brian Walker and his team at the Lyall house used the same approach as Burnett. He'd been impressed at how Burnett found the key. Thought he could do a lot worse than just mirror Burnett, since the two houses had the same security features.

In common with many others, Walker saw Burnett as brash and too young for his level. But also agreed the lad was very bright, and most likely to succeed Porritt.

The raid had been a big success, and he could now prepare the case against Lyall.

***

Porritt glanced at his watch. It was 2.24. He couldn't wait any longer and called Alison.

'Hi Alison, Any word your end?'

'Nothing so far, sir. All quiet.'

'That's us on the way to Belfast office. I'll call again when we get there. Oh, and just to let you know, we've got Jane here safe and sound. A bit traumatised and tearful, but otherwise fine.'

'Good news, sir. Give her my best wishes.'

'Alison sends her best wishes,' Porritt whispered to Jane as he hung up.

Tears welled in her eyes again. 'Thank you, sir.'

Twenty minutes later, they arrived at Belfast office. McGowan was waiting for them at the door with a woman dressed in civilian clothes. He introduced her to Jane. 'This is Beth Calvert. She works with us as an associate. We don't have women police officers over here, at least not yet. But Beth will look after you while you're here, and make sure you get to your hotel.'

'Come on,' Beth said with a smile. 'Let's go.'

***

Porritt, Williams and McGowan entered the conference room next to McGowan's office. A man with a big smile and a shock of white hair introduced himself. 'Hello, sir. I'm Doc Russell.'

'Good to meet you.' The men all shook hands. 'Could you just excuse me a minute? Can I use your phone please, Alan?'

'Yes, sir. In you come.' McGowan opened the door to his office.

Porritt called Alison again. 'Any news yet?'

'Yes, sir. I've had calls from CS Burnett and CS Craig.' She gave him a summary of their reports.

'Good. I like Craig's. That's the one I was worried about. I'll call again later.'

He went back next door. Williams raised an eyebrow and he nodded in return. 'Going well so far.' He smiled at everyone. 'Right, I'm going to work with Doc Russell now. Mike, will you plan to take Brown and Henry back to Lincoln Prison on the plane later? Say about seven. And Alan has a man he wants us to hold for him as well. Put them in the segregation unit as usual, under false names. We don't want their info to leak out.'

Williams and McGowan left the room. Doc Russell leaned forward. 'You want help with an analysis, sir?'

'I do. It concerns this.' He lifted the small brown case onto the table.

Russell studied it. 'Is it booby-trapped, sir?'

'Don't know. Could well be. What do you think?'

Russell examined the locks with a magnifying glass. 'If it is, it's not obvious. Do you have a key?'

'No.'

'Let's take it along to my lab and we'll cut it open.'

They laid the case on a lab table, and Russell used a more powerful magnifying glass to study the locks again. 'Don't see anything suspicious, sir. But let's not take a chance.' They both put on safety glasses.

Russell then lifted a tool box onto the table, and drilled a hole in the lid about an inch in from each corner. He then pulled out a thin, sharp knife, cut through the leather between the holes, and peeled off the cut section to reveal shirts, all neatly folded.

He used the knife to lift the top shirt out of the case. Then did the same with the next shirt to reveal a cloth bag in the centre of the case, surrounded by folded underwear. The bag carried a logo: 'Lyall Shoes'.

'Looks like these clothes protected the bag, sir.'

'I think what we want is inside these shoes.'

Russell cut open the cloth bag to reveal a pair of black shoes. Porritt thought they looked the same as the ones he had seen at the hospital in Skegness.

Russell lifted the magnifying glass again and examined the shoes. 'If there *is* anything inside, it must be in the heels. And these heels are not normal.'

'How do you mean?'

Russell took off one of his shoes and held it up to the magnifying glass. 'You see this heel? It's made up of layers of leather and then buffed smooth. But you can still just see the layers.'

He pointed to the shoes they had found. 'Now, on *these* shoes, you can't see the layers of leather. They're covered with a fine skin, maybe rubber or plastic, to seal the heel. Now, why would someone do that?'

He picked up one of the shoes again and examined the heel under the magnifying glass. 'You see this, sir?' Porritt bent over to peer through the glass. Russell took the point of the knife and indicated a faint line running across the heel from side to side, about half an inch in from the instep. 'I think this heel might be in two parts, and the tape holds the two parts together.'

Russell took a finer knife, like a scalpel, and cut through the tape down the side of the heel. He then pulled the tape off all the way round, and they saw that the faint line across the bottom continued up each side.

'I think this back end must slide off, sir.' He tried to pull it off, but it wouldn't come. 'Need to use a bit more force,' he said, and opened up a gap with the point of a screwdriver. Then he gripped the heel and slowly worked it off the shoe.

Inside the heel, a cavity held a small cylindrical container. He lifted it out and gave it to Porritt, who unscrewed the top. A roll of film dropped out. 'Bingo. Well done, Doc.'

'Got a microfiche reader over here you can use, sir.' Porritt loaded the film, and the first page came up on the screen, with 'Top Secret' stamped across it.

'I'll get the other shoe open for you, sir.'

The document was the minutes of the War Office Strategy Review Committee from last week. Porritt felt sick. Bloody gold-dust for the Germans. But now he checked the third action step he took after meeting Halton five months ago.

The front page of the minutes had a blank sheet over the 'X' column on the distribution list, but the secret dot that Porritt had added showed clearly at the fourth line of text. And the fourth person on the distribution list was Sir James Dunsmore. This was a photo of *his* copy.

'Gotcha,' he said, under his breath. Now all he had to do was link Dunsmore with Lyall Shoes and their case was complete.

Russell came over with a roll of film from the other shoe. It was a continuation of the same minutes.

Porritt put the rolls of film into an evidence bag. 'Later today, I'd like to print a copy of the page I just looked at. Can you do that for me, Doc?'

'No problem, sir. Just come back when you're ready and we'll print it off.'

'Good. Thanks for your help. We'll probably repeat the exercise this afternoon. I hope to pick up the body of a lad who fell from the ferry tonight. I want to see if he's got anything in his shoes.'

'I'll make sure I'm available for you, sir. In the meantime, will I just bag up all this stuff?'

'That would be good. But keep the shoes separate.' Porritt headed back to McGowan's office.

Beth Calvert caught him in the corridor. 'That's Jane tucked up in her hotel room, sir. We've put a police guard on the door. I've told her to call room service for breakfast. The hotel will let me know, and I'll go over and join her.'

'Good. What did the doctor say?'

'She's exhausted, but in good shape. He gave her a sleeping pill and reckons she'll get a good eight hours.'

Porritt glanced at his watch. 'Okay. Have her back here by midday, and we'll debrief her then.' He went back into the conference room.

Williams was checking paperwork, and looked up as he entered. 'How did it go?'

Now that he was back with his number two, he could relax. 'There was a pair of Lyall shoes in the case. Doc Russell worked out the heels were false. They contained rolls of film. The minutes of last week's Strategy Review Committee.'

Williams' eyebrows shot up.

'That bastard, Dunsmore. Thank God we've now got him in custody. Malcolm says he's got masses of info on Dunsmore, so we should be okay on that front. What else is happening, Mike?'

'Well, we're all organised for the flight at seven. But Alan got word from Alison on the agents over here, and he's not happy. You should have a word with him, sir.'

'So, Alison is sending out the agent info. That's good news. Let me call her.'

He lifted the phone and connected.

'Hey, well done. I hear you've now got the agent info out. What does it look like?'

'Right, sir. CS Craig has identified the agents run by both Lyall and Kay. In summary, we have a total of fifteen agents for Lyall covering three agents in each of London, South-East, and South regions; two agents in both East Anglia and Central; and one each in South-West and South Wales. And for Kay we have a total of fourteen agents covering two agents in each of West Midlands, Lancashire, Yorkshire, West Scotland, and Northern Ireland; one in each of East Midlands, North Wales, North-East, and North-West; none in East Scotland or North Scotland. I've given the regional heads names and addresses for the relevant agents.'

Porritt took notes as she spoke.

'I've now just got the info from CS Burnett and Superintendent Walker, and the agents' names match up. They have a lot more detail on what the agents actually did, though, and they've also got a further seven names of associates that seem to be involved with them in some way. CS Burnett asked me to tell you that one name on that list seems to be an explosives expert in Lincoln. He said you'd want to know that. He also asked me to tell you that Wadsworth's name was on the list. I'm just about to send these last details to the regional heads as well, if you're happy with that.'

'Yes, I'm delighted. Well done to everyone.'

'Thank you, sir,' she said, and rang off.

Porritt checked his notes, then turned to Williams. 'That's twenty-nine agents in total, Mike. Seems a hell of a lot, don't you think? They must have gathered a vast amount of information. Bloody hell, this was bigger than I thought.'

There was a knock on the connecting door, and McGowan popped his head round. 'Ah, sir, you're back, so you are. Could I have a word with you?'

Porritt stood to go into the office, but McGowan came into the room. 'No, I'm happy to talk here, sir.'

He sat down again and waved for McGowan to take a seat. 'Got a problem, Alan?'

'I have, sir. Alison passed me the names of the agents over here, and as I feared, one of them is Charlie Flynn, whom we spoke about earlier. We've to lift him under breaches of the Treachery Act, 1940, the penalty for which is execution. Now I dread to think what will happen in that community if they think Charlie Flynn faces the death penalty.

'So I'd like to know how serious his involvement is with the organisation. I mean, if he's just running a taxi service for them, we wouldn't execute him for that. So, my question is, sir, how do I get details of what he's done, so I can feed the right info to journalists and keep the lid on this?'

Porritt sat and thought. He had to trust McGowan, who knew what he was doing over here. And it sounded a reasonable request. 'Okay, let's see what we can get for you.' He picked up the phone and got through to Alison. 'Can you patch me in to CS Burnett, please?'

A few minutes later, Dave Burnett came on the line. Porritt explained the situation and asked him what info he had on the activities of the NI agent, Charlie Flynn.

'Hold on, sir. Need to look through this info here.' There was a pause. 'Right, sir, I've got a copy of a contract between Flynn and John Kay of Aquila that details the work required and payments. All the agent contracts seem to be the same, but have a local twist. I can also go through the eleven reports we have from Flynn detailing the work he did for Aquila.'

'That sounds great, Dave. I'll put Alan on and he can take details.' He handed the phone to McGowan and watched him write several pages of notes.

Eventually he hung up and turned to them. 'I feel happier now, sir. A lad called John Mooney seems to have written the reports that Flynn signed. If it's who I think it is, he's an engineering graduate from Queens, and the son of one of Flynn's lieutenants. Some of the reports are pretty general, but there's some valuable stuff too for the Germans. There are details of British troop positions and movements in the border region; an assessment of vulnerabilities at the giant Harland & Woolf shipyard here in Belfast; an analysis of the issues associated with attacking and neutralising Aldergrove Airport, the main ferry links, and power transmission centres; and the possibilities of safe houses for a covert invasion through the province. Enough there for me to feed snippets out through journalist contacts and hopefully calm the situation.'

He went on, 'And Dave suggests you read a copy of that contract. I'll get it typed up for you, sir. He says Kay charged the Germans a twenty percent fee on top.'

'Okay, Alan. I'd like to see it.' McGowan got up and left the room.

'He's a lot happier now, sir,' Williams said.

'Yeah. He was right to raise the matter, though.'

A few minutes later, McGowan came back and handed Porritt a typed copy of the contract. "Agreement between Flynn Enterprises of Falls Road, West Belfast, Northern Ireland, and Aquila Organisation of Great Britain. This agreement states that Flynn Enterprises will use their best efforts and endeavours to help Aquila organisation in their aims of expanding the interests and influence of the Third Reich within Great Britain. In particular, though not exclusively, this agreement focuses on such activities within Northern Ireland, which may ultimately lead to the achievement of a united Ireland. In return for such assistance, Flynn Enterprises will receive a retainer of fifty pounds per month. For assistance provided by Flynn Enterprises in assessing or assisting in specific actions to help the aims of the Organisation, Flynn Enterprises will receive one hundred pounds for each instance. For other routine assistance, for example, from the taxi business, Flynn Enterprises will charge pro rata. Signed 23 March 1939. Charles Flynn, Owner, Flynn Enterprises. John Kay, CEO, Aquila Organisation of Great Britain (North)".

Porritt passed the contract over to Williams.

Williams said, 'Don't like the bit about a united Ireland, sir. That's sneaky.'

'Yeah, I'll bet that's the local twist for Flynn. I'm sure the other contract over here won't have that. But just think about the money for a minute, Mike. That contract has been running for four years at fifty pounds a month. Plus eleven reports at a hundred pounds each. A total of three thousand five hundred pounds. That's about nine hundred pounds a year. Great money for the agent for not doing very much. And assuming they're all similar, then multiply that by twenty-nine agents and you get a total of over a hundred thousand pounds. And Lyall and Kay charged twenty percent on top. The more agents they have, the more money they make. They were each earning well over two thousand pounds a year. These guys were raking it in.' Porritt shook his head. 'They took the Germans for suckers as well as us.'

'Well, it won't do them much good in prison, or once they're executed.'

'That's true. But let's make sure we trace as much of that money as we can, and get it into our country's coffers, huh?'

***

Porritt took the call from Alison just before seven. All Regions had lifted their agents at six with a few snags.

One agent in the West of Scotland had a heart attack and died as the team entered his house. But they lifted his wife for taking and sending photos of Jane's kids.

The agent in Portsmouth turned out to be away sailing with friends. The SB team planned to catch him when he returned on the Sunday evening.

Porritt asked Williams to prepare the case against the Aquila group. He also checked with McGowan that the sea search had begun to find Brenner's body. Then left word for Stevenson and Maxwell to join Jane's debrief.

By just after seven, he was on his way to the hotel to grab a few hours' sleep.

***

By twelve, Porritt was back at Police HQ ready to start again. He'd had about four hours' sleep, a quick shower and breakfast.

Stevenson and Maxwell, already in the conference room, handed him a copy of their report. He flicked through it before Jane arrived. Her hair and make-up looked more like usual, and he smiled to put her at ease.

Stevenson operated the recording machine. 'Debrief of Sergeant Translator Thomson, at RUC HQ, Belfast, Saturday 10 April, 1943. Time 12.07. Commander Porritt leading, CS Stevenson and DI Maxwell present.'

'Good afternoon, Jane. I hope you're feeling better after your ordeal. We'd like you to tell us what happened after Brenner kidnapped you from Station 19 on Wednesday, so we can gather further evidence to prosecute these people. After CS Williams and I left the interview room at the sound of the explosions, what happened next?'

'Thank you, sir.' She described the escape through the fence; the long journey to Kay's house; her abortive attempts to get away; her realisation that she had to keep in with Brenner to save herself; and his apparent love for her, which she thought had sprung from her spontaneous action in holding his hand in hospital.

'I'll never show compassion to a stranger again. Or at least not before I know more about what drives them and have thought through what might happen.'

The others nodded and smiled wryly.

Porritt said, 'That sounds like a good lesson for everyone in these troubled times.'

She told them how Brenner's attitude changed once the photographs arrived, her mistake in telling him about her brother, and how Mrs Kay had protected her from rape and left her the knife.

He asked if she still had the photographs, and she handed them over. He studied them. 'Can you just say for the record where these pictures were taken?'

'The children's photos at my mother-in-law's front door. My father's in a room at Glasgow University. We did a lot of business there, and I've been in that room before. But I don't remember the customer.'

The photographs were good evidence. 'May I keep these pictures?' She nodded, and he put them in his folder. 'So, what happened next?'

She described their long journey to the ferry and the events on board when she realised Brenner was going to kill her. But he then fell overboard.

'So, let me ask about that. You thought he was going to kill you because the guards hadn't come with you on deck. Is that correct?'

'That's correct, sir. Never left alone before that.'

'And you felt he was gripping you too tightly and forcing you over the rail?'

'Yes, sir.'

'So, you were ready to use the knife to kill him, to defend yourself? Is that correct?'

She nodded. 'Yes, sir.'

He studied her. She had answered promptly, and had a strong case for self-defence. It didn't look like Brenner had 'turned' her, which sometimes happened in hostage situations. 'But then he became violently sick and leaned over the rail to vomit. Is that correct?'

'Yes, sir. That's right.'

'And then he leaned over even further?'

'Yes, sir.'

'If you had wanted to, could you have grabbed him and stopped him going overboard?'

'Yes, sir, I could have.'

'But you didn't.'

'No, I did not. He was going to kill me,' she said, indignantly.

'But using a knife can get very messy. In the circumstances, wouldn't it have been easier just to give him a wee push in the back?' He moved his hands slightly to emphasise the point. 'Just to help him over? In self-defence? I think that's what I'd have done in the same circumstances. Is that what happened?'

'No,' she said, even more indignant. 'No!'

Just then, McGowan's secretary knocked and came into the room. She passed him a folded piece of paper.

He laid it on the table without reading it, and smiled at Jane. 'Okay, Jane. I think we should leave it there.' He was comfortable she had kept her integrity. He would have a chance later to interview Brown and Henry, and find out more about Brenner's intentions.

There had been tension in the room until the interruption. Now everyone sighed and relaxed.

He lifted the paper and read the typed note. 'Body matching description picked up off Antrim coast. On way to Belfast. ETA 14.30. CI Quinn.' He folded the paper and put it in his pocket.

'I'd like to update you, Jane, on what's happened while you've been in the clutches of Herr Brenner and his happy gang.'

She looked at him with widened eyes.

He told her about the Aquila organisation, of which Brenner was a part, and how difficult they were to catch. He then explained that when Brenner kidnapped her, he'd thought she wouldn't cooperate, and they'd have to put her under pressure by threatening her family. So he'd put a watch on her family and, as a result, he had now caught the agents who took the photographs, and had arrested the three leaders of the organisation and a total of thirty-six agents around the country.

'Brenner made an error kidnapping you. He let his heart rule his head without a reality check. Big mistake. If he hadn't done that, we might never have caught them. Let's hope his hero Hitler makes the same mistake. We'll always defeat people like that.

'I do sincerely apologise to you, Jane. While you've had a really rough time of it, we've been able to use your position to smash this whole German spy organisation. I hope you agree it's a good result for us all.'

Jane looked bewildered. 'My God,' she whispered.

'Now, I have to ask you a big favour.'

'Well, if I can.'

'We've arrested the couple who owned the house where you stayed, together with their driver, and we would like you to formally identify them for us. You're our only independent witness to these people, Jane. And so, until we've got that over, we want to protect you twenty-four hours a day. We think we've got everybody in this spy organisation, but we won't be sure for a few days. Is that okay with you?'

She nodded.

'Good. And now for a much more difficult one. We think we've recovered the body of Herr Brenner, and we'd like you to identify him for us this afternoon. Could you do that, please?'

Jane's hand flew to her mouth.

'We'll be with you all the time. Nothing will happen to you, I can assure you.'

After a moment's pause, she murmured, 'Okay.'

241

'Thank you for that. I assume, now this is over, you'll want to get back to Glasgow and check in with your family. Is that right?'

'Yes, sir. That would be good.'

'CS Stevenson and DI Maxwell will take you back to Glasgow on the six o'clock ferry this evening. How would that be?'

The look of relief on Jane's face spoke for itself.

***

Just before three o'clock, Jane, Porritt, Stevenson, and Maxwell, with Beth Calvert, arrived at the City Mortuary. An attendant showed Jane and Porritt into a bare room with tables round the walls and a large space in the centre. She could see the others through a window.

The attendant then wheeled a trolley into the room. Jane felt her hands shake and her breath came in quick gasps. Porritt asked if she was okay. She took a deep breath and nodded. The attendant lifted the sheet to show the body's face. She looked down at him. He had a bruise on his forehead and his nose looked broken. After a few moments, she nodded to the attendant. 'That's him,' she whispered.

Porritt asked, 'Do you formally identify him as the man you know as Karl Brenner?'

'Yes, that's him.'

The attendant replaced the sheet over the body and wheeled the trolley out.

She stood still. Tears welled in her eyes. She had never seen a dead body before. Now she realised what mortality was all about. Life was transient. And she had helped end this man's life early. She imagined him entering the water and flailing his arms, trying to get air. And then everything went black.

***

Porritt grabbed her before she fell. The others rushed through the door. Maxwell and Calvert helped carry her to a seat outside and got her a drink of water.

He gave Stevenson a wry look. 'It'll be hard for her, Jim. Make sure she's okay for the next few days.'

They went over to a side table where the attendant had laid out Brenner's clothes. Porritt picked up the shoes and studied the bottom of the heels. They had the same faint line across as the ones he and Doc Russell had worked with. He put them in a bag to carry back to the lab, together with a key that looked like it belonged to the small brown case.

He studied a passport and ID cards beside the clothes. The passport and one ID card were in the name Daniel Gallagher, with papers in German in the name Karl Brenner. The other ID card was in the name Jane Thomson. He kept that, and put the others into a bag. He asked the attendant to send the remaining clothes over to McGowan's office.

He and Stevenson left the room and joined the girls. Jane had recovered, though still looked pale. He gave her the ID card, and she burst into tears again.

Porritt had told Maxwell to use some petty cash and clothing coupons to buy new clothes for Jane if she needed them. The women left to visit the shops on Royal Avenue for an hour before going out to Larne to catch the ferry.

Porritt and Stevenson went back to the Police lab, and Doc Russell opened the shoes. They also held rolls of film. The minutes of the previous meeting, with the secret dot marking them as Dunsmore's copy.

Porritt called Halton and told him he now had proof the mole was a committee member. They agreed to meet on Monday to discuss the details. Halton called back later to tell him Churchill had invited them both round for a drink on Monday evening to hear all about it.

Porritt felt drained. He arranged to piggyback on an RAF flight to London and planned to spend a precious day at home on the south coast on Sunday before going up to London on Monday. *Roll on Sunday.*

***

The ferry to Stranraer was much quieter than the one they had come over on, and Maxwell found space to relax in the upper lounge. Jane wore a new pretty blue dress they had just bought.

Stevenson went off on a wander. Maxwell leaned over, 'Would you like a drink, Jane?'

'No thanks. Don't drink now.'

'Oh? Why is that?'

Jane gave a wry laugh. 'Took a couple of drinks one night and look what happened. Got stuck with Tommy and two kids. That's one hell of a price to pay for something I didn't even enjoy in the first place.'

Maxwell was astonished at her candour. She hadn't realised Jane had such a cynical side. Or maybe it was just a reaction from her Aquila trauma. 'What about a cup of tea, then?'

'Yes, thanks. That would be good.'

244

Maxwell came back with the teas a few minutes later. She tried to keep the conversation light, but Jane kept asking questions about the agent who had taken the kids' photos. Eventually she said, 'I'm sorry, Jane. I can't talk about it. I was there when it happened, and your children were never in any danger.'

'What'll happen to Elizabeth Kay?'

'I don't know, Jane. That's for the courts to decide. But I believe we've got a lot of evidence from the house that she was an expert forger, so she could go to jail for a very long time.'

Maxwell talked about her sister's family and the scrapes the children got up to. But Jane didn't respond. She just sat and listened.

After their arrival in Stranraer and drive to Glasgow, they dropped Stevenson off at his home in the West End. Jane then asked if they would take her to Cambuslang to see her children, even though it was late.

Jane's parents-in-law were surprised to see them. Jane explained she was on a sudden visit to Glasgow and just wanted to see the children. Maxwell watched as she went into the children's bedroom, leaned over and kissed them gently on their foreheads. 'My darlings, I'm so glad to be back with you again,' she whispered.

Maxwell agreed to drop Jane off at her parents' house. 'On a Saturday night, Tommy will be well drunk, and I can't face that.'

The car stopped on Lawrence Street and both Jane and Maxwell got out. 'There's no need for you to come up, Sandra. I'll be fine now.'

Maxwell smiled. 'Remember Jane, we want to look after you and keep you safe. I'll just see you up and wait until a uniformed policeman gets here.'

'All right.' Jane thanked the driver, and they both went upstairs to the door.

Jane pressed the bell and waited. Maxwell could see a shadow coming towards the door through the frosted glass panel. Then the door opened to reveal a woman in her forties. 'Oh, Jane. I'm so glad you got the message,' she said, her eyes filling with tears.

Jane's body stiffened beside Maxwell. 'Mrs Bryce? What message? What's wrong? What's happened?'

'Oh, Jane,' Mrs Bryce said through her tears. 'It's your brother. His plane crashed into the Channel. He's missing, feared dead.'

Jane slumped against the wall and let out a plaintive wail that cut right through Maxwell. She grabbed Jane by the shoulders and held her tight. Maxwell thought Jane's cries were like the howls of a wolf she had seen in a recent film. Suddenly, Jane broke free and ran into the house. Maxwell followed.

Jane's parents, seated in adjoining chairs in the living room, looked utterly broken. Jane knelt into their arms, her loud wracking sobs mingling with their own.

Even Maxwell, hardened from years of such events, felt tears rise and turned to Mrs Bryce. 'Should we make a cup of tea?'

Mrs Bryce stood, tears running down her cheeks. 'They don't want tea, dear. They just want their boy.'

'Are you staying?'

Mrs Bryce nodded. 'Yes. I'm their shop manageress. I'll stay for a while.'

Maxwell wrote her name and number on a pad of paper. 'If there's anything you need, like a doctor, or just anything, please call me, and I'll get it organised for you. Will you do that?'

Mrs Bryce looked at the paper and nodded. 'Yes, I'll do that, dear.'

'I'll leave you to it. Now, we'll have a policeman outside the door overnight, just to make sure Jane's safe. He'll help as much as he can. And would you tell Jane I'll come round tomorrow morning?'

Maxwell turned and looked at the group again. Jane knelt on the floor between the chairs, her arms around her parents, with one grey-haired head on each shoulder, all wracked with sobs. The image stayed with her all the way down to the car.

On the way downstairs, she met the policeman coming up and told him the family had had devastating news and that he needed to treat them a bit more gently than usual.

Chapter 12. Aftermath

Maxwell got back to Lawrence Street just before eleven on Sunday morning. The policeman on duty said it had been quiet, apart from neighbours asking about the Wisemans. He had told them about the son, which seemed to satisfy most of them. Only one person had asked why that required a police guard, and he replied the lad had been on secret work with the RAF, and they just wanted to protect the family for a few days.

He also said Mrs Bryce had left at 01.40 and told his colleague at length all about the family. 'Such a nice young man with a great future. Another terrible loss in this horrible war.'

Maxwell rang the doorbell. A few moments later, Jane appeared, pale-faced and trying to smile, and waved her inside. She admitted she'd had a rough night, with nightmares of people drowning. First Brenner, with arms flailing. Then her brother, beating his hands on the Plexiglas cockpit of his bomber as it slowly sank. The images had flip-flopped, and after an hour, she took a sleeping pill and managed to get some sleep.

Jane's parents sat in the living room, blank-faced. It would take them a long time to recover, Maxwell thought. She told Jane that she had a car downstairs for her to visit the children and her husband, if she wanted. After talking quietly with her parents, Jane went away to tidy herself and get ready to go out.

On the way out to Cambuslang, they discussed what Jane should tell her in-laws about why she was back in Glasgow after only a week away. Maxwell advised against any mention of the Brenner experience, and Jane agreed. They would explain her reappearance by the sudden loss of her brother and the need to console her parents. And Maxwell's presence as necessary because Jane was working on a series of sensitive documents that required her protection.

The car stopped at the gate of 11 Brownside Road, and as they got out, Maxwell glanced up at the bedroom of number 18 opposite. She was astonished to realise she had last been there only three days earlier.

Mrs Thomson was surprised to see them again, and the children jumped up and down when they saw Jane. She knelt and hugged them both, but within a few moments they broke free to play with their toys again. Maxwell thought the older boy, Stephen, was very like Jane, and seemed quiet and thoughtful. The younger boy, George, was much livelier.

They all went through to the kitchen where Mrs Thomson prepared lunch, and Jane told her why they were there.

Mrs Thomson's eyes filled with tears, and she hugged Jane. 'Oh, my dear. I'm so sorry. We're losing so many precious ones these days.'

They had lunch at the kitchen table. The boys were typical four- and five-year-olds, playing up to strangers. Then Mr Thomson arrived back from the golf course. He gave Jane a big hug when he heard the news.

After lunch, Maxwell and Jane took the boys to the park to let them play on the swings while they sat in the sunshine watching them. Maxwell recognised a couple walking a dog nearby as two of her team on watch.

'You know something?' Jane asked. Maxwell turned and raised her eyebrows. 'When I lay trapped in that house, and Brown brought their photos up, I almost fell apart with fear. I vowed then, if I ever got out of that situation, I'd never leave them again.' She had tears in her eyes. 'But I can't do that, Sandra. This is not me here. I have no identity. I'm Tommy's wife. Or I'm the children's mother. But I'm not me.' She paused and took a deep breath. 'When I'm in Lincoln, working for Commander Porritt, translating German documents, life has a purpose. And when he took me over to Station 19 to translate the interviews, it was even better. I was doing something valuable. They appreciated me. I contributed. I was me.'

She paused again. 'I have to go back there, Sandra, at least until the war is over. I need a purpose in my life. I can't come back to this life with Tommy and the kids. I just can't do it. It's maybe what I *should* do, but I can't. I need to get back to that purpose. Am I so terrible?'

Maxwell smiled and thought for a moment. She put her hand on Jane's arm. 'What about your parents? Don't they need you too? Perhaps more than ever now?'

Jane nodded. 'That's true. But Mum and Dad are very resilient. They'll come through it. They'll have changed, of course, but they'll get through it. I just can't have my life defined by other people, Sandra. Whether it's Tommy or even Brenner. Or my parents. I need to be me. Commander Porritt said it's a mistake to let your heart rule your head without a reality check. And he's right. Well, *this* is my reality check.

'Back there with Grandma Thomson, I saw it. I saw my life here stretching out in front of me. And I don't want it, Sandra. I want to be free. I know I'm thinking only about myself, but I really did not want this life in the first place. It was a bloody accident. My own stupid fault. But the price is too high, Sandra. It's just too high for me.' She paused again and glanced at Maxwell. 'Thanks for listening. I appreciate it.'

Maxwell smiled. 'Give it a few days. You've been through a terrible ordeal. It's been a hard experience and you need time to adjust. Just try to relax and think about the children. Then you'll maybe feel better about it all.' But Maxwell was surprised at the hardness in Jane's attitude compared with the shy, nervous woman she had first met just a few weeks before. The experience with Brenner had clearly left its mark. Jane's newfound freedom had given her the determination to live her life the way *she* wanted. The traumatic events of the last few days had unleashed a new confidence.

Jane smiled back, with tears in her eyes. 'Thanks for trying. But I know I won't. Anyway, I think we ought to get them back.'

***

Jane said her farewells and got into the car with Maxwell to drive back to Glasgow. On the way, they came past the Stewarts & Lloyds factory and across the Dalmarnock Bridge. She asked the driver to pull up at the side of the power station. It all looked so normal. The red sandstone building across the road. The oriel window of her house. A number 30 tram sitting at the terminus. The Boundary Bar at the next corner. She turned to Maxwell. 'I suppose I better go up and say hello. Otherwise, I'll never hear the end of it.'

'You want me to come with you?'

'Yes, please. He won't say too much if you're there.'

They got out of the car, crossed the road, entered the close and climbed the stair. She took a deep breath, mentally shook herself, and rang the bell.

Tommy opened the door. He was still in his vest and unshaven. He looked hungover from the night before. Not a pretty sight, she thought.

'Oh, it's you. What are you doing here? You're not due back for another couple of weeks.'

'Can I come in?'

'Oh, yeah. Of course.' He opened the door wider, and she led the way into the kitchen / living room. It smelled musty, and there was a pile of dirty dishes in the sink over at the window. She sat at the table.

'Who's this?' he asked, pointing at Maxwell.

'This,' she said, 'is Inspector Maxwell of the Glasgow Police. I'm doing some very sensitive work, and she's protecting me while I'm up here.'

He raised his eyebrows. 'Sensitive work? Protection? Sounds very important.'

'Just to let you know, I'm up with my parents right now.' She felt a lump in her throat and swallowed. 'My brother's plane crashed into the sea. He's missing, presumed dead.' Now it was out, she sat up straighter.

'Oh, Jeez. I'm really sorry to hear that.' He came over and gave her a hug.

After a few seconds, she realised he hadn't washed since yesterday and pulled away from him, wrinkling her nose. 'So, I've just popped in for a minute to let you know. I'm only up for a couple of days to make sure

Mum and Dad are all right. So far they're coping, but not very well.'

'Oh, so I won't be seeing you, then?'

She glared at him. What he meant was that he wouldn't have her in bed. 'That's right. Back down Tuesday or Wednesday.'

'Well, it's important work you're doing.'

'Right.' She stood up. 'We'll get on our way and leave you to it. See you in a couple of weeks.'

'Yeah, see you then, doll.'

Jane and Maxwell left the house and went back to the car. 'Now you see what I mean? I can't live with *that*,' she said, with a snarl. She wasn't going to kowtow to Tommy any more. She would take back control of her own life.

Maxwell pursed her lips and nodded. 'Yes, I can understand that.'

As they drove back over to the West End, Maxwell asked, 'Are you serious about going back south Tuesday or Wednesday?'

'I don't need to be here any longer.'

'All right. What we've arranged is for Jill to stay with you until you're back in Lincoln. You may remember Jill. She was one of my team on the ferry. She'll be with you from tomorrow morning.'

'That'll be fine.'

'What I'd like to do then is to assume you're going down Wednesday, and organise for you to go to York for the formal identification of the Kays and their driver. Then you're clear to go back to Lincoln for Thursday. How does that sound?'

'Sounds good. Let's do that.'

***

Porritt had planned a rest day at home on the Sunday.
But the call from Halton about seeing Churchill on the
Monday evening meant he had to be even more certain
of the case against Dunsmore before then.

He called a close friend. A top fingerprint expert.
And met him in Portsmouth Police HQ at noon on
Sunday. The expert examined the four small film
containers and their contents, and found a partial print
from one roll of film. Porritt cheered when it matched to
Dunsmore. Now he had a rock solid case against him.

But Porritt wanted to know more. He asked Craig to
check the findings from the eight-week survey on the
SRC members and assistants they did months ago. See if
they could link Dunsmore with the Lyall shoe shop. Also
to check Dunsmore's diaries from the thirties to find out
his activities in Germany.

On the Monday morning, Porritt went up to London
early and met with Craig at Scotland Yard.

'Here's the eight-week survey report, sir. Dunsmore
went to the Lyall shoe shop three times. Normal visits.
Each time, the shop owner served him. He made two
purchases. Nothing suspicious.'

'Yeah. That's when he handed over the films.'

'Also checked the diaries, sir. Lots of meetings with
people. Uses only initials. No aims or outcomes. We'd
need to check official records for those. And that would
take time.

'A1 appears in '36. I assume that's Aquila 1. Many
meetings after that. A3 and 4 appear in '37. But I also
found this at his house, sir.'

He passed over a photo. It showed five men at a swimming pool, laughing and raising glasses of beer and champagne.

'That's Dunsmore on the left. And I think the guy on the right is Martin Bormann, one of Hitler's inner circle. Saw an article about him in the paper. Dunsmore mixed with some top Nazis over there, sir.'

'Wow. Well done, Malcolm.'

Porritt then met Halton at his club in late afternoon. They planned to have a light dinner before going round to see Churchill. Porritt had not told Halton who the mole was in his phone call. As soon as they were alone, Halton said, with eager eyes, 'Right. Who is it?'

'Sir James Dunsmore.'

Halton's eyes opened wide. 'What? Are you sure?'

'No doubt about it.'

'Blimey. I always thought he was a bit of a sleazy bugger, but I never suspected this. Where is he now?'

'We arrested him in the early hours of Saturday. He's in a secure cell in Pentonville.'

'Come on. Tell me all about it.'

Porritt gave him a summary of Dunsmore's arrest and what they found at his house. He told him about the shoes with the secret cavities holding rolls of film. And showed him the front sheet of the SRC minutes with the secret dot.

At the end, Halton said, 'And you got all the leaders and thirty-six agents? I'd mark that as a huge success, Jonathan. Got to tell the PM.'

At seven o'clock, they went round to 10 Downing Street and to Churchill's private quarters. He welcomed them and poured them each a large brandy. Then teased them that they still needed him to tell them where the moles were. They laughed and settled down on the sofas.

Porritt ran through the summary much as he had told Halton earlier. Churchill nodded. 'Really impressed, Jonathan. Great result. I'm relishing that pompous ass opening his door to a tipsy toff and wife. And your lot piling in behind them. That's a good one. Take him all the way, Jonathan. Show no mercy.'

'Right, sir. Will do.'

'However, I'm worried about your comments on our signal-gathering. We have great decoding now at Bletchley Park. But we shouldn't miss signals like that. Can you two think about how we can do it? Tack it on to Bletchley? I know you're both busy, but let me know your views as soon as you can, please.'

Porritt nodded. 'Will do, sir.'

'Good. Well, great to see you again, Jonathan. Well done.' Churchill chuckled. 'And I'll savour the girl in the ball gown shouting, "Any joy, John?" Brilliant.'

They all laughed. 'Thank you, sir.'

How lucky they were to have a leader like that at this time, thought Porritt, as they walked back along Downing Street to Whitehall.

***

Porritt's team worked with local prosecutors in each SB region to prepare their case against Aquila. A huge task that took almost a year.

He ordered no publicity. Kept it all very low key. They heard offences under the Treachery Act in closed courts. With the penalty being death, the accused quickly admitted guilt to get a prison term.

In the main, the accused were just political activists who had jumped on a lucrative gravy train. But the evidence from the Kay and Lyall houses damned them.

Porritt tracked each case. The big ones went first. Dunsmore. Then Lyall. Then Kay. Each hanged in Pentonville. Lyall and Kay's wives got ten years. Mrs Kay's reduced by a third for her help to Jane.

The agents, including Mary Brady and Dr Mair, all got ten years. Ted Richmond, Kay's driver, got five. This gave his family a major problem. His disabled son became so upset at losing his father.

Wadsworth, the fishing boat skipper, got ten years. And the crew five years. Also caused family problems. Joe Armitage never saw his wife alive again.

The two brothers on the south coast, identified from papers found in the Lyall house, each received ten years.

In NI, Charlie Flynn got ten years. Within days, turf wars broke out as others tried to take over his patch. Six weeks later, prison officers found Flynn garrotted in his cell. For McGowan it was all just normal.

Porritt also told his SB heads of the weak points found in the agent's reports so they could take action.

***

In 1945, after the Allies won the war, the July election swept Churchill from power. Attlee took over with an agenda for change. But behind the scenes, the wheels ground on.

The new regime asked Porritt to help set up the trials of former Nazi leaders at Nuremberg later in the year. Then, after his analysis for Churchill, they asked him to help set up the new signals unit called GCHQ the next year. He also got a knighthood. And took over Sir John Halton's duties when he retired.

He was really proud of his SB team, and passed his baton to Dave Burnett. He promoted Sandra Maxwell to the Glasgow lead role when Jim Stevenson retired.

***

A few days after her traumatic return to Glasgow, Jane visited York to formally identify the Kays and Ted Richmond. She then returned to her work at Station 19. Everyone welcomed her back, and she settled into the routine much as though nothing had happened, though she needed sleeping pills for several weeks to help with recurring nightmares.

She never went back to live with Tommy. Whenever she returned to Glasgow, she lived with her mother in Lawrence Street in the West End. Her father died in early 1945, from a broken heart, her mother said. After the war ended, they sold the business. Jane's mother did some dressmaking from her home, but it was more of a hobby to keep her active rather than a business. Jane continued to pay Mrs Bryce a salary for caring duties with her mother.

At the end of the war in May 1945, she went back to Stewarts & Lloyds. The company, now involved with German reparation work, required a German interpreter on the executive floor. Jane fitted right in.

However, in September 1945, Porritt called and asked her to join him in Nuremberg as part of the British team's translator group.

'It's going to be very different, Jane. Because of the massive workload, we're going to have to introduce simultaneous interpretation. That's where you'll have to listen to the speaker through a headset, instantly interpret what he said, and speak it into a microphone. It's the first time anyone's done this, and it's going to be very demanding. We think some translators will have problems with it. We're going to need our best people, and you're one of our best. What do you think?'

Her heart leapt at the opportunity. It sounded super, and she wanted to say yes. But she had now settled back in Glasgow with her mother. And with Grandma Thomson now not coping with the children, she had brought them back to live with her and her mother. Tommy couldn't care less about what happened to them. She was conscious of her long silence. Her heart was saying yes, but her head was saying no.

'Have you got a problem with it, Jane?'

She tried to pull her thoughts together. 'I have, sir. I've now got my children back staying with me and my mother, and I don't want to leave them again. I loved working with you in Lincoln. It was great. But for over two years I hardly saw my kids. Nuremberg sounds wonderful. I'd love to do it. But I just don't want to leave them again. Sorry, sir.'

'I thought that would be your answer. So I've got a proposal for you. Would you like to hear it?'

Her heart leaped again. 'I certainly would, sir.'

'Well, if you sign up for at least a year, I'll relocate you, your children and your mother to Nuremberg, and set you up in your own apartment, rent-free. I'll provide a local nanny full-time for the children, and pay for them to attend the International School. Oh, and one other thing. You'll be our senior German to English translator, and we'll pay you at an enhanced Captain rate. How does that all sound now?'

It was such a generous package, and she felt tears well up in her eyes. This was what she really wanted. To do the job she loved, but have her family with her. They could easily visit Prague to see her Grandma Bilova, and could go and see her Grandma Weissmann in Dresden as well. She missed them both so much. The tears began to flow. Tears of joy. She just had to go for it. 'Okay, sir. That would be wonderful. I accept. Thank you so much.'

'You're welcome, Jane. Glad to have you back.'

A Note from James Hume

Thank you so much for reading Hunting Aquila. I hope you enjoyed it.

If you have a moment, please leave an honest review at Amazon. Even if it's only a line or two, it would be *very* much appreciated.

I welcome contact from my readers. If you'd like to hear about new releases in advance, send a brief email to james@jameshumeauthor.com

Or if you want to comment on any part of the storyline, then please also send an email and I'll happily respond. But first, check out other readers' comments below to see if I've covered your subject there.

I won't share your email with anyone else, nor clutter your inbox. I'll only contact you to respond or when a new release is imminent.

James Hume

Technology in the World War 2 Period

In my storylines, I use the technology of the time as authentically as possible, based on family and friends' experiences, (since I was just a young boy during ww2), or from deep research.

Like most authors, I also use artistic licence to help tell an interesting story, and provide my readers with the best possible reading experience.

However, some readers challenge me on aspects of the storyline that don't ring true to them. In a couple of cases, where they proved their point, I've changed the text so other readers don't have that same experience.

But most of the issues they raise <u>could</u> have happened as described in the story. Let me illustrate with some of their challenges.

Tape Recorders?

The 1930s was a decade of great technical innovation, though it's hard for us to see the full impact looking back from today.

Recording machines using magnetic wire were available from the mid-thirties, and used by law enforcement for evidence gathering. The end of the decade saw portable versions of these machines available. But their use was largely limited to special applications, such as broadcasting or law enforcement, through the 1940s.

The widespread use of recording machines only took place after the war with the development of magnetic tape. So I agree, tape recorders were not available at the time of the story.

In my first draft, I used the term 'wire recorders' to describe the machines of the time. That is technically correct, but has an entirely different meaning today.

Therefore, to avoid confusion, I changed that term to 'recorders' or 'recording machines' for those machines that used magnetic wire. But not tape recorders.

Filming for Research?

By the mid-thirties, film was used routinely for analysing industrial and commercial processes. This included traffic planning of crucial hubs and junctions.

London continued its urban planning activities during the war, with limited use of film cameras during peak times. Did they analyse traffic flows round Trafalgar Square on that day in April, 1943? I don't know. But they could have done.

Also, please note, it certainly was not an early version of CCTV as one reader commented.

Frequency of Short-Wave Radio?

Another reader challenged why the comms guys had to set up special equipment to identify the frequency of the spy's signal when they could simply have read it off the old man's radio set. This is not true, since the spy's signal came through as interference.

Also, triangulation was a common practice at the time to establish transmitter location, as it still is today.

Out-of-Car Communications?

The Empire Exhibition of 1938 in Glasgow (similar to the Festival of Britain of 1951 in London) was intended to showcase the technology developments of British Empire countries following the great depression earlier in the decade. It was a huge statement of optimism for the future, which as we now know, was strangled by the outbreak of war a year later.

At that Exhibition, in the Canada Pavilion, the RCMP demonstrated a rudimentary out-of-car personal communications system as described in the story. It was the highlight of my father's visits as a young man. From various comments at the time and subsequent research, I believe this system was first developed at the request of the NYPD.

The advent of in-car radio telephones in the mid-thirties had transformed policing in New York City. But that then highlighted the lack of communications when officers were out of the car. Trying to find a solution,

NYPD approached the Aircraft Radio Corporation (ARC), who made most of the aircraft radio equipment in the US, to see if their technology could help.

A small team at ARC came up with a solution that was expensive, bulky, uncomfortable to wear, and had a limited range. But it worked. A few other North American PDs also bought systems. It was this system the RCMP demonstrated in Glasgow.

In the late 1930s, ARC paused this project because of the huge build-up of aircraft production in the US. After the war, ARC, now owned by Cessna Aircraft, sold off the out-of-car technology.

Now, did the Glasgow Police buy one of these systems when they saw it demonstrated at the Empire Exhibition? I don't know. But they could have done, and then used it to apply the innovative 'follow-from-the-front' technique.

Boots the Chemist?

Another reader challenged why the spies would go to Boots for their photos.

In the 1920s, Boots had the highest footfall on the High Street after the Post Office. This factor drove much of their business strategy over subsequent years, even into the 1990s. They aimed to be number one in the High Street for each of their services.

Hunting Aquila

During the war years, they maintained all their services as best they could, including a photo developing service, which was expensive and intermittent. I was a young child then, but remember visiting the local Boots store depicted in the story. We also have family snapshots taken during the war years to prove it.

Now, did that Rutherglen branch have a photo service available on Thursday, 8 April, 1943, at the time of the story? I don't know. But it could have done.

In the first draft of the story, I had the spies develop their own films. But, on editing, I felt the story lost pace at that point, and since the spy had to catch the afternoon post, going to Boots was the better option.

Orange Juice for Breakfast?

I was just a young child during ww2, but clearly remember getting orange juice most days. It came in a small bottle, was concentrated, and needed to be diluted.

On checking my research, the British Government distributed Welfare Orange Juice for children from 1943 under the LendLease programme. Like every other commodity at the time, it found its way onto the black market. So, the incident could have happened.

Female Police Inspector?

There were certainly some females at senior rank in the UK police services at the time of the story. According to my research, the first female police inspector in the UK was Florence Mildred White, of the Birmingham City Police in 1930. And there were female Chief Inspectors and Superintendents in the Met from 1932.

I hope you accept these points, and they allay any concerns you may have over the rigour of the story. I always aim for accuracy. The storylines are fiction, but could have happened. That's how I use artistic licence.

I learn so much from my readers, and love to capture every nuance of their reading experience if I can. So, please contact me with any points you wish to make.

See below for my other books. Happy reading,

James Hume

Chasing Aquila (Sequel to Hunting Aquila)

Just after World War 2, Superintendent Sandra Maxwell, Head of Special Branch in the West of Scotland, checks if a suspicious death in Glasgow is linked to Aquila, a German spy organisation that flourished in the UK during the war. She finds that Aquila has now morphed into a sinister new organisation. Can she and her colleagues in London catch the killer by chasing him across Holland and Germany, capture the head of the organisation, and smash their new activities before they spread to every major UK city?

This deftly plotted, action-packed thriller is full of twists and turns. Carefully weaving fact and fiction, it provides powerful and intriguing lessons that still apply in today's changing world.

"Great sequel to his first book. Closure at its best. The story will keep you reading and at the edge of your seat. Great character development that brings the reader into a relationship with the main characters. A great combination of action, story, characters and intrigue. This book is a masterpiece. Keep writing, James. These books should be movies." (US Kindle Customer)

Link to amazon.com - https://amzn.to/2ObOMrQ

Link to amazon.co.uk - https://amzn.to/2Cq8eyi

Killing the Captain (A post-WW2 crime drama, with a twist)

Book 1 of the Captain Trilogy, in which a dispute between two businessmen in the UK escalates into two US CIA v Soviet stand-offs. This book sets the scene.

Just after World War 2, partly deaf Adam Bryson lip reads a conversation between two businessmen planning a murder. It then sets off a series of events that involve Sandra Maxwell, Head of Special Branch in the West of Scotland and her colleagues in London. Can she identify the target, capture the crooks and deal with the aftermath before anyone gets killed?

"A well-researched and accurate depiction of a rather difficult time for Britain. A good story, well told, and kept me busy reading! I have read all three of this sequence of stories and much look forward to the next one. Soon, I hope." (E.A.M)

"I really enjoyed reading this book. I read the last few chapters really slowly as I didn't want to reach the end. Great characters and story lines." (Alan))

Link to amazon.com - https://amzn.to/3gRPHKn

Link to amazon.co.uk - https://amzn.to/2ZWGVUo

Avenging the Captain (Sequel to Killing the Captain)

Book 2 of the Captain Trilogy, in which a dispute between two businessmen in the UK escalates into two US CIA v Soviet stand-offs. This book has the first minor clash.

Just after World War 2, Gary West, Head of CIA Operations in Europe, is puzzled by sinister activities of staff at Soviet Embassies. Their latest seems to focus on Glasgow, Scotland. Can Sandra Maxwell, Head of Special Branch in the West of Scotland, her colleagues in London, and Colonel Chuck Campbell, Head of CIA Operations in Scotland, help him solve the puzzle, capture the crooks, and deal with the aftermath before anyone gets killed?

"Good story. Great sequel to Killing the Captain"(Cary)

"I enjoyed the characters and the plot. It was a fast-moving story with real-life twists and turns. I look forward to reading more stories by James Hume." (Rick)

"Mr Hume was able to transition through all three books without losing any of the players. Highly recommend these books." (Amazon Customer)

Link to amazon.com - https://amzn.to/36p7J6H

Link to amazon.co.uk - https://amzn.to/3GYIiFF

Finding the Captain (Sequel to Avenging the Captain

Book 3 of the Captain Trilogy, in which a dispute between two businessmen in the UK escalates into two US CIA v Soviet stand-offs. This book has the final major clash.

Just after World War 2, Gary West, Head of CIA Operations in Europe, is faced with horrific demands for a prisoner swap from a secret Russian group. He has no choice but to agree. Can Sandra Maxwell, now Head of Special Branch in London and her Glasgow colleagues, help the CIA to find this group, capture them, and deal with the aftermath before anyone gets killed?

5 ★ AMAZON REVIEWERS ON JAMES HUME

"These ww2 stories are really great, even if fiction. Although adding real history takes it to a new level of enjoyment." (PW)

"The "...Captain" series is a very easy to read set of novels. Great plot. Hume doesn't get hung up on unnecessary details. Moves the story blithely along." (Carmine Di Giacomo)

"Well developed theme and characters. Highly plausible story, with intrigue and personal stories to make it seem real. Excellent read." (Jane H Kelley)

Link to amazon.com - https://amzn.to/3ZkICbW

Link to amazon.co.uk - https://amzn.to/41zW39g

Hunting Aquila